The Liberation of the Jew

Albert Memmi

THE LIBERATION OF THE JEW

Translated from the French by Judy Hyun

The Viking Press   New York

To all those who fight for their freedom

Contents

Part Three: The Way Out

Preface
to the
Compass Edition

This book was written before the Israeli-Arab Six Day War, which means that it owes nothing either to immediate political preoccupations or to passions aroused then in each of us.

I had published previously another work, *Portrait of a Jew,* wherein I attempted to do a systematic inventory of the condition of the Jew through a particular existence—my own. Later it became necessary to examine the different results of the oppression of the Jew: thus the origin of *The Liberation of the Jew.*

In spite of subsequent events, I have not changed a single line, because I believe that a book corresponds to the truth at the time. And especially because the events themselves confirmed the essential points of my conclusions:

—The Jew was, and largely still is, oppressed—the continual object of a potential menace.

—Like all those oppressed, the Jew has the right to be liberated.

—The liberation of all people, including Jews, has taken the form of national, as much as social, liberation.

—All other measures after all are only compromises with the oppressors.

—Finally, aside from the Jew, the mechanisms of liberation described in this book apply to the majority of oppressed peoples everywhere.

Paris, 1973   ALBERT MEMMI

preface

"Many a time have they afflicted me from my youth
May Israel now say:
Many a time have they afflicted me from my youth:
Yet they have not prevailed against me."

Psalm *129: 1-2*

Preface

I am keeping the appointment I made three years ago when writing *Portrait of a Jew*. I will not evade, as you will see, the promised answer. Having come so far, I must now decide: what do you do if you are a Jew? Is there a way out of the Jewish fate?

To find the answer I will use the same method used in my earlier book: I will continue to tell of my own life. Having established the inventory of what I am, it is now my intention to discover how best to manage my life with a view towards surmounting this fate. Naturally I do not rule out the possibility of delving into the lives and experiences of others in order to clarify my own. I continue to believe that my own itinerary rigorously followed, is to a great extent typical. But above all I needed to see clearly into myself and to put order into my own accounts. If you recognize yourself in my mirror, so much the better! What then did I do when I clearly understood that I belonged to the anxiety and the hostility, to the humiliation and the threat—to the oppression? How did I react to my Jewish fate?

For the sake of clarity I thought it was a good idea to group together the periods of rejection followed by the periods of affirmation. Through a systematic analysis of myself and my efforts I hope to arrive in both cases at the extreme limit of the inventory, and perhaps discover, through the process of elimination, what attitude is possible today for the Jew who wishes to put an end to the shame of his existence.

Thus in one sense this is an optimistic book since it describes a liberation, while the preceding one, *Portrait of a Jew,* described a misfortune. I do not necessarily believe that an author specifically proposes remedies; it is enough that his description of reality be correct, though it be imaginary. It is up to the reader to draw his own conclusions. In this case, however, it so happens that the search for a way out was an integral part of Jewish reality. Throughout history the Jew has almost always hoped for a solution to his problem, whether it be in assimilation or in the myth of "next year in Jerusalem." Rarely do the oppressed accept their oppression. In varying degrees they resign themselves to it, organize their lives to the best of their ability within its limitations, deceive the oppressor and themselves, invent and listen to ideologies which divert their attention, fool them, or help them to live. But in the final analysis liberation is inscribed in every oppressive situation, so that the groping efforts of the oppressed, his different defensive moves against his destiny, his defeats and his never-extinguished hopes, are still a part of himself. The portrait of the Jew is not complete with the description of his misfortune, the myths which accuse him and the deficiencies to which he submits. We must also add his more or less courageous, more or less effective response to this misfortune. Only then is the picture complete, and that is what I am attempting here.

However, I prefer to warn the reader that, for the most part, this is neither a more joyous nor a more tranquilizing book. The price paid for liberation is rarely small. Of course, I expect the same emotional reaction—the same approbation I hope, but also the same anxieties—which my earlier book aroused. This is not surprising! I would be too naïve if I believed that I could discuss such a touchy subject without shocking Jews and non-Jews alike.

Though the fact that those who profit from an oppression, willfully or not, do not like to hear about it is easily understood, one is more surprised at the protestations of the victims themselves. But it is the truth: the oppressed find the description of their servitude even less bearable, as if the description itself increased their anguish. If necessary they will allow themselves to be pitied, they will allow others to lament with them, but only on the condition that the others pretend to believe them proud and irreproachable; in that way, the inevitable results of their long oppression—their wounds, their inner deformities and destruction—are not too closely revealed.

I do not want to say hypocritically that I regret this commotion over my work. On the contrary, I see in it proof that I have honestly and effectively done my duty as a writer as I understand it. It may seem to the oppressed that I am adding to his troubles by reviving them or that I am insulting his misfortune by revealing it. Not at all: I find it necessary that he become courageously and completely aware of his oppression. Otherwise I do not believe in the possibility of a cure for such a long illness. How can we say that the drama of his existence has left no mark on the soul of the Jew? Or on that of the Negro? How can we minimize the drama, even during the periods of relative calm?

In the one month following the publication of *Portrait of a Jew,* while people were telling me that I was exaggerating, several events occurred which unfortunately confirmed my doubts. In Argentina the swastika was carved on the thighs of a few Jewish students. In England neo-Nazi meetings were held in which "Jews get out" was heard again. In America they continued to pillage the synagogues: twenty-five in two years. Here and there the Fascist International was being brought to life. And in North Africa, one of those great historic migrations of a Jewish community in its quasi-totality began. Of course, they were in a hurry to explain that all that was without significance and of no importance. Moreover, the English Fascists were, it seems, dispersed by the country people themselves; the Argentine government promised to punish the guilty parties; the African refugees were welcomed. What did we have to complain about? Of not much, effectively, except this: in the final analysis Jewish history in the Diaspora continued to repeat itself to an astonishing degree. . . .

Here I can only repeat myself: the description of this itinerary is of no value except in its absolute severity. Yes, the Jew remains essentially oppressed. In any event it is thus that I have, most often and everywhere, lived with my Jewish condition. My successive departures have never finally resolved anything. Other experiences which were at least as disquieting as the ones I had experienced awaited me elsewhere. And everywhere I believe I have met with a heavy negativity in the existence of most Jews. In varying degrees, but everywhere, the Jew is objectively separated from the others; in the minority, living under a more or less serious threat, periodically struck by catastrophes which at the very least wrench his heart. The result is that he is also *inwardly* threatened, anxious, separated from himself, living a culturally and socially abstract and amputated life.

It is this double oppression, interior and exterior, which must be our point of departure. For what chance has a liberation whose difficulties have not been foreseen? What possibilities of success has it if we do not begin by eliminating all the false solutions?

part one

SELF-REJECTION

"I have powerfully assumed the negativity of my times."

FRANZ KAFKA, Diaries

"You are a Jew, Dobrouch," Menahem once said to him. "Never forget it."

"Why remind me? Do you think I don't remember it myself? It would be better if I didn't. It terrifies me! It is as if you said to me: 'You are sick, Dobrouch, you are going to die, Dobrouch' . . . I'm not anything anymore! I am nobody! I am the wind! a tree! a ray of sun!"

MENDEL MANN, The Fall of Berlin

Does the Jew Exist?

1

Towards the end of my adolescence I had had enough of being a Jew; or so I dared tell myself. It was, at first, not so much anger as it was impatience and irony. The details of my life in the ghetto which had so pre-occupied me suddenly seemed laughable: "Lilliputian problems," I noted in my diary at the time. "To be Jewish: above all, a narrow and constricted fate." Why, when my life was just beginning, should I accept this limitation? Why should I forsake so many splendid adventures to remain vanquished among the vanquished? I wanted to taste every food, enjoy every pleasure; I would be proud of my body and sure of my mind; I would practice every sport and understand every philosophy. . . .

Moreover, the entire world seemed to invite me to a marvelous wedding celebration. It was 1936. The Popular Front was in power in France: once again the French were giving all peoples an example of social justice. In Tunisia the colonial administration was slowly opening its doors to us; in joyous open-air meetings, miraculously tolerated by the police, we rubbed elbows with Arab peddlers, Sicilian bricklayers and French railroad workers, one and all dazzled by these new feelings of brotherhood. In Spain, however, the war was beginning, never to end. Yet, in the evening, before disbanding, we cried out joyously: *"No pasarán! The Fascists will not pass!"* Our worthy Spanish brothers could not lose our common battle for prosperity and liberty.

Even the general unleashing of the catastrophe a little later did not greatly upset me. On the contrary, I am ashamed to write, I recall its beginnings with a kind of happiness. During the first air raids we almost enjoyed jumping into the hastily dug trenches. The world was animated by extraordinary historical stirrings: so these men with mythical names really existed—Indians, Japanese, Australians. . . . It was all proof that the world was infinitely rich, diverse, full of surprises and infinite promise. What importance could Jewishness—so fragile, so special and so superficial—play amidst the turmoil of my blood and of the universe?

Here it is important that I recapture the proper tone of this period. Today it is almost in bad taste to hide one's Jewishness. I have been told that in the United States being Jewish has ceased to be inconvenient. Jews proud-of-being-Jews are found even in Paris drawing rooms, which pleases me greatly and irritates me a little. Thus, a socially well-connected writer who, during a long career never depicted a single Jewish character in any of his books, spoke calmly the other day to an interviewer about his Jewish origins. The publisher of a large French newspaper of moderate views dared reveal to his astonished readers that he was born a Jew. These are signs of peaceful times and I hope with all my heart that they last. All this proves

that for the moment there is no immediate danger in proclaiming oneself a Jew.

But such has not always been the case. On the contrary,
since the time of the French Revolution the most common
reaction of Western middle-class Jews has always been to
cover up, camouflage their Jewishness. Even after the publication of my last book, *Portrait of a Jew,* many well-
meaning friends told me of their misgivings: I should not
have labeled myself a Jewish writer! And, I might add,
they were not completely wrong. What Jew, at some point
in his life, has not been moved to regret or revolt at not
being like others?

I am not trying to justify myself; I do not need to defend a period of my life which was but fleeting and from
which I have completely recovered. Today I am perfectly
opposed to self-rejection, to all disguises, to all these attitudes of self-torture. I can scarcely hide my irritation at
the piteous and useless efforts of those dissimulating Jews.
I simply wished to note that my rejection was not solely
marked by flight and recantation. The Jew who denies
his Jewishness is not always a cowardly and tricky chameleon deserving of nothing but derision and anger. In my
opinion, this judgment is too sweeping and too easy.
Among those who reject their Jewishness are to be found
the worst and the best. The careful and the vanquished,
yes, those who have chosen to play a lifelong game of hide-
and-seek with their contemporaries in order to preserve
their possessions and their well-being. But there were also
authentic rebels who dared question their fate. There
were at the same time the grotesquely bourgeois and men
of sublime stature. Self-rejection can be a shabby trick, a
final surrender, a plea for acceptance completely lacking
in nobility. But it can also be a first step towards revolt,
the first awakening gesture of the oppressed, the furious
rejection of that which he has become in his servitude.

In short, at the time, I sought not so much to reject my-self as to conquer the world. I rejected myself as a Jew because I was rejecting the place assigned to me, and in which my people were content to remain. I felt my Jewishness to be a collection of odious harassments and ridiculous rites. I sorted out my ideas into two main categories: on the Jewish side, a skein of outdated customs, with neither truthfulness nor effectiveness; on the other, a system of accusations and injustices. I thought I had to extricate myself from these absurd nets; and, of course, I felt capable of demolishing everything with a few heaves of my adolescent shoulders. When we graduated from the lycée at Tunis many of us decided to cut ourselves off from the past, the ghetto and our native land, to breathe fresh air and set off on the most beautiful of adventures. I no longer wanted to be that invalid called a Jew, mostly because I wanted to be a man; and because I wanted to join with all men to reconquer the humanity which was denied me.

Why, then, did I not continue along this path? Why, at a certain point, did I once and for all abandon this attempt? Of course, the world, temporarily filled with a spirit of fraternity, had slipped away again, and it was preparing to show us its most atrocious side. But that was not the only reason; I am quite sure that the awful catastrophe which followed those years was not the determining factor. The Jewish destiny is such that one massacre more or less, as monstrous as it might be, only vindicates a history already full of gloom. Nor was it because of weariness or for moral reasons. I slowly became convinced that this way out was a deception, a door painted on a brick wall. I had to admit that a simple negation of self did not exist; that I had to go much further or I would resolve nothing. That pure and simple transparency was an abstract, illusory solution and, in the final analysis, untenable.

TWO

My reasons stemmed from my own past. From time to time some fine gentleman from France or Italy would come into my father's shop. Most of the time it was only a matter of a small service: a stitch on his wife's pocketbook, a briefcase handle to replace, an extra hole for his belt. Then, as we were friendly and curious, he would sometimes talk with us. After a moment, having sized him up, my father would ask the fatal question, but backwards as a precaution in the improbable event of an embarrassing mistake:

"You are Christian, aren't you?"

This, if the signal was understood, translated into:

"You're a Jew, of course. . . ."

Invariably the gentleman answered with one of these expressions which so delighted our artisans' milieu:

"I am of Jewish *origin;*" or, "My parents were Jews;" or "I am a freethinker. . . ."

This we ourselves translated without the slightest hesitation. We called these delicately modest Jewish visitors the "of origins," and after a while, like my father, I learned to ferret them out and, I admit, to feel contempt for them. Since that time I have never believed in anyone's transparency.

Later on, in Europe, when I had met dozens of these "of origins" I was already well prepared. I discovered that in Europe they bore another name: they called themselves, among themselves, Israelites. They were even successful in having themselves called Israelites by others, especially when the latter had reasons for wanting to please them. Their highest ambition was that no one might find anything to say about them at all; nor, moreover, about any Jew in the world. The Jews? What Jews? What are you talking about? They didn't see a thing. They spent their whole lives laboriously trying to make everyone believe in their non-existence. And, for a time, unfortunately all too fleeting for their own hopes, they could almost believe in their own success: when they appeared completely out of context, without past, if they succeeded in not opening their hearts, if their interlocutor had not had the time to delve too deeply into their personalities, finally if they had sufficiently ceased being. . . . Then, for a moment, they might really give the illusion that the Jew did not exist; that they, at any rate, had nothing of what was generally understood as Jewish. They are, I repeat, respectable Israelites, not dirty Jews. . . . Again I am being sarcastic but I am sincerely more indulgent today. It was, after all, too difficult to be a Jew and everyone tried to remedy the fact as best he could. The only trouble was that these contortions were perfectly useless. The "of origins" played at being invisible, but everyone saw them except themselves: and yet, were even they really fooled?

The unfortunate truth is that it has never been enough to affirm "I am not oppressed" in order to cease being oppressed. Neither in one's behavior, one's mental habits nor in one's concrete existence. The story of the little Jewish tailor is well known: on arriving at the Paris station a Polish refugee declares to his wife:

"And now, wife! No more gefilte fish, no more goulash! We are going to assimilate. . . ."

Whereupon he proceeds directly to the Jewish section of Paris. The anecdote might have added that since the majority of little tailors were Jewish, and that these Jewish tailors were clustered in a few streets, he could hardly do anything but join them. And that, worse still, his bad French was pronounced with a strong Yiddish accent, and that he needed the help of the Jewish community, etc. . . . In short, the Jewish fate cannot be reduced to words. So the Jewish fate is too difficult to live? Well, I make it vanish, I deny it: see, no more Jewish fate! But no one is deceived by the trick, and Jewish fate continues to stare the spectators in the face. In the final analysis they refused to give a name to their misfortune in the magical hope of seeing it thereby disappear.

Above all, what our hero did not realize was that his game required two players: the Jew and the non-Jew. For its ultimate success the two partners had to accept the rules. Obstinacy on the one side was of no use as long as the other disdainfully refused to co-operate. I have been told in France, that far from being humiliated or disheartened by this solitary comedy, the old French-Jewish families persevered to the death. In the concentration camps, in front of the crematory furnaces, the Franco-Israelites repeated, like Saint Paul: "I am French. I am a French citizen!" With this firm constancy they would finally win. They would baffle their executioners, and finally gain the esteem of their fellow citizens. What a triumph to earn at last a diploma such as this!

"For me he will always represent a certain type of French Jew. Nothing, neither the war, nor the unjust persecutions could change his idea that he was of purely French tradition, therefore bound to Europe by centuries of political affinity!" (Gaston Berger, *In Memory of M. Alexandre.*)

(In passing let us admire the "bound to Europe" and "by affinity;" is it a slip or is the Jew not quite a part of it?)

It is debatable whether this tireless love is grandiose or humiliating. But one cannot refrain from timidly objecting, "All the same it didn't prevent them from being burned!"

Certainly, they would reply, but we were wrongly burned! By a misunderstanding! They wanted to burn the Jews, and we have proved that they burned the French. By our courage, our unity, we have demonstrated the foolishness of our persecutors.

On the eve of his arrest, the same French-Jewish philosopher, M. Alexandre, urged to flee by his friends, told them with supreme logic:

"What do I risk? To die a Jew? *It's absurd. . . .*"

It certainly was absurd to arrest this Jew who didn't exist. Yes, but was a man arrested, tortured, killed? But . . . all those bodies? Well, it was an error of history. Not even of history, a deception perpetrated by the Nazis, an hallucination, nothing. Really, what small satisfaction! One can prefer less misery and less logic, for what kind of unity is this which leads you to the furnace for no reason? It is a fact that the Jews were condemned in any case, whether they thought of themselves as Frenchmen, Italians, Poles or Jews. But was that not the real absurdity: that of the Jewish destiny, which leads him to torture and to fire; from which nothing, neither reasoning nor philosophy can save him, because the Jewish fate is not a matter of position or principles or reason or philosophy?

THREE

This attitude presupposes an implicit philosophy which furnishes the Jew with his obvious unity and his letters of nobility. In talking with a Jew who repudiates his Jewishness, whether he is a middle-class liberal, a youthful rebel or a systematic revolutionary, you always meet with the same love of abstraction. Another French-Jewish philosopher, usually a discerning thinker, earnestly declared to me: "I am against the distinction between Jews and non-Jews." As if it were a matter of a dispute about methods! A Russian-Jewish sociologist, learned and perspicacious in his own field, objected to me: "I have never considered my Jewish birth of any importance . . . except," he added proudly, "when it is necessary to fight persecutions." As if persecution were not also a *social fact,* heavy with meaning, which partly determines Jewish existences. A politician, whose courage I usually admire, tried at length during a discussion to demonstrate that one ought not to do more for the Jewish victims than for the others. A fine way of disguising the poison!

Of course, I too have saddled a great many wrong horses, taken their lovely shadows for substance. Encamped on the pink clouds of the Universal, for a long while I passionately asserted that man, in his heart, was one, that all men were brothers, generous and equal. Down on earth, however, a real and difficult battle was in progress, whose blows I was hardly able to avoid and hardly ever able to return. These incidents are but transitory, I assured myself; the mistakes of a humanity which still had rough edges. All I had to do was to despise those savages: weren't they killing each other too?

I had convictions: one day the swords would be turned into plowshares, and this miraculous morality would be adopted by all, conquerors and conquered, oppressors and oppressed, and all human nature would shine forth as evidence of Justice and Love. But meanwhile? Meanwhile, it was only right that we take the first step, that we preach the example. We proudly proclaimed that we did not exist.

As Jews of the Left we had at our disposal a method of reasoning which we used against any too-tenacious adversaries. It was a peeling-off tactic comparable to eating an artichoke. We started out with Stalin's definition of a nation; then we considered each trait mentioned in this definition. We asked ourselves: do the Jews have a common language? Obviously not. Do they share a common territory? Not that either. Do they even have a religion?

No! No! Most Jews can't even remember the names of the important prophets! The only trouble was that when the peeling was finished, contrary to the artichoke, the Jew always found himself intact. It reminded me of the traditional discussion of the existence of the outside world, which so astonished and irritated me when I was a philosophy student. Our professors, after discussing one by one the characteristics of what we saw and touched, concluded that the visible and tangible universe did not exist. With rage I told myself over and over that their reasoning had to be faulty, since it led to such an absurd conclusion.

What was this logic which led us to doubt our very existence? As if it could ever be reasonable, coherent or even respectable to deny our concrete existence! If there is a conflict between reasoning and existence, then it is the reasoning which is bad. The existence in question probably surpasses any accepted definition. It was our habitual frame of reference which was wrong, politics and philosophy which were not capable of understanding everything.

Thus I rapidly had to abandon these views. Rather than stagnate on a definition, assume the existence of a make-believe community of human spirit, I decided to take for my starting point this fact: *my separate existence as a Jew.* I might become impatient with this existence; I had the right to rebel, to question it. I knew that I might in turn be embarrassed: What is this existence? What is Jewishness? I willingly admitted that numerous problems were still extant; I saw perfectly well that the majority of Jews were ignorant of Judaism or barely conscious of their Jewishness; that one's Jewishness was certainly not convenient, badly adapted as it was to the world in which we live, its arteries hardened by its values and its institutions. But the fact remained and I had to recognize it as such; I had to understand it and, to a certain extent, accept it.

The reader will protest that at one and the same time I am making a great fuss about Jewishness and also stating that it is only an incoherent survivor, a sort of historical monster, a fossil. The Jew does not live, he survives. He is not a normal being, but an historical phantom who still haunts the world because his harassments, his persecutions and his sufferings endure. Without these exceptional circumstances, happily on the road to a solution, he would have disappeared long ago.

This thesis contains both some truth and enormous ambiguity. I will return to the undeniable fossilization of Jewish culture. It seems to me quite useless to cry out in indignation like the traditionalists every time a courageous Jew or a non-Jew (Toynbee) dares suggest it. Nevertheless, the problem of the Jew's existence cannot be confused with that of the value of his cultural heritage. The Jew exists, whether he is beautiful or misshapen; whether his spirit is adapted to the real world or completely submerged by it. A living fossil—is he any less a living creature? Does this state keep the fossil from eating and drinking, from rejoicing and suffering and from fear of death?

Dare I stretch the paradox any further? As a Jew I exist more than non-Jews! My uniqueness makes me exist more, because it makes me more cumbersome, more problematical to others and to myself, because my conscience is more painfully aware, because the attention of others is more directly focused on me; like the giraffe, an animal who has also tarried on in history, whose presence is felt more and who is more disquieting than the ultramodern dogs and cats of our apartments. His picturesque and inconvenient long neck often causes him to die of hunger or condemns him to circuses or forces him into cages.

Three times cursed, alas, but the Jew does exist and his existence is more weighty and worrisome than that of others; he has, up to this moment, led the existence of a giraffe.

Name-changing

2

ONE

I was never able simply to deny my Jewish
fate. I had to accept it or reject it, fight it or
assume it, but never without misgivings or
ambiguity. When I wished to dissimulate,
it was with laborious stratagems; when I acknowledged it, it was with passion. Which-
ever solution was adopted, for me at least,
the price was high.

I again admit that it was a matter of temperament and personal background. I could
never satisfy myself with the cautious, head-
in-the-clouds attitude of many of my coreligionists who wavered between lukewarm affirmation and passive rejection. With the
same passion which motivated all my actions I preferred to push my rejection to
extremes, even to a mixed marriage, even to
the rupture with my people . . . free to return to them with the same violence. Appearances to the contrary, I sincerely believe
that few Jews, whatever they say, are ever

able to remove themselves from their Jewishness for very long.

Why, I often wondered, did our partners in the little comedy acted out in my father's store not simply lie to us? Why didn't they calmly say: "Yes, I am Catholic."

For, as the police well know, the only way to remain unnoticed is to avoid complicated and naïve efforts to become invisible and, on the contrary, to assume another identity; to become a bricklayer, a plumber, to possess a real body with ordinary habits, not to become a ghost. By merely denying themselves, so awkwardly at that, they allowed us to guess at their identity. One is led to believe that they did not completely want it or that they were unable to go any further. But for the Jew who wished to forget himself and be forgotten, it would have been indispensable to go a great deal further.

Name-changing is a well-known and much-discussed act. Its results are pitiful. It was in Europe, in France to be precise, that I discovered its extent: the Jews from Eastern Europe, North Africa and Asia are desperately anxious to pass unnoticed. So are old French-Jewish families, who have realized, perhaps as a result of some alarm, the Hebraic or Germanic consonance of their names. Since Jewish destiny is surely one of the most troubled in history, one can understand that this is certainly a very old and familiar Jewish tactic. Here again my first reaction was one of severity, until I understood the meaning of this other disguise of the hunted man. If the idea never occurred to me in my own case, I do not wish to appear more virtuous than I am. Had I been called Levy, Cohen or some other more revealing name, who knows if, at some period of my life, I too might not have been tempted? Why wouldn't I have discarded a banner-name, a brand-name which would have immediately designated me as a member of a minority, separated?

On the other hand, I maintain without hesitation that the non-Jew's irritation or derision on this subject is either monstrous gall or an extraordinary lack of perception: that of the oppressor who accuses his victim of the crime of which he himself is guilty. "You must admit that it isn't loyal!" I was resentfully told by an otherwise well-meaning friend. One of our professors at the university had what he thought was a most humorous habit. He systematically translated the names of his Jewish students: "Klein? Do you know what Klein means? In *German* it means little. You must have had a little ancestor, etc. . . ." Naturally he accentuated the German pronunciation of Klein. Thus translated and illuminated by etymology Jewish names can perhaps seem comical; Blumenfeld which means field of flowers or Zilberberg which means mountain of money can be funny. But no joke is just a joke. The anger or the aggressive irony of the non-Jew faced with the camouflage of the Jew might be explained, I admit, by simple uneasiness. All masks produce that effect. Also, one feels a certain apprehension when faced with disguises. These disguises have certainly played many a trick on non-Jews, who, believing they are dealing with a Gentile, have spewed forth their hatred into the lap of the astonished Jew. When all is said and done, however, in attacking this verbal screen behind which the Jew hides, one is again hunting and excluding him. In camouflaging his identity the Jew hopes to avoid attention, in other words to become an ordinary citizen. In translating Klein or Blum, our witty professor literally unmasked the outsider; he destroyed his actual social being, so painfully acquired. He proved that he did not have an ordinary French name; he sent him back to his foreign origins.

I do not believe in the innocence of this little game. I am even convinced that there is no fundamental difference between this amusing manipulation of Jewish names and one of the extreme forms of anti-Semitism: pure and simple denunciation. A collection of Jewish names, enumerating their various transformations, periodically appears in French bookstores: in every case it is an attempt to prevent the victim from escaping his destiny, to mark him more certainly as a target.

But I have already pointed out this astonishing reversal of accusations in every oppressive relationship. Yes, name-changing is a means of defense, a flight, almost a fraud. Nor is this step specifically Jewish. For every insecure person it is one of the simplest means of escaping the clutches of others. A non-Jewish friend, of White Russian descent, honestly admitted to me that it was disagreeable for her to give her name in department stores or to the police, for each time she was obliged to spell it out. But if the oppressed disguises himself, whose fault is it? He certainly does not do so with a light heart! It is not especially aesthetic, courageous or loyal. Is it then more beautiful, more loyal to force men, in order to live, to wear a permanent mask? To tremble with anxiety when they believe themselves discovered? How dare anyone reproach them for using this pathetic defense against a hostile world? Once again, the unnatural efforts of the Jew only condemn the society which oppresses him and not the Jew himself.

TWO

On closer inspection one is amazed to find that this effort is never pushed to its conclusion. Of course, there are Jews who change their names radically and adopt one at random from among those of the majority; but they seem to be extremely rare. In perusing one of the numerous anti-Semitic volumes (and on this point they can be believed), one discovers that it is almost always a question of half measures, almost never a complete rupture.

A case in point is that of a Jewish doctor from Central Europe, obliged to relocate. Many patients, he thinks, would rather not be attended by an alien and a Jew. In these professions where public opinion carries such weight, where one daily relies on the client's confidence, why not avoid these negative factors? He therefore decides to change his name. It was Kalmanovitch; what will he be called from now on? Smith, Jones? Not at all: his decision will be charged with a significant ambiguity. After going through a great deal of red tape and money, he obtains official permission to call himself . . . Kalman. Certainly Kalman is less obvious, less exotic than Kalmanovitch; but still he will not remain completely unnoticed. In the final analysis this camouflage is but a veil through which it is easy to see if one cares to look. Thus Davidovitch is content with David or Davidson, Silverman with Silvers, etc. There were enough of these changes at the end of the war to give rise, in France, to the humorous expression: *mutilated names.*

Some decide to go beyond this simple amputation. But though they want to change their countenances completely they nevertheless choose one which is *equivalent.* A Jewish publicist from Morocco whose name was Benamar decides to sign himself Emmanuel. He gains a little, of course, for it might conceivably be a Protestant name, and doubt is possible. But while he was at it, why stop at a name that is half-camouflage, half-revealing? At times the make-up is very thick, at times very superficial, but it is almost always make-up and not a true transformation. Aron becomes Nora: which is equivalent *in reverse,* hardly a disguise. Schwartz becomes Black, Bronstein becomes Brownstone and Grünfeld, Greenfield: all that is neither arbitrary nor complicated: it is an exact *translation!* The translation is often very approximate. For example, when Napoleon forced the French Jews to choose a surname from among the French names, they forged themselves conventional equivalents. The Haims decided on Vidal, because Haim means "living" in Hebrew, and Vidal comes from *vitalis*. Often a *simplification* seems to suffice, for reasons pertaining to euphony. Like many foreigners, many Jews do not say their name, they spell it out quite spontaneously.

Sometimes the game is even more subtle, the effect more opaque. The construction seems inspired by pure fantasy. One of my readers explained to me that he had decided to call himself Solvi, instead of Schlomovitch. At first I didn't see the connection. He assured me that there was none (or he did not wish to reveal it).

"Solvi sounds better, doesn't it?" he confided. "I just like it. . . . Schlomovitch is really impossible to pronounce, even to write!"

I felt, however, that there must be a link between the two names. Some time later I wrote them down side by side and discovered it. It was then clear that all the letters of Solvi had been taken from SchLOmoVItch. It was an anagram. The anagrams are often accompanied by a *simplification:* Israel becomes Alsi (ISrAeL). An Algerian-Jewish journalist is called Moneva. I was surprised: it is not a North African name, and I know almost all of them. At my request he willingly told me his first name: Adda. I saw no connection and told him so. But there was really none. Then why Moneva? He explained: "My two daughters are Monique and Eva, therefore MO-Nique plus EVA." This time the old name is completely abandoned; but the rupture is not complete because the continuity with himself is assured through the intermediary of his children. Observe that the two men whom I have just cited both seemed courageous and relatively relaxed; the former has been financially successful and the latter is a journalist greatly admired by the Moslems whom he defends; but both of them felt it necessary to cover up their tracks.

One might multiply these examples and perhaps discover other processes which I have overlooked, such as *complete transformations,* but accomplished in two or three stages such as these French examples: Block first becomes Block-Morhange, then Morhange alone; Weill-Curiel will become, I suppose, Curiel; Levy-Lebar: Lebar; Grunenbaum-Ballin: Ballin; and Block-Dassault: Dassault. (Yes, even one of the richest men in France deemed it necessary to change his name.) The change, slowly carried out over two or three generations, permits them to get used to the new uniform until it is almost a part of the family silhouette. Then, in spite of a complete exchange, the rupture does not appear absolute.

THREE

Why these masks? Why this timidity, this half-hearted concealment? Such an effort merely to fabricate a transparent disguise is not without significance. It is a complicated dialectic, influenced in each case by personal motives. But essentially it seems to be a double contradiction: self-rejection immediately counteracted by a profound resistance to this rejection. The camouflage is at the same time wished for and not wanted, decided upon but not desired. As if it were necessary to hide, but not too well; to allow one's identity to be guessed at, but not announced. As if one were afraid of completely disappearing under another skin, into another being. That is precisely why the disguise fails.

The Moroccan Jewish publicist who exchanged Benamar for Emmanuel obviously did not want the North African Jewish connotation of his name to handicap him in his profession. But at the same time he considers this a weakness, a little cowardly and condemns himself for it. He well knows that neither his friends nor others will approve. In short, he acknowledges guilt towards the group, a difficult feeling to beat when one is Jewish, when one belongs to a menaced group, and is thus responsible to its members and prompt to accuse them of treason.

So he compromises: he chooses a name which might be Jewish, without having to be Jewish. Of course, he will only have the benefit of a doubt, but he will have ceased being, irretrievably, a North African Jew. Those who translate or reverse their names are more clever still. They feel that their inner security has been preserved. Henceforth shielded from non-Jewish eyes, they nevertheless remain intact, since they have abandoned nothing of themselves. Better still, they save their self-esteem, since they have conceded almost nothing to their oppressors.

Whatever the disgrace of his condition, in every victim lies an ambiguous desire, both ardent and shameful, to resemble his persecutor. It is a legitimate temptation: for to overcome his difficulties the oppressed must often identify with his oppressor. A scandalous temptation: for this identification is relatively treasonous vis-à-vis his own people. "Really," a young Jewish doctor told me with a sigh, "they ought to force us to change our names!" He forgot that if such a decision were taken in spite of us, it would give rise to martyrs.

How do you resolve this contradiction? How do you preserve your self-esteem, that of your fellow Jews and still obey one of the imperatives of life among the non-Jews? Well, you remodel yourself in their image, you dress in the latest styles; you abandon Bronstein, because Bronstein is a symbol of oppression and because it is troublesome; nevertheless you try basically to save it: you call yourself Brownstone.

In other words, behind the new clothes, the facial contortions and the make-up, you remain the same. Better still if you give your children Christian first names, their religious names, in reality their true names, will be those of their grandparents: Moses, Abraham or Sarah. On their official documents, they will come second, behind the other, but will in secret link them to Judaism. The change of name is truly a mask, a tactical measure, and not an auto-da-fé. It is only the first step in self-rejection, but as can easily be seen, it forewarns of further difficulties and troubles.

Of course, too, these efforts, half-finished disguises, nostalgic, therefore revealing, flights, are not always entirely conscious. When questioned, those concerned hesitate or rationalize. Benamar, in calling himself Emmanuel, wishes only to show that he does not want to be mistaken for a Moslem (it was during the Algerian War). But, he affirms, he did not in any way wish to disappear as a Jew. It is plausible. However, had he had in mind only the erasure of his North African origin, then why did he not pick a resolutely Jewish pseudonym such as Levy or Cohen? Why this ambiguous Emmanuel? Why does Davidovitch content himself with an equivocal David or Davidson? In effect, if this hypothesis is true, whether conscious or instinctive, the intention is twofold: it was necessary to remain Jewish, but not too Jewish; it was necessary to loosen the link with the self, but not too much. And so we get Emmanuel, which, moreover, is similar to Benamar in its sonority.

When Heinrich Heine wanted to make fun of this Jewish custom, he chose the name Hirsch for his hero. He then transformed it into Hyacinth: was it deliberate or by chance or through the marvelous intuition of poets that this was doubly successful since his own name, Heine, also begins with "H"?

". . . because Hirsch is a Hebrew word and means Hyacinth in German, I've let the old Hirsch out to pasture and I now sign Hyacinth, Collector, Operator and

Appraiser. With that I have the added advantage of an "H" already stamped on my seal and I do not need to have another engraved. I assure you that in this world it is important how one is named, the name means a lot. When I sign Hyacinth, Collector, Operator and Appraiser, it has a very different ring than if I wrote simply Hirsch. Now nobody can treat me like an ordinary tramp." (*Pictures of Travel.*)

One might object that I am drawing exaggerated conclusions from an ordinary procedure. I don't think so. On the contrary, I am convinced that a whole psychology of name relationships might be evolved and that I but touch on it here. The name literally sticks to the person, and most people suffer when they hear theirs mutilated, as if it hurt their very being. It is doubtless the old magical fear of losing one's soul. A number of incantations, maledictions or benedictions are made, through the intermediary of the real name. It would be easy to show the affective and symbolic importance of the name in the family group and in any adherence to that group. To abandon the family name is to leave the family, to break away; which is precisely what happens to girls who marry. The fact is that the Jew never abandons his name without regret and remorse, in other words without grave distress. If he finally does decide on this course of action, it is because it can aid him considerably in his difficult existence. But such is the equivocal nature of his action, the laceration of every self-rejection: one is brought to it for protection against non-Jews, but one cannot resign oneself to pay for his security at the terrible price of one's own destruction.

Israeli Jews furnished me with a surprising proof of this phenomenon, only in reverse, for there too people change their names; it is apparently a custom for anyone wishing to gain an administrative or political post. Now, although the *intention is exactly the opposite, the mechanisms of transformation are identical.* The Jew of the Diaspora tries to cover up the too-visible signs of his attachment to another culture since they arouse hostility in others. The Israeli Jew, on the contrary, no longer living in fear amongst non-Jews, has no need to camouflage. Better still, regaining what he considers to be his fatherland, rediscovering his lost liberty, he wishes to find a spectacular way of affirming himself. He rediscovers his true name, a name more Jewish still, more revealing in the eyes of others. Now, far from simply selecting any name from the immense Biblical reservoir, he often carefully chooses one which in some way recalls that which he bore during his oppression. The ex-Prime Minister Shertok called himself Sharett, which is very similar. François, Francis and Alfred are simply transformed into Ephraim. At best, they adopt the Hebraic first name of their own father preceded by the traditional Ben according to the rules of Semitic onomastics. Why these hesitations when the Jew's return to Israel is experienced as a veritable *Entry in Glory?*

It seems that, even in triumph, an absolute rupture with the self is not always desired. The Jew of the Diaspora seeks, at least in appearance, to loosen the ties which bind him to his group and to himself. But he is ashamed and suffers in denying a part of himself; he dares not go too far in his flight. For this useful front seems at the same time proof of his defeat and a guilt-ridden weakness. The Israeli Jew wishes, on the contrary, to pick up the scattered pieces of his people, he wishes to rebuild the great lost Jewish community. Far from wanting to camouflage, to veil his Jewishness, he accentuates it, he claims it. Therefore he too will change his name; but this time in the opposite sense. He returns triumphantly to himself, to his group, to the ancient time when his was a free nation. He disdainfully dismisses the fake name of his exile borrowed from non-Jews, symbol of his long night of oppression. Never again will he be a Bronstein or a Block, a Vassilovitch or a Benillouche, these masquerade names in which he dressed himself for centuries to please either the Russians or the Arabs or the Germans. At last he will find his true self again. . . . It is then that he hesitates: just how far can he go in this direction? The exiled Jew he condemns, whom he definitively rejects, was, all the same, himself—is still a part of himself. The sadness, the bitterness is still caught in his throat. He cannot, without unbearable loss, totally deny the memory of his misery. So he in turn will not dare go all the way in his transformation.

Thus, even in his new-found glory, the oppressed does not immediately cease being one of the oppressed. Even in the path of his liberation which must undo what the oppression did, one can see how he compromises with any self-rejection, one can see the mechanisms of resistance to self-rejection come into play. Finally, whatever the case, one is not so easily freed from so many centuries of oppression.

The Humor of the Jew

3

One more of these examples will suffice, but it is almost too good to be true: Jewish humor. Here, even more clearly defined, are the same tension, the same rejection and the same impossibility of self-rejection which characterize most of these Jewish measures. And if all Jews do not change their names, what Jew does not repeat or does not willingly listen to "good Jewish jokes" with the same special pleasure, a strange mixture of jubilation and embarrassment, of provocation and complicity?

When I compared a number of themes from these amusing little jokes or stories, I was struck by an obvious fact: they are in no way to our advantage; the portrait of the Jew which emerges is not at all flattering. One might almost say that they reflect many characteristics of the accusation. Is it said that the Jew loves money? This theme seems to be a veritable obsession in Jewish humor where stories of debts, deals and a host of financial worries abound. Is the Jew accused of cunning? There are endless stories in which the hero reveals the fertility of his imagination and the far-fetched ingenuity of his inventions. Is the Jew made out to be a coward? His humor expands the situations in which the Jew trembles before a more powerful non-Jew, or before all of society. Although he is indulgent and somehow an accomplice the storyteller clearly does not approve of his hero's monetary preoccupations, his tricks or his cowardice. The humor of the Jew is undeniably directed, in part, against himself.

Could we be influenced by non-Jews in our repetition of these stories? Every oppressed person, I repeat, adopts as his own a part of the charge instituted against him: it is one of the internal dramas of oppression. But only in part. The humorous tradition of the Jew is too rich, too old, and too integrated a part of his folklore and his literature. It begins with the Talmud, and that itself is no coincidence, and there are Judeo-Polish, Russian, Belgian, French (Judeo-Provençal in the South of France and Judeo-Alsatian in the East) sources of it. We even have a Judeo-Tunisian variety in which the hero's name is simply J'ha like his Arab or Turkish homonyms. I had thought that this was essentially a people's humor, but I was amused to discover that it was just as popular in the most assimilated drawing rooms of New York or Paris. Jewish humor is, without a doubt, the permanent product of collective creation: the anonymity of the inventors; the variations on the same theme; the subtle references to conventions hardly known to non-Jews and, on the other hand, the immediate complicity on the part of Jewish listeners. It is part of all Jewish considerations, it utilizes all the tools of language, adapts itself to every culture and flourishes at each step of the long wandering.

Some people have tried to disarm the virulence by endeavoring to distinguish real Jewish jokes, which would be fundamentally benevolent, from the others which would, they maintain, be more or less plagiarisms. But the distinction cannot be pushed very far. I have rarely seen complete absolution on the part of Jewish humorists; and in any case, since the Jews willingly repeat the stories of non-Jews, they adopt them in part. No, you must accept this fact: Jewish humor, adopted or invented, contains a strong dose of auto-aggression.

The truth is that the Jew's self-questioning reappears in his humor. Whether he expresses it in Yiddish or in Arabic, his humor translates the difficulties of his life, his inner distress and the concrete, daily manifestations of the hostility of the non-Jewish world. Because, of course, his self-questioning echoes that of the rest of the world. It is terrible to admit, but the Jew's self-rejection and his rejection by non-Jews are so intertwined that it is sometimes difficult to distinguish between them. If jokes about money are legion it is because the Jew is preoccupied by the economic aspects of his existence and because he knows that he is accused of this very trait. If the Jew's ingenuity in getting out of tight spots is so often described and made fun of by the Jew himself it is because it is undeniable, heart-breaking and necessary; he confuses it and in a way regrets that such intellectual outlay, such efforts should be necessary to achieve results which are often so minimal. In making fun of himself, by this very mockery, the Jew reveals his absurd preoccupations, the acrobatics to which he resorts to face them, his complicated and ludicrous adaptations to life in a too-harsh world, one which he can't face unprotected. It would be amusing to classify these little stories by subject matter following the lead of Charlie Chaplin and his films: one would discover in them a complete repertory of different situations lived by the Jew: the Jew in trade, the Jewish soldier, the Jewish neighbor, the Jew and the police, the Jew in the street. The Jewish hero always appears ill at ease, badly integrated, anxious and fearful of a rather vague menace. In short, Jewish humor tells of the fundamental lack of adaptation of the Jew to non-Jewish society.

In passing let me say that this explains why it is almost never gratuitous, why one rarely finds the simple joke, the pure witticism, the play on words or the farce, dirty allusions or enormous exaggerations. It is not by chance that Freud, in his obstinate investigation of intellectual mechanisms, thought of his people's humor and was so often, I believe, inspired by it. Jewish laughter is bitter and full of meaning. It is based on a painful awareness in the Jew of his real condition, perhaps opposed to, or complementing the glorious and mystical description offered him by his tradition. I venture to say that the basic negative aspects of the Jewish fate such as I have tried to describe it are to be found in Jewish humor: objective oppression and accusation; concrete deficiencies which circumscribe his life and mythical image. And, more or less disquieting, they are adopted to a greater or lesser extent by the Jew himself. Jewish humor is above all an expression of the negativity of the Jewish fate and of the impatience of the Jew with this negativity.

TWO

One problem obviously remains unsolved: why does the Jew, so easily wounded, so eager to avoid any discussion of his existence, so gifted at self-protection by means of universalization and abstraction, why does he choose in this case to place himself on stage with such cruel precision? Because the confession is also an exorcism. Jewish humor is certainly an unveiling of Jewish misfortune, but it is also an effort to counter this misfortune.

"Why does the Jew laugh?" wonders Nathan Ausubel in *A Treasury of Jewish Humor,* and he answers with the saying of the old sages of the synagogue: "When you're hungry, sing; when you're hurt, laugh."

Now, in the history of human misery few peoples have been hungrier than the Jewish people or more hurt. And it was misery without hope of change—despair. But then Jewish humor appears like a salutary reaction. The avowal of sadness, the self-revelation is immediately counter-balanced, attenuated by a bitter pleasure. To question one's harsh destiny helps, in a way, to make it bearable. It is rejected and reaccepted with the same gesture. As with name-changing, Jewish humor is both an admission of defeat and an attempt to mitigate it.

This retaliation by humor hopes to achieve a double result: lessen the Jew's anxiety and take the edge off the non-Jew's hostility. The Jewish storyteller never tires of describing the failures and weaknesses of the Jew, his difficulties in living and his wry faces. Making fun of his own misgivings, the Jew analyzes them, examines them, detaches them from himself. Certainly he makes them more obvious and reveals them, but also he gets used to them and reassures himself. By the same token, in the witty description of his habits and his ridiculous aspects he solicits a benevolent complicity, he disarms his interlocutor. So, you accuse me of being an avaricious, greedy, go-getter? Well, I too describe myself as someone preoccupied with money, ingenious, etc. . . . See what a good sport I am! Then you must admit that it can't be very serious, since I am the very first to joke about it. What is funny cannot be very dangerous.

Then let us examine, if you please, the difficulties of my life; my cleverness makes you laugh (or irritates you); what, I ask you, would I have done without it? My daily livelihood, that of my children, sometimes my very existence depend upon it. How could little David have defied the huge Goliath had he not thought of using his slingshot? All of non-Jewish society remains a Goliath for the

Jewish David! You accuse me of being afraid? Certainly I am often afraid! But who would not have trembled in my shoes?

In short, Jewish humor is a barely disguised plea addressed to Jews and non-Jews alike. And when pleading one's case, it is sometimes more clever to admit the facts. The confession permits the plea. And while we are at it, one small revenge: we may take advantage of an amusing confession to throw into the non-Jew's face a few little truths concerning them which we had been saving up. These complicated machinations are all a little ridiculous, of course, but a sharp mind is still a prerequisite for their success! Can the non-Jew say as much? More favored by fate, this Polish officer, or that little Oriental pasha need not exert such efforts in order to live. But, poetic justice, their minds have been left fallow. The Jewish storyteller jubilantly insists on the non-Jew's stupidity. I remember the childishly touching joy of our artisans when they thought they had nailed, in two logical thrusts, an often amazed buyer. It created in the store an extraordinary impression of complicity, even the best kind of complicity: it was, after all, a victory for Jewish intelligence.

One can now see where the real distinction between true Jewish stories and those invented by non-Jews lies— not in any disclosure, self-criticism or negativity, for they also appear in the Jewish story, but in their counterpart: explication and defense. The Jewish story is of more complex intent; its context is almost always benevolent or tacitly understanding. Here, for example, is a good story which I have just heard:

"Do you know why," asks the narrator, "there are two Tablets of the Law? Obviously not! Well then I will explain it: God, when he had completed his Ten Commandments, engraved them first on one stone. This was the normal thing to do. Then, his masterpiece tucked under his arm, he set off to offer it to the different nations.

"Do you want it?" he asked the French.

"First of all, what's in it?" the French asked him suspiciously.

"Rules of conduct: for example: Thou shalt not covet thy neighbor's wife . . . "

"Oh, no thank you," said the French. "How on earth would we ever have any fun?"

Then God went to see the Germans:

"Do you want it?"

"What's in it?"

"Rules of conduct. For example: Thou shalt not kill."

"Heavens!" said the Germans, "then how would we make war?"

God then went to the English, the Italians, the Greeks, the Arabs and the Chinese: nobody wanted his masterpiece, and God was very upset. It was then that he offered it to the Jews. The Jews immediately asked him:

"How much?"

"Nothing," said God quickly. "Nothing, it's free."

"Well then," said the Jews, "in that case we'll take two."

This amusing story is certainly not very malicious and its Jewish origin cannot be doubted. However, it clearly reflects traits of the accusation: immediate concern with the economic aspect, readiness to get in on a good deal, obtain the maximum benefit. I have heard variants where the Tablets of the Law are replaced by other objects such as clothes or utensils and where the Jewish hero appears even more greedy and shrewd. On second thought, however, one quickly realizes that this story expresses more than avariciousness and shrewdness. It contains a message, an extension which the teller wished to suggest. In accepting this present, in extracting two Tab-

lets of the Law from the divine partner, the Jews thought
they were getting in on a bargain. But was it really a
bargain? Is it not disquieting that the other nations had
refused the present? Over and above the apparent gratu-
ity of the deal, wasn't the price finally paid very high?
Not to have fun, not to court the neighbor's wife, not to
make war. . . . One might enlarge on the true meaning
of this bargain which was, in fact, purely spiritual.
Beyond the joke, the bitterness of the Jew faced with the
austerity of his life is evident. In any case, it goes far beyond a purely amusing description of the Jew's
shrewdness in trade, although that too is to be found in
the story.

I would like to suggest that the same story can be either anti-Semitic or self-justifying, depending on the background which gives it its true meaning. To return to a
statement for which I have often been criticized, I would
even say that almost all Jewish jokes told by a non-Jew
are more or less anti-Semitic, and every Jewish joke told
by a Jew is a plea. I have verified it a hundred times: the
same story, which makes me laugh, which delights me
when among friends, makes me ill at ease when I hear it
in a night club. Under cover of laughter, of this game
enjoyed by all, the non-Jewish comedian can manifest the
hostility he bears the Jew without an excessively bad conscience. Merely hearing him announce a Jewish joke, the
non-Jewish audience begins to laugh in a certain way;
they anticipate a preconceived image of the Jew, at best
unfavorable. A Jew, telling almost the same story, unveils
the same Jewish weakness but only to explain and exon-
erate.

THREE

In short, humor is one more defense mechanism of the
Jew. This explains its richness and constancy throughout

history and geography. The Jew has few means at his disposal which permit him to arrange or get used to or make less difficult his difficult destiny. But, like the other Jewish defense mechanisms, its efficacy is mediocre and the Jew knows it. He will agree willingly that his wiles do not get him very far, that he has never definitely triumphed, that everything must perpetually be recommenced.

The other day two Jewish merchants, partners in the same textile business, both decided to change their names. You must understand them—they were called Zoberman and Moscovi! And that combination didn't look at all well on the sign over the door! . . .

After much thought, Zoberman decided to call himself Smith. Yes, Smith! What could have been more unobtrusive?

Then Moscovi thought for a long time and had an equally marvelous inspiration: he would call himself Smith too!

"Smith and Smith!" What a happy coincidence! How could one be more socially acceptable? Find a sign more discreet?

Only here is how it worked out in the course of their daily routine: A client telephoned:

"Hello? I would like to speak to Mr. Smith!"

"Smith? Yes, he's here . . . but which one do you want? Zoberman or Moscovi?"

Jewish humor is both a defense mechanism and an admission of impotence. Obviously I do not intend to make an exhaustive study of Jewish humor. However, I believe that that is its fundamental significance. All of Chaplin might be interpreted in the same manner, the little man who defends himself as best he can with a sleight of hand and a pirouette, but who reveals at the same time his sharply painful marginality, his bewilderment and the brutality of the world. Even when Jewishness seems to be accepted, it always contains a large measure of self-questioning and rejection. Thus, in those marvelous Hassidic stories which belong to what is apparently such a positive Jewish universe, the hero is squashed by man and nature. True happiness must be sought in ecstasy and union with God, outside this cruel world. The little peddler, humiliated and insulted, hurries on icy roads to get home before nightfall; the little artisan hurries to finish his work before the arrival of the Sabbath. At home, basking in the light of his own people's respect he unveils himself: he was a saintly man disguised as a peddler, a shoemaker. But first he had to overcome his own anguish, pass through the shadows, the cold and the hostility. The truth is that a totally isolated and preserved Jewish world, even in a ghetto, has never existed in the midst of a non-Jewish ocean, except in our nostalgic and retrospective imagination.

That is why I do not think that Jewish humor is, as has sometimes been said, an expression of unshakable Jewish optimism, a manifestation of Jewish positiveness, or even a creation born on one of those rare days of fairly cloudless happiness. Although that is not completely false, it is unfortunately not that simple. In the dreadful chronicle of the Warsaw ghetto, found by chance in the sinister ruins, the diarist Ringelblum could not refrain from jotting down the good jokes which made the rounds of the ghetto. Thus, besieged, starving, bombarded, condemned to death, the Polish Jews continued to tell jokes. One would have to be blind not to see that it was precisely the sense of the comic which permitted them once again, thanks to this long conditioning, to face a practically unlivable reality; that all the salt, all the learned and varied spices of the ingenious Jewish mind were necessary in order to endure such a continually destructive fate.

Like every storyteller the world over, the Jewish storyteller relates the human comedy. But the human comedy, lived and told by a Jew, is particularly uncertain and uneasy. Surely one of the best expressions of the relationship of a people with itself is to be found in its sense of humor. Jewish humor tells of this complex and particularly serious drama of our relationship with non-Jews and with ourselves. It also illustrates the cruelty of the Jewish fate, the futility and the unending effort to come to grips with this cruelty.

In short, Jewish humor is an attempt to correct Jewish destiny, a half way measure, a safety valve. This is already something, but in the final analysis not very much. My life is absurd, the world hostile and my own people crippled by misery. The world is unacceptable for the Jew and I should reject the existence which it offered me. But what can I actually do about it? A long history has taught me the uselessness of certain gestures, the danger of certain words. Moreover, it would be impossible to live in total self-rejection. Therefore I adjust: when the oppressed cannot revolt, he laughs. He can at least show that he is not taken in, that he is not totally submissive, that he continues, in spite of everything, to reject his stupid destiny. So he laughs, but this laughter is directed as much against himself as it is against his oppression; he makes fun of himself as much as he flouts his destiny. Basically the Jew does not believe in the effectiveness of his revolt and he prefers to be the first to joke about it.

Explained, denounced, rejected, the Jewish fate seems disarmed, becoming almost bearable. Revolting through words, forcing others into a kind of partnership by making them laugh, dreaming of imaginary triumphs, I am somewhat comforted by these amusing psychodramas. My uneasiness is not so profound, since I can joke about it; my misfortune is not so great since it can be ridiculed. My life is not this unlivable despair which would have demanded an absolute rejection. Wouldn't it be better then to take the world as it comes and the Jew as he is?

A confession of uneasiness, an attempt to alleviate the burden of being a Jew, a plea to non-Jews and to oneself, a smoke screen against the hostility of the world, Jewish humor is certainly an attempt to come to terms with negativity—wherefore this double impression of embarrassment and relief. But for precisely this reason, self-rejection fails once again. Self-questioning through humor could only be ambiguous. It was condemned by its necessary caution and extenuation to remain an irresolute tension, an incomplete revolt. A verbal response, tactical measure, a rejection ceaselessly turned back, Jewish humor has never been anything but a symptomatic remedy, a light salve for a profound suffering.

Assimilation

4

The time came when I had to admit that
little tricks would be useless, that half-dis-
guises could only procure a half-peace. I
thus discovered one more fact of life. Camouflage was an insufficient adaptation to life
among non-Jews; it was actually necessary
to resemble them. In short, I had to try to
assimilate.

The word is now out. Assimilation! How
we argued the question in our anxious adolescent discussions! To assimilate or not to
assimilate? Had we the right? The obliga-
tion? Could we? Would it be a catastrophe
or the cure for all our ills? At times we maintained that assimilation was the worst kind
of cowardice, at times a duty. We had to
lose ourselves in the society of men! Before
we go any further, let me say that I no
longer feel that assimilation deserves either
the excessive honor or the indignity then
heaped upon it. What was it all about anyway?

I persist in thinking that Jewish conduct, Jewish destiny, cannot be understood without reference to the Jewish condition. This condition differentiated and separated us; we were oppressed. Basically, our painful problem, whether hidden or avowed, was simple: how to alleviate or eliminate the oppression? Certainly we could fight and try to return blow for blow. And we have done so! Some day I will describe certain episodes where, for the first time in centuries, young Jews learned how to use firearms and grenades, not in the service of some army which despised them, but for their own good. It is well known that the Kibbutzniks, whom the world now admires, were trained in our obscure Jewish communities. We were but a handful, and revolt was not yet possible. The people as a whole instinctively adopted the other tactic of every oppressed person—trickery. To escape being too tempting a victim, one had to distract the attention of the persecutors. Wasn't a change of identity the best means to this end? A seeming identification with the men in the other camp? I must confess that our anger, which was healthy and which I do not regret, contained a great deal of hypocrisy. Far from being shocking or unusual, assimilation was but one further and even necessary step on the road to self-rejection.

In any event, in our stormy discussions we forgot that assimilation is first of all a fact. Jewry has never been an absolute, an impenetrable block; it is also the sum of relations with non-Jews. What Jew, living among non-Jews, has not been assimilated to some extent? When I look back and try to understand our history as North African Jews, at a glance I discover one long, thwarted striving towards conformity. Before striving so ardently towards the European model, we were Phoenicians, then Berbers, then Arabs, in language, costume, and eating habits. And traces of all these successive vicissitudes remain.

I have told of the ironic or angry scorn which we felt for the assimilated. I now see that it was tinged with a good deal of class spite. For the assimilated were to be found first of all among the rich who often moved to the newer sections of town where the houses and the cars were depersonalized. They sent their children to French schools, dressed in the latest Italian fashions, and traveled regularly to Europe. We were hurt by this too-willing and too-rapid change; to us it appeared a kind of treason. We felt abandoned by our middle class who mingled with the non-Jews in fancy places called Tennis Club or Governor's House. But the change was general, and sooner or later the result identical. Our parents, uncles, and aunts no longer dressed as their fathers and mothers had before them, in white or blue burnooses and wide Arab trousers. And we were so far removed from our parents in our dress, in our language, and our technics that we were frightened and embarrassed in our relations with them. Even our rabbis timidly tried on the robes of the Catholic priests, and in that they were only imitating the French rabbis. In short, assimilation went on in any case. It was simply a question of time and osmosis.

One can, of course, deplore this. One can loudly proclaim that true courage is demonstrated by fidelity, that imitation is too easy, that true non-conformist behavior today is the affirmation of one's Jewishness, etc. . . . I myself sustained these arguments for years, and even now I take them up again under the influence of the same emotions. However, here I would like to state my doubts. To what exactly was one being faithful? What is a specifically Jewish custom? Leaving aside for the moment strictly religious rites and values, could one fail to see that most of the so-called Jewish customs have been borrowed at random from surrounding peoples following the fluctuations of our migrations? Ah! I have too stubbornly defended the *couscous,* an Arab dish which has become our Sabbath dish, not to know how dubious a cause this is! How could I have taken the Ashkenazic delicatessen, beet juice with cream which is Russian, or sweet stuffed carp which is Polish, any more seriously? The oppression has lasted too long to leave the Jew with many sure landmarks; and he no longer knows what is his own and what he has copied from others. One has only to think how much of Africa has been left the American Negro! When I gave it some thought, when I tried to encompass my past, my history, I was overcome by the same dizziness, for they had dangerously crumbled. . . .

Leaving these considerations aside, since I wish to start from the present, I thought that there must surely be a real, recognizable countenance for each Jewry. The *couscous* was Arab; it became mine. The stuffed carp was Polish; it became Jewish. Today we love *couscous* and carp and this transition is in itself significant. All these things have become Jewish during one of the numerous laps of the journey. What will the next dish be? The next costume? To prohibit assimilation is to deny steak and French fried potatoes to Jewish immigrants in France. It is to prohibit a permanent, generalized, and inevitable aspect of the majority of Jewish communities.

In short, for a Jew, assimilation cannot be judged by exclusively moral criteria. It was very silly to talk of taking the easy way out, treason, abandoning the ship, when history has regularly forced us to abandon our sanctuaries one after the other, to move elsewhere, with new neighbors and under new regulations. On the contrary, assimilation was very often one of our most healthy reactions. It is thanks to the much-ridiculed imitative ability of the Jew (which has often outraged me) that the German Jews ended by resembling the Germans so astonishingly; that the children of American Jewish immigrants play baseball as if they had never practiced any other sport since the destruction of the Temple. At the

moment I write these lines, in 1966, I cannot help thinking of the North African Jews, suddenly finding themselves in Paris, Marseille or Nice. Is it not eminently desirable, for these unfortunates and for their best relations
with the French, that they not be an object of daily astonishment and thus inevitably of some degree of conscious hostility?

Soon, in any case, I no longer made it a point of honor
to reject assimilation, and I stopped asking myself if I
ought to or if I could assimilate. In *The Pillar of Salt* I
recounted how passionately I admired my philosophical
mentor and how I developed the supreme ambition of
transforming myself into a Western philosopher. And for
a while I firmly believed that from such a transformation
I would obtain an inner harmony and peace with the
world.

TWO

However, this is where the impossible Jewish destiny
raises its ugly head. Assimilation was necessary and, as
long as the oppression lasted, assimilation had to fail. In
this there was no mystery. The same dilemma can be
found in all oppressive situations. I pointed it out in the
case of the colonized, and it would be a simple matter to
discover it with regard to women and Negroes. Insofar as
the oppressed is driven to despair, he is led to reject and
imitate his oppressor simultaneously. It is the same dynamic process. The colonized admires and copies the colonizer before he combats him. The Negro, even in the
midst of his revolt, reveres white values and tries to realize them in himself. But the process never completely succeeds because the colonized must remain colonized and
the Negro must remain in his place.

If it is true that assimilation had to be tried, that it has
obtained for the Jew a few adjustments in his life among

non-Jews, it is equally true that it has sadly failed to resolve the Jewish problem. What is the cause of this failure? I have spent a long time in searching for its underlying reasons. What Jew (and in former times, what
colonized) has not heard, without knowing just how to
defend himself, the friendly or bitter reproach "Why
don't you assimilate? Why this insistence on living differently?" But the question, apparently so simple, is confus-
ing when one examines it. To whom is it addressed? Does
it have in mind my conduct as an individual responsible
for my own destiny, or that of the entire Jewish group?
For the half-benevolent, half-aggressive reproach to be
justified, assimilation had to depend on good will. But I
was convinced that no matter how willing the spirit, one
cannot accomplish one's assimilation alone: that, as long
as the group refuses it, the individual remains powerless.

In effect, how could I pass unnoticed if my parents, my
friends, my relatives, continued to reveal my identity?
And how could I have lost myself in the crowd if I remained so different and separated from them? Constantly
held back, reminded by so many painful echoes, I would
have had to lose all memory. Up to now, when one of
their cries resounded somewhere in the world, I listened
with all my might and with a beating heart. How could I
have traveled my road alone when the awful relay which
prevents my sleep has not been interrupted for a second?
For assimilation to succeed, it had to be a possibility for
the entire Jewish group. Until now, apparently, history
has not permitted it.

The truth is that even on a collective scale, assimilation is still not a matter of simple good will. To propose
assimilation globally to a group is, in the final analysis,
absurd. As the philosophers would say, it contradicts its
own essence. In order to assimilate, a group must consent,
if only confusedly. Now it is clear that a group, inasmuch
as it is a group, cannot want to assimilate. It cannot want

to go against its own existence, for then it would be rejecting itself. The disappearance of an individual, then of another individual, or even of many individuals can irritate the group, diminish it, but it does not seriously attack its life nor, more importantly, does it signify the group's accord.

Does this mean that no Jewish community has ever disappeared? No, of course not. Whatever their rarity, history has furnished a few examples of mass assimilation. But if I dared formulate a kind of law in this difficult matter, I would say that a human group voluntarily accepts its formal death only to avoid total death. Jewish communities have only been assimilated when their only choice was between extermination and metamorphosis. So they submitted with the tenacious hope of saving themselves in spite of everything; from this stem the disguises and the masks and the Marranos. One cannot ask a group to renounce its own existence in order to save itself since this formal existence coincides with its very life as a group. Outside of itself, it is literally nothing since it becomes something else. I do not say that this is good or bad; but it is evident that a Jewish community which dissolved into the non-Jewish milieu would cease to be. What hope is there that it should do so of its own free will?

Were violence, terror, and drawn daggers the only ways out? Obviously a better solution existed: to let the slow trap of time take its course. But there had to be a trap and there had to be time. And time requires a long period of drowsy tranquillity before it can wear down a group to exhaustion. The uneasy vigilance of the unreasoning beast must be put to sleep, its defenses sufficiently mollified, so that it will allow its individuals to fly away one by one like the swallows. The death must be so sweet and easy that the beast falls asleep or can no longer summon the strength to resist. Perhaps one day it will have at last forgotten the distinctive traits of its identity and will no longer recognize itself as different from the majority. A group could never consent to it otherwise, could never relinquish life of its own accord. Conversely, that is the reason why an oppressor can almost never swallow up another people by violence, for violence, unless it is too extreme, awakens the oppressed and keeps him on the alert. Up to now, each time Jewish communities started to let themselves go, they have always been assailed head on, pricked, poked, bled, and exasperated. Indeed, it would have been strange had their consciousness not been constantly alerted. They could hardly have failed to keep at least one eye open.

I know full well that assimilation has recently again become a popular topic of discussion. I have been told that in America, Jewish leaders are no longer primarily preoccupied with anti-Semitism, but with disappearance through conformity. Has the time of decisive relaxation come at last? Although my intention in this work is to examine an itinerary already taken, I will, nevertheless, answer sincerely. I believe that people are deceiving themselves on this point, even in America. This vision has always appeared when the calm was of any appreciable duration, but each time it has been a myopic vision. During each period of relative peace a great hope rises in the hearts of all Jews; a great hope, but also a great disturbance. Can it at long last be possible for us to settle permanently in this country, to lead exactly the same life as our fellow citizens, without ever having to fear them again? It soon becomes clear that in order to accomplish this, one must force oneself to lead their life, resemble these men as faithfully as possible. At that moment, faced with this progressive amnesia, the Jewish community seems gripped with panic, dizziness, as if on the brink of an unknown abyss in which it will be engulfed without recourse.

Assimilation, which was so ardently desired, soon turns into a mortal peril. A compensatory mechanism is then set into motion. These same American Jewish leaders, so convinced of the American Way of Life yesterday, are today extremely anxious to slow down a movement which they had fostered. And what is more, who dares say that we are completely through with anti-Semitism? I fear, alas, that the Jewish conscience has not been awakened for the last time. On the contrary, happily, hasn't the state of Israel interested more Jews in their own future? If for a long time assimilation was premature, today it is perhaps too late.

Until now, then, Jewry has had neither the ability nor the desire to assimilate completely. What is to be done before such profound resistance? Before an essentially collective phenomenon possessed of its own rhythm and its own intensity? Even had I participated fervently, the conduct and the destiny of my group were beyond my control and dominated me to a great extent. Only my youthful arrogance could have made me believe for a moment that we could get very far away from the ghetto. Like our Tunisian middle class, we were only the vanguard of troops which were pushing us from behind as much as we were clearing the way ahead. The whole body had to advance for the head to permit itself the slightest progression. Of course, we could discuss this point at length, approving or condemning, fuming with impatience or insolently braving the world which surrounded us. But whether we played the role which had befallen us, or gave it our own interpretation, I realize today that we had not in the least transformed the meaning of the fundamental themes of the drama.

THREE

I know very well I haven't finished with this difficult chapter.

"Forget about the ghetto," one might say, as I have sometimes said to myself. "Why don't you go your own way alone? You pretend your intention was to put your Jewish fate to the test completely, rigorously examine the different solutions. Assimilation seemed an acceptable way out to you. Are you then afraid of taking this path alone? Because your group did not follow you, because of masochism, stupidity!"

So be it. Let us suppose I had been able to go the road alone, far ahead, without looking back and without worrying about my people. Suppose I had had this strength or this indifference. I would still not have succeeded in assimilating. For here is the second objective impossibility of assimilation. In oppressive situations assimilation runs counter to the profound wish of the oppressor as well as that of the oppressed.

It is true that the candidate for assimilation continuously hesitates; he takes two steps forward and one back. It is true that, from the beginning, I wanted to preserve a private domain of my own. I was quite willing to pluck my feathers, to dye them if necessary, but only in order to deceive. I would have given up on the surface, so that I could better save myself more profoundly. Not through any particular weakness or cowardice (I can judge myself when necessary), but because the necessity of tearing oneself away from the self is never convincing, because self-rejection is surely one of the most revolting of gestures. I might have consented to a lot more than this; I might have succeeded had I not discovered what an exorbitant price I had to pay for my entry into the non-Jewish community. And—the supreme humiliation—without any guarantee of ever being tolerated.

In Paris I lived in the same building for several years. I could only be well satisfied with my neighbors who were quiet and courteous people. From time to time I exchanged a few words with them and, little by little, I found out who they were. I, on the other hand, instinctively refrained from revealing too much of myself. In this fashion they must have thought I was one of them, and I finally believed it vaguely myself. The fact is that only their reality filled the space of our relations; my own, I conjured away, repelled, rounded at the corners. But it was convenient and we lived in harmony together. I could at last tell myself that I was assimilated with my neighbors.

One day a new tenant moved into the building.

"Did you know," he said to me, troubled and scornful, "that the people across the hall from me are Jews? Polish Jews!" (Three months later we were North African Jews.) "The peace and quiet in this building are lost! You can't imagine how noisy these people are, how dirty and familiar. In the building where my sister lives, there is a Jewish family from Central Europe, and can you believe it . . . etc."

Suddenly, I was brought back to my senses, outside of this easy, apparently peaceful relationship which I had had with my neighbors. This man, with whom I was partially able to identify, brutally reminded me of the abject image he had of my people, an image which was an integral part of his universe, of this universe which I wanted to adopt. And now what was I to do? Was I to be silent or did I speak? Speak! A dignified protest. "Watch your step! I am a Jew myself, etc. . . ." But then, once again, there I was out in the open, a Jew! A Tunisian Jew! The disguise was over and the assimilation stopped. Would it have been better for me to keep silent? To say nothing? No, because even if the disguise remained, the assimilation had still been arrested, identification suddenly became impossible. How could I continue to identify with people who despised and insulted me? Inside, at least, I again become distant, different, and separated as usual.

Of course I might have insisted, pursued identification at any price, but one can see the cost. In order to reach my destination I would have had to ratify this condemnation of my people and myself which the non-Jewish universe proposed. In order to assimilate, I would have had to assimilate not only the model, but also the accusations and the injustices. I would have had to swallow the poisoned fruit.

I retreated, it is true. At this precise point the oppressed generally retreats—but it is because he comes up against the others. In order to assimilate it is not enough to accept one's own laceration, this game of hide-and-seek with oneself and with others. One must consent to the scorn and the accusation; one must appropriate them; and finally, become the accomplice of the insulters and the persecutors. One forgets too often that if assimilation fails, it is more because of the oppressor than because of any reticence on the part of the oppressed. The refusal of the colonizers rather than the hesitation of the colonized was responsible for the failure of colonial assimilation.

Why did he refuse? I am not drawing the portrait of the non-Jew here; a book about the oppressor is equally necessary. I have, however, tried to answer this question in another book, *The Colonizer and the Colonized*. Oppression is too advantageous. Privilege is certainly the pivot of the colonial relationship. Why would the colonizer abandon a position in which he found so many benefits? If the privilege of the non-Jew is often more subtle, it is no less certain.

By assuaging the negativity of the non-Jew, the existence of the Jew permits the non-Jew to exist more strongly. He is surely not the most unhappy nor the most despicable of men since the Jew is even more unhappy and more despicable. He is surely not on the lowest rung of the social scale since the Jew is even lower. And if it sometimes happens that the Jew is not there, it is an anomaly and a shame which needs rectification; hence legitimatized racism. The scapegoat process fits into this mechanism. It is too convenient to have the Jew to crystallize all social, metaphysical, and individual evil. In short, the misfortunes of Jewish existence must help support and compensate for the misfortunes of non-Jewish existence.

And that is not all. Relative to the Jew, the non-Jew's positivity increases; he reasserts himself, enjoys more fully that which he owns and that which the Jew is not supposed to have. Stateless, the Jew serves as a reminder to the non-Jew that he has a country, without which he might not see its value. He rediscovers a past, a history from which the Jew is excluded, and must remain excluded. And there again, I remind the reader, it is not merely a question of purely verbal or psychological privileges. In an economic crisis or simply in the competition for jobs, the Jewish rival is thus actually eliminated.

If the Jew did not exist, then he would have to be invented. No society deprives itself of the pleasure of inventing its own Jew, be he the foreigner, the gypsy, or actually the Jew; in other words a different being, therefore excluded and separate, therefore suspect, therefore presumed guilty, therefore a most suitable choice for the crystallization of collective anxiety—an expiatory victim. That is why no oppressor can consent to the assimilation of the oppressed. For him it would be an imposture and a frustration. And in a way, it is; for even though the Jew still exists, the non-Jew is deprived of his most convenient scapegoat. This is the explanation of the rage caused by the Marrano; and what Jew is not, to some degree, a Marrano? The non-Jew is under the impression that he loses on all fronts: as a Marrano the Jew continues to exist, a foreign body, disquieting, all the more frightening because he is no longer mistrusted and, at the same time, he is no longer even useful.

In short, assimilation was one more half-measure, on my part and in the opinion of the non-Jews. So at last we must dare to formulate the decisive question. For anti-Semitism to be disarmed once and for all, would it not be necessary for the Jew to disappear? To end the Jewish condition, would it not be necessary to end oneself as a Jew? And since anonymity is an illusion, since one can hardly be nobody, a frank metamorphosis was in order. Was it perhaps necessary to transform myself into a non-Jew?

Conversion

5

In Christian countries real assimilation was called conversion. Could I have sunk to this degradation? In all honesty I don't think so. In any event, I would never have had the strength to take this step. But how could it be avoided? Conversion had to be faced if a definitive solution to this impossible destiny was to be found.

For after all, the world which oppressed us, periodically killed us, was Christian. Was there a better method for ending this absurd battle in which we always got the worst than our transformation into Christians? But, the reader may object, the *Christian* world was not the only one. Moslems occupied a large part of the globe, not to mention the Buddhists! Naturally one had to become Moslem if one lived among the Moslems, Buddhist among the Buddhists. Nothing was to be gained by dodging the issue in this way. Like assimilation, conversion was a fact;

Jews had been converted and were converting daily.

Assimilation was only a half-measure; it failed because it didn't go far enough. The unkind comparison of the assimilated person to a chameleon is more profound than it might at first appear; for however well he reproduces the color and the shape of his surroundings, however well he imitates their immobile rhythm, sooner or later he makes some surprising movement and reveals his presence. So he is not this greenery with which he hoped to be confused after all: he is not this brown soil whose contours he simulated; he is himself, an exotic animal, strange and a stranger, thus particularly vulnerable. And so he is soon captured or killed.

Moreover, conversion was the logical conclusion, the profound psychological truth of assimilation. Assimilation was an orthopedic operation on the body and the soul. It required constant refocusing and painful adjustments. That is one reason why the face of the candidate for assimilation was so often ridiculous or irritating. In principle, conversion would put an end to these odious contortions, close the gap between public and private life. Since Jewishness could not be lived harmoniously in alien surroundings, why not seek another unity? Of course such a total gift, the complete suppression of one's private domain, was a kind of symbolic suicide. But it was an optimistic suicide. If I must die, it is to be reborn in the image of my conquerors, in harmony at last with the universe which surrounds me. Wasn't the main point to live in peace among men? To love them and be loved? And wasn't the shortest route to this end to become perfectly identical with them?

Alas, this peace gets off to a bad start. In Tunisia each year there were a few cases of conversion; the example was hardly encouraging. Local snobbism dictated that the middle-class families send their daughters to study with the Catholic Soeurs de Sion. Consequently, from time to time, some little girl thought she was undergoing a mystical crisis and wished to be baptized or even to take her vows. The result did not make a pretty sight. The unhappy parents resisted, cried, threatened. The girl was exasperated by the obstacles placed in her path, and her tenderness often turned into hatred. A sort of cataclysm descended on the family who lived through several miserable years. Why this panic? Because the parents took upon themselves the convert's extraordinary condemnation of their group. The entire collectivity vaguely considered the convert as dead, having died an infamous death. The price exacted by conversion was an appalling struggle, the most painful there is; against one's own people.

I remember the extraordinary passions which were aroused at the mere mention of the name of a Jewish pharmacist from Bizerte who had been baptized a Catholic. He was known only as "that filthy X." They spoke with bitterness of his baptismal name. (He had chosen Christian, and with redoubled cynicism, they said, he decided to call his son Christophe.) They accused him of I-don't-know-what machinations with the diocese. One has only to think of the suspicious scorn with which renegades are viewed, even among those who welcome them. Do you know that "Marrano" means "pig"? One always suspects the convert of some sordid, if not downright evil, calculation. If the assimilated provokes some irritation, the convert calls forth fury and hatred.

Obviously this violence can be explained by the finality of the act of conversion. Assimilation is a gradual process of varied aspects, at once underhanded and necessary. Basically, every Jew undergoes it and, to some degree, gives in to it. Conversion is a unique and decisive act, a jump, the irreversible passage from one community to another, from one ideological universe to another. Moreover this irrevocable adoption of a new order seems

to condemn the old once and for all. In one stroke the
convert seems to want to assure his own salvation and to
proclaim the failure of the group from which he origi-
nated. In abandoning the group he labels it as unlivable
and unredeemable. Worse still, by effectively depriving it
of his own participation, he contributes to its approaching death and accelerates it. That is why even very powerful groups are upset by the act of conversion. They
resent it as an injury and a defeat, an attack on their
being. In brief, in the eyes of the original group, the convert is a traitor who deserves every punishment.

I rejected the convert's unconditional condemnation
on principle. Not that everything is false in this collective
intuition. Numerous conversions certainly endanger a
group. But they are symptomatic, a sign of the group's
anemic condition and not a sign of the convert's perversity. Later on I met the converted pharmacist from Bizerte. He was an unhappy man, terribly troubled at being
the object of all those attacks. He was obsessed by the
Nazi adventure and above all preoccupied with saving
his children from a new cataclysm. Now, just how mis-
guided was he? By some miracle, had Jewish existence
ceased to be menacing? The convert seemed to believe
that his group was bound to disappear. And if he were
objectively right? We know the answer: even if the group
were condemned to death, one ought to remain for the
sake of solidarity. This is debatable. Of what use is this
negative solidarity? Why persist in this collective misfortune? To save what? The values of the group, we are told.
But the convert has ceased to believe in them, or at least
he no longer cares about them. Why demand his fidelity
to something he no longer values? By temperament, I do
not like to join in these collective violent condemnations.
I suspect them because they are too easy. The fury and the
cruelty of which some believers, led astray in their faith,

are capable have always appeared suspect to me. Perhaps some day, for a change, one might examine the deeper motives of these zealous opponents of the convert and discover not simply heroism, moral rectitude, and purity.

No matter how much I argue the point, however, I know what self-repugnance I would have had to overcome. In the name of liberty and personal salvation, I absolve the convert as I do the assimilated. Perhaps with sufficient effort, I might have been able to imagine myself in the role of a convert. But here again, how could I have ignored the price of this liberty? My memory would never have been short enough to escape the burden of this terrible Jewish history. Above all, I could never have overlooked the despairing panic of my own people in the face of my conversion. Whether legitimate or not, I could never have discounted their angry and horrified bewilderment. At times I deplore their lack of adaptability down through the centuries, their eternal refusal when the door has been left ajar. But conversion has not been the historical solution to the Jewish destiny. This is another fact which I can regret, but most platonically. How could I have abandoned them to the dangers which threatened? How could I have kept them from interpreting my gesture as criminal treason? Nor could I have blamed them. Their anger would only have been the expression of their anxiety. In order to escape the hostility of the non-Jews, should I have accepted henceforth that of my own people?

There is a possible objection:

"Of what importance would the hostility of your people have been since they would have ceased to be your people? In leaving them you wished to end your involvement with them and their cruel destiny. Your doubts and your scruples were comprehensible before conversion, but afterward?"

As if it were that simple! As if one could leave a group as one does a railway station! And particularly the Jewish group which is a threatened minority and therefore demanding and exacting. Several converts have described this apparently paradoxical feeling. They did not feel they had left Jewry, nor had they ever wanted to.

"In adhering to the New Testament I do not feel that I have abandoned my people." (E. G. Berrebi, a Protestant convert.)

In fact, if the convert wishes to find his salvation, if he wishes to save himself from the Jew, he hopes to save the Jew which is in himself as well, and even to save other Jews; if not all Jews, then at least his own descendants. And if Jewry is impossible to forget, in this case there is an objective explanation: the nature of Christianity and the relationship between the two faiths. (I leave aside conversion to other religions, which for the moment would be theoretical.) The Jew who becomes a Christian does not completely break with the world of his past. He finds a new perspective, one which is cursed and abhorred by his people, but which unquestionably derives from his past. He opens a condemned chapter of the same book, and a main chapter at that, since it gives another meaning to the common history. On the contrary, far from having finished with Judaism, he is led to dig more deeply into it, more than he ever has until now. Most converts know the Jewish tradition better than most Jews. They reread the Bible, or read it for the first time; for the first time they become interested in Jewish ideology and history in a thoughtful way. These have always been profound and dogmatic Christian preoccupations, but the converts take them to heart more anxiously than the ordinary Christian, as ex-Jews and brand-new Christians. The paradoxical result is that the converted Jew feels more Jewish than the Jews and more Christian than the Christians.

"I have never been as Jewish as I am since I have become Christian," a convert told me.

"I am not more Christian than Jewish, nor Christian although Jewish. I am essentially Christian because I am Jewish. . . . Each day my Christianity reveals to me a little more the Judaism rooted deeply inside me, and my rediscovered Judaism, reviewed in the light of my Christianity, illuminates it with all its brightness." (Denise Aimé, a convert to Catholicism, in *Les Ténèbres Extérieures*.)

This hallucinating reminder, in the very midst of her new values, prevents her from forgetting the old, and the fate of her ex-coreligionists. The convert rarely allows anyone to speak ill of his ex-religion. He lends an attentive ear to everything favorable to the Jews in the texts and declarations of his new leaders. The famous Papal affirmation, "We are spiritually Semites," is a favorite pronouncement of converts who delight in it and cite it on every possible occasion. Nor do they have to look very hard. Christianity furnished them with all the ideological material necessary for this burning interest which they henceforth entertain for their ex-community. The origins of Christ were Jewish; the role of the Jews in Christian eschatology is everywhere abundant. And now they even discover the golden key to their terrestrial and celestial existence. To be authentically Christian, one must necessarily integrate Judaism and the Jews.

"This clearly shows what the convert's first duty is, not only to deny nothing [of Israel] . . . but to prove by one's whole attitude that one has denied nothing." (Denise Aimé, *ibid.*)

Alas, conceptual subtleties cannot resolve the real cleavage between two conflicting communities. In fact, only after he has left them does the convert discover that salvation comes from the Jews. He imposes on himself the new and imperious duty of looking after the Jews. But in so doing he only projects his own separation. In spite of himself, he becomes living proof that one cannot forget a too-tenacious past, nor decide upon a future chosen with such difficulty. In insisting on the Jewish genesis of Christianity, he strives to convince everyone, to bring together the two inimical parts of his being; he wishes to reassure himself twice.

The result is that he becomes odious to both parties. He insists on proposing a salvation to the Jews which revolts them, which inflames them all the more against him. In his desire to show them that he is not the egotist and renegade they imagine, since he returns with full hands, he only succeeds in arousing their suspicions of some added perversity. He is no less unbearable to those who have received him. The severest criticism of Christians I have heard came from the mouths of converts. They are like disappointed lovers. They accuse their new coreligionists of ignorance, indifference, and lack of purity. Their fondest wish is to restore their new brothers to the Truth Faith, that of the source! After a passionate indictment, one convert explained himself in these terms: "In every authentic Jew there is a prophet." And he sincerely believed that this time the true Jew was himself. In brief, the convert wants at one and the same time to be the true Jew and the true Christian. Won't he suffer henceforth from being neither one nor the other? Isn't this, in fact, what happens?

TWO

Conversion has never really tempted me. I have simply envisaged it as a logical, terminal stage of rejection. Self-rejection as a solution can only succeed in and by complete acceptance by others. In the Christian world such an identification presupposes conversion; our societies remain too deeply religious in their mental outlook, even in their institutions which on the surface seem the most removed from religion. But I was personally never able to go that far. When, in moments of great despair, I cried out, "Oh, to be Jean Dupont, French and Catholic!" I really meant, "Oh, to stop not being Jean Dupont!" I wanted above all to shed my Jewishness, this extraordinary presence in me, with ramifications in my smallest gestures, my slightest thoughts, indefinitely nourished by the sarcasm, threats, and aggressions of non-Jews. I did not sincerely imagine myself in their skin, nor more importantly, in their religious form.

When I thought about the Church and Christians (as Christians, of course), the predominant feeling was immediately one of revulsion. I know that I will wound many Christians whom I like or esteem. I also know that many Jewish readers will be glad to contradict me. It is because of such pivotal moments, among other things, that this book could only be written as a personal statement. I do not wish to involve anyone in my personal itinerary which I will continue to define as precisely as possible. However, I am convinced that these feelings exist to some extent in every Jew, just as they exist in every oppressed person in relation to his oppressors. And for a serious comprehension of Judeo-Christian relations, in the hope of their eventual improvement, it would be necessary to take this into account.

How can I explain just what the Church represented for me, a Jew? In Tunisia, I used to admire its organization, the powerful means at its disposal, and the flexibility of its methods. The whole Carthaginian Hill was its property; the statue of Cardinal Lavigerie stood at the entrance to the Arab town; the school system of the Soeurs de Sion; the Pères Blancs and their innumerable "Houses," set in the heart of the Medinas and their impeccable command of Arabic; the way it took care of its men, and resisted all political changes, even after the independence of the country. But I could never like the Church or even trust these too-enterprising, too-effective, too-constantly-underhanded men who were interested only in their own cause.

On occasion I have been struck by the calm of a chapel, but I have never been moved. In the midst of these kindly statues, the forest of tremendous columns, the superb organ, the golden richness of the altar, I have at times felt pangs of desire for the peace and security which emanate from a cathedral. Certainly it would have been good to have been inside and no longer outside with the tempest and the threat. But I could only dream of such things by forgetting who I was, in ceasing for a moment to be a Jew, in evading my habitual and historical relations with the Church. As soon as I had returned to my senses, as soon as I thought of the Church in relation to me, a Jew, I rediscovered this mixture of rancor and revolt, of irony and irritation against such overbearing pomp, an ideology so contrary and so triumphant, a power so pervasive. Far from abandoning myself, I found myself once again on the defensive.

Purely personal feelings? Because I was abnormally distrustful and offended? Or because Christianity as such was particularly repugnant to me? I don't think so. As I have already said, I had been educated by Christian philosophy through the intermediary of those great Western philosophers whom I so admired. And I did not regret either the education or my respectful admiration. It was my actual day-to-day relations with Christianity and with Christians which were tainted.

I have often noted similar stories in the works of Jewish writers. One of our Catholic professors at the lycée in Tunis had founded a sort of club ("Crossroads," he called it), open to all, "Moslems, Jews, and Christians." The point of the association was officially very vague, and I did not understand it too well. But I became attached to the founder until I realized suddenly what its real aims were. One night, when I was especially disturbed by one of those obscure youthful anxieties, I confided in him. I spoke of my family, myself, my problems, and the difficulties of my life in general. Did he deem that the propitious moment had at last arrived? Suddenly he showed his cards, and eschewing the amiably neutral tone which he affected ordinarily ("Moslems, Jews, and Christians") . . . with eyes shining, he uged me to give myself at last to Christ, the only way out, the only hope, etc. . . . I was flabbergasted. Although my reaction was perhaps exaggerated, as is often the case at that age, I felt he had tried to take advantage of me. The meetings at the Crossroads turned out to be a method of leading us all into a single path. A few years later I relived that same scene, an echo of the first. I was in Algiers, hungry, almost ill, when I was told to go to a priest who, they told me, often gave work to impoverished students. Voluble, confused, probably intentionally to drown the poison, he ended up all the same by putting his cards on the table. I never saw him again, but I have never forgotten him.

These were ordinary episodes and a constant propensity of the Church. During a chance conversation in a weak or abandoned moment, they propose Christ, suddenly revealing that all their friendliness was but a means towards an end pursued through you. I have never been able to overcome the disgust with which I regard this aspect of the Spider-Church, lying in wait for its prey. And my first reaction was almost always one of distrust and retreat, to look for the meaning underlying the charity and the apparent good sentiments of such and such gesture of the priests and the faithful. Why *Catholic* Aid? Why l'*Abbé Pierre?* And why *Christian* Aid to the little Negroes, and *Christian* Aid to the little Chinese? I asked myself why, if their good deeds were really for the benefit of others and not a calculation, did they entitle their aid "Catholic" and assign a priest, in other words, a uniform?

I realize that upon reflection and with some good will, all these charges can be minimized. Their seriousness is debatable; it is possible to consider it all a matter of personal taste; that, if the result is worth it, the revulsion and resentment are unimportant. As the reader can see, I am not trying to dramatize at all costs. But it is obvious that to leave Jewry would not have been enough for me, that I had to be able to enter Christianity. In the state I was in, the second half of the road was just as painful as the first.

My revolt attained its height during and after the war. It has often been said that the horrors of the last war convinced many Jews of the necessity of conversion. What has been less noticed, however, is how firm in their differences and separation many Jews have become since then. What good Jewish soul could take a single step into the Christian world? The hair-splitting discussions of whether or not Pope Pius XII knew or did not know, was or was not silent, make me laugh. As if, at the time, we had entertained the slightest hope of seeing the Church lift its little finger to save us! It never occurred to us, and we never dreamed of asking it to. Without suspecting the Church of being on the side of the assassins, we confusedly placed it among those indifferent powers which, at best, ignored our existence. Today I realize that distinctions must be made. There were generous priests, as there were Vichy collaborators. And if the Church has by and large taken a neutral stand, it was a matter of self-preservation and saving its own flock. But then, whether it was guilty, in agreement, or simply neutral before the awful death of so many of my people, how could I have dreamed of becoming part of it without shame, without dishonor?

"Once more the Cossacks attacked Poland; once more they slaughtered Jews in Lublin and the surrounding areas. Polish soldiers dispatched many of the survivors. Then the Muscovites invaded from the east and the Swedes from the north. It was a time of upheaval. . . . Entire communities of Jews turned Christian and though some later reassumed their own faith, others remained in darkness. . . . But the moment the Jews caught their breath, they returned to Judaism. What else could they do? Accept the religion of the murderer?" (Isaac Bashevis Singer, *The Slave*.)

The best and the worst elements, accumulated throughout history and by the successive needs of men, are to be found in Christianity, as in all important doctrines. Albert Camus once wrote that to discuss Christianity one had to consider it in its most beautiful and most consummate expression. I would have liked nothing better! Unfortunately, my relations with Christianity and with Christians were not limited to texts and ideology. Between Jews and Christians was it really a matter of debate in which the best man won? Was it really a question of books and arguments or of fire and armies? When we faced their hostile troops, of what importance to our lives were the thoughts of distant promoters or the present doctrinaires of Christianity?

Of what importance was Christianity in its original state, or doctrinal purity (And what does this purity

mean? Where does it end? Where does the soiling begin?)
if the majority of men living under Christianity have
prevented me from living?

The matter was both simpler and more serious: one of
life and of honor. An oppressed person cannot, without
decaying, without walking over his own heart and over
his pride, completely adopt the values and the customs of
his oppressor, however beautiful and strong in themselves, however superior to his own. For a long time the
sight of a Christian priest aroused in me the same anxiety, the same potential aggression, as that of a policeman.
He personified, in his own way, the same iniquitous and
all-powerful order. For too long, the Church has given a
free hand to its persecuting or murdering offspring, as
well as arming them from time to time. It has too long
legitimized injustice; it has weighed down my existence
as a Jew, until it has irrevocably deformed it. Whether it
wished it or not, the Church has become the sum total,
the condensation of the hostility of the world which surrounds me, one of the symbols of my oppression.

THREE

If I have not yet mentioned the doctrinal aspects of conversion it is because I did not feel they were the most
important. A theoretical condemnation of conversion by
itself would probably not have prevented the disappearance of the Jew. The concrete conditions of the life of the
Jew among accusing and aggressive non-Jews made conversion unbearable, though these conditions seemed to
demand, call for it.

Having said this, however, the logical difficulties inherent in conversion are not any slighter. To use a philosophical term, there are two serious aporias of conversion,
one for the non-believer and one for the believer.

I have already spoken of my attitude toward religion

in general. I freely acknowledge that it occupies an enormous de facto position both collectively and with innumerable individuals. But I personally had no philosophical use for it whatsoever. On the contrary, I felt that the philosopher's main aim should be to elucidate our actual relations with the world, and thereby help men to overcome their need for religious and magical beliefs. In short, I am definitely to be counted among the non-believers (among Jewish non-believers, because for me Jewishness is not only a belief but an objective condition). What kind of intellectual juggling would have been necessary for me to reconcile what I wanted to be with what seemed so unacceptable to me? I am amazed that the mystical significance of conversion is so often overlooked in this debate. For conversion to another religion is, after all, first and foremost an act of faith! To respect, to adore a God presupposes at least a belief in his existence! And why would I have gone out looking for another system of beliefs when I had already discarded that of my own people?

I did not reject Christianity in toto because total rejection of such a great and complex doctrine would have been over-simple. But how much more difficult it would have been for me to accept it in toto! There are good and bad elements in Christianity, but how the bad outweigh the good! How could I swallow these dogmas and "mysteries" which to me were nothing but insoluble obscurities of doctrine? Or at best, the mythical expression of our ignorance and the difficulty of living? How could I endure this incoherent mixture of clerical decisions, made over the centuries by men and imputed to a God? The brilliance of the Christian doctrine stems from the historical position it occupies. In the Occident everything speaks of it, so that its voice is amplified by thousands of echoes. But when I reflected for a moment, when I took the trouble to delve more deeply into the social and historical glory, to go beyond the contingent splendor, I found so many half-truths, hasty conclusions, and such feeble reasoning that the philosopher in me lost patience and soon became contemptuous.

My attitude was, of course, that of a non-believer for whom truth is a cardinal value. Would I have been easier to please if I had been a believing Jew? Would the habit of bending my mind to sacred propositions have made me more understanding, better disposed towards a similar mental attitude? Not at all! The act of conversion is more serious for the believer than for the non-believer. The mystical aspect which is debatable for the non-believer, in this instance becomes terrifying: God is betrayed, not only men or logic. Conversions are frequently accompanied by morbid phenomena. Many converts, whether believers or not, end up on the psychiatrist's couch. "When I was baptized I had hallucinations," one of them confided to me. "I thought I heard my father crying in the back of the church." The long Jewish martyrdom was, among other things, the price to be paid for this inability to adapt. A true believer cannot renounce his eternal salvation for a miserable and temporary carnal rescue. Faithful Jews have generally preferred to let themselves be slaughtered and burned rather than to abandon themselves to this mystical treason.

The Jewish believer, if he is sincere, cannot even have my relative and relativistic indulgence for Christian values. For him, aside from the deception and the cruelty of a heresy which has so harshly triumphed, the Law has already been stated and Christianity adds nothing new. What would he do with a doctrine of which he already possesses the best elements and which contains, on the contrary, so many erroneous embellishments? Our most humble artisans expressed their scorn for what appeared to them fairground paganism with its carnival-like processions, the adoration of a plaster of Paris god, human skeletons, fetishes, and even the bizarre trinity, inconceivable to a Jewish mind.

And I must admit that I didn't think them absolutely wrong. What is fundamental in the Judeo-Christian experience is an insistence on the moral betterment of humanity and, on this subject Judaism has said practically everything. For me the mysteries and the imagery of Christianity were above all of poetic or symbolic interest. Am I, in spite of myself, insidiously contaminated by some cultural chauvinism, by the well-known Jewish pride? Perhaps, but whether it was naïve pride or lucidity, acquired through contact with the great Christian documents, I could not concede to Christianity the slightest spiritual superiority.

In both cases then, conversion seemed to me degrading, absurd for the non-believer, a sacrilege for the believer, a disaster for both. Even today I do not see how these two aporias are to be resolved.

By grace, they told me! One day, some converts say, they experience an extraordinary psychological upheaval. They are caught up in a sort of wave which carries them away in spite of themselves, sweeping everything before it, the old faith and the old ties, and throws them powerless and enthusiastic into the arms of the new truth. It has even happened to rabbis who have, I understand, immediately asked for Christian baptism. I do not want to open a supplementary philosophical or clinical discussion here. I reserve my own opinion on this discovery or pseudo discovery of the self and the world. Not that I doubt the sincerity of those who have experienced this type of conversion which is, perhaps, the only one which interests me. But as this experience does not depend in any way on one's own will, it is clear that we often cannot expect solutions by this means nor envisage it as a way out for all. At best it is a happy experience reserved for the few.

In spite of everything I might still have been able to convert by overlooking the irrationality and the sacrilege and without awaiting grace. The reader may feel that I have exaggerated the significance of conversion; that it could be simply considered as a tactical measure. But if conversion is nothing but this empty act, a simple ruse, who cannot see the indignity increased by such a decision? For then one goes from degradation to deception, which for me is another form of degradation. Was it necessary to become unworthy in my own eyes to escape being unworthy in the eyes of others? But we are caught in a vicious circle. It is obvious that such a position is uncomfortable. Did I have to live a life of lies and affectations? Was that the peace I had paid for so dearly?

I promised myself, and I dared promise the reader, the utmost precision in this recital of my itinerary. I know perfectly well that for this conclusion to have been completely convincing I would have had to have experienced conversion myself. But I could see perfectly well who I was! And I knew enough converts whom I questioned intensely. They had almost never found peace. Far from abating, their difficulties had generally increased, or at least changed form. Almost always their conversion complicated rather than simplified their relations with themselves and with both the old and the new groups.

Christ did order his new disciples, "Leave your families!" But in fact they can never be completely left behind and the convert lives a new drama. A terrible feeling of guilt prevents him from blossoming in the destiny of his choice. Simone Weil's extraordinary severity is common knowledge, as is the furor of other converts. It is because the Jewish group's obstinate existence endlessly bears witness to its own defection. The convert would have had to take along with him his wife, his children, his ancestors, his friends and acquaintances, in short, all Jewry!

His relations with the adopted group are no less painful. A converted university professor explained to me the painful distinction by which he lived. "I belong to the Church, but not to the mass of Catholics. . . . Of course, I find them again in God! But here below, I remain in conflict with them." A woman who converted after her marriage to a Catholic writer told me, "Intellectually I agree, but how can I say it? The heart . . . the heart does not follow." Rarely, in effect, does the convert give himself completely; partly because he does not feel completely adopted. I am not speaking of the systematic a priori anti-Semitic rejection. The odious Drummont's incontrovertible judgment is perhaps familiar: "A converted Jew may make one more Catholic, but not one Jew less." The flair for hatred has in this instance hit upon something: the converted Jew, although a statutory Christian, feels and remains different in his own eyes and those of non-Jews. "No, it is not a solution, " a converted friend of mine wrote to me. "If I say that I am a convert, that complicates everything; if I don't say it, people speak in front of me and very often some anti-Semitic phrase pops out . . . it reverberates in me and has repercussions on my husband and on our life. And it is the little everyday details that make up a life. The truth is that I live in apprehension. The truth is that I am saved from nothing."

Far from being an act of economy, a liberation or an improvement, conversion seems to aggravate the torments of the convert. Far from liberating him from his Jewishness, in most cases it makes it even harder to bear. The convert can't win for he exchanges one anxiety for another, perhaps a more subtle one. Just what did he hope to find in conversion if not appeasement and reconciliation with the world and with himself? Why would I have converted if conversion could not liquidate my odious fate? In conclusion I might add that the failure of conversion appeared more significant and more dramatic to me than that of assimilation. Like assimilation, conversion was and proved to be impossible. But it was also the ultimate gesture which I could have made in order to change the course of my destiny.

Mixed Marriage

6

And so we come to mixed marriage. I should have dealt with this after assimilation and before conversion; in the dynamics of rejection it occupies a position about halfway between the two. If I have not spoken of it until now, I must admit that it is because my own involvement has been a stumbling block. It so happens that I myself have a mixed marriage and that I published a novel, *Strangers,* in which I was imprudent enough to describe, in the first person, the drama of a mixed couple. I knew that everything I wrote would run the risk of appearing suspicious and attributable to my experience alone; that I would hardly be believed if I stated that the story was not exactly my own; and that the use of the first person was nothing but one literary device among many. In fact, I almost gave up on this whole chapter.

But I told myself that dropping this chapter would be contrary to my pledge in undertaking this whole study, and I do not wish to dodge any issue which can serve to bring it to a successful conclusion. So I will plunge right in. Yes, I have a mixed marriage, and this entire account is based on personal experience. But I continue to believe that to live through an experience, overcome it and think it through is the best point of departure for an understanding of a situation.

This said, it is still not easy to discuss mixed marriages —an immense problem for the human race and its future. I will limit myself here to marriages between Jews and non-Jews, although numerous difficulties and hopes are common to all mixed marriages. For every oppressed person, in effect, mixed marriage can seem like the ideal solution. By marrying the oppressor's daughter, he places himself on an equal footing with him. Between partners so diversely treated by fate, this solemn and equalizing act is a triumph for the weaker. It is a promotion and a brilliant revenge. Willy-nilly, he creates, and imposes on his powerful adversary, unquestionable ties of the most intimate nature—those of flesh and blood. "Right is won when the bed's undone." Henceforth, even despite his own embarrassed objections, the oppressed will benefit from the advantages of his new relationship with the privileged clan, even if these are indirect. With a little luck, he can even gain their respect and esteem. In short, mixed marriage can seem the royal road to liberation for the oppressed. Unlike most of the other solutions which demand his submission, self-rejection and respect for prevailing values, mixed marriage obliges his new ally to accept him as he is.

With my own mixed marriage I did not seek to resolve such a clearly defined problem. I was twenty and I fell in love. I am, however, convinced that one's marriage choice is not haphazard. I was Tunisian, Jewish, poor, unknown, having just arrived in Paris, the city I had dreamed of for twenty years. I married a blonde, Catholic French girl whom I had met at the Sorbonne. (The only thing I forgot was money—she had no more than I, but I was, in this respect, totally unconcerned.) By my marriage, in one fell swoop I created solid and multiple ties which joined all my disparities to this prestigious universe I was burning to conquer. I might add that in a way I succeeded, because I made the best marriage possible considering what I was and what I still am.

I have had to conclude, however, that mixed marriage is no solution to the difficulty of being a Jew. It was experience that convinced me of this; and not only my own. I have discussed the problem with dozens of men and women who have lived the same adventure; I have witnessed many dramas in which this conjugal difficulty was the basis of all conjugal difficulties. On the other hand, I have almost never seen a mixed marriage alter an oppressed condition and very rarely have I seen it subjectively help someone.

I will not again go into the conflict which inevitably arises with the original group. No visible attempt at assimilation—and mixed marriage is obviously one—can be accepted without anger by the Jewish community. Is the community wrong? Perhaps; I have already said that I don't consider assimilation a catastrophe. On the other hand, it would be hypocritical of me not to state the facts: mixed marriage means disappearance in the long run, or else it is a futile effort. This explains the agreement between believing Jews and atheist Zionists in condemning it. In other respects, arguments are not lacking for a lessening of the condemnation by the synagogue. On close inspection of the texts, it appears that this doctrinal rigidity against mixed marriages probably only dates from Esdras; in other words, from the return from Exile. Solomon marries the daughter of the Pharoah, and the Bible finds nothing particularly bad to say about this: Abraham marries his servant Hagar; and Ruth was a Moabite. In any case, the angry condemnation of mixed marriages serves little purpose, as they have always been frequent in Jewish history (from which, among other things, stems the insistence on their condemnation), and today, according to some Jewish leaders, they have reached alarming proportions. Nonetheless, the doctrine of condemnation has prevailed. A constant exogamy, infinitely more important than admitted, exists alongside a tireless, almost visceral rejection on the part of all Jewish groups.

The reason for this duality is always the same: the members of a minority group are always tempted to lose themselves in the majority, and the menaced group can never happily accept such a hemorrhage. In the past few years most of the associations of colonized students have taken a violent position against mixed marriage. Anyone who contracts one is almost considered a traitor. This is absurd. The colonized who marries outside his group does not necessarily accept the oppression but wants, on the contrary, to circumvent it—in his own way, it is true. At most, one might say that the act of mixed marriage comes before that of revolt, at a time when the oppressed still believes that imitation of the oppressor can save him. One can still understand, in any case, that it is not always possible to bear the firm and profoundly anguished reprobation of one's own people, even when it is unspoken or ironic.

The best advice which can be given to a young mixed couple is not to live in either the husband's or the wife's native city. Once the first blush of enthusiasm passes, the number of young couples who are totally ruined by beginning their lives together in the midst of family and friends is enormous. But moving from one's home town is obviously a serious step, and why get into a situation which requires such an extreme remedy? If I had to choose between the safety of the group and the happiness of the individual, by temperament and by philosophy, I would choose happiness. Had I been convinced that mixed marriage could procure peace for the soul of the Jew, an end to his anxiety, and a better adaptation to the non-Jewish world, I would have extolled the virtues of mixed marriage, no matter how serious this choice. But all things considered, I have not noticed that it simplifies the fate of the Jew, nor that it helps him in bettering his relations with other men—Jews or non-Jews—or with himself.

For mixed marriage doesn't even satisfy the Jew's great desire for reconciliation with the world. In fact, the fruit he so eagerly sought can have a strange, almost unbearable taste. What had often been an ambiguous wish, a vague hope, will be realized to the point of obsession. Henceforth, the marriage partner will embody the non-Jewish presence which thus becomes continuous, daily and obligatory, even in their intimacy. The reader will protest: if from the start I consider the partner in a mixed marriage as a representative of a strange and hostile group, the game is lost before the dice are thrown. Why stigmatize the marriage partner and his group a priori as strangers, as adversaries? In this way, doesn't every marriage become impossible?

I don't want anyone to think that I take a pessimistic or defeatist view of marriage. On the contrary, I rate marriage and the couple very highly. The couple is probably man's best chance; his second and last chance; which permits him to find anew, or best approach, his lost unity; to overcome the separation which is to me the cruelest misfortune of mankind. Every marriage is a drama; the highest hopes are placed in it, and therefore it must always fall somewhat short. Every marriage brings together beings who are separate and distant from one another; that is why each marriage is a difficult and perilous undertaking. For this reason, wouldn't it be better not to further complicate it? Isn't it wiser to shorten the inevitable distance as much as possible in the beginning? Every marriage is difficult, and it is a simple fact that a mixed marriage is much more difficult than others.

TWO

I have already underlined the importance and significance of the family for the Jew. I did not hide its dangers, the debilitating warmth which insulates the Jew from the turbulence of the outside world, thus making him all the more vulnerable. But for this very reason the family remains his surest sanctuary, a private domain and a last retreat in a hostile world. In his efforts to appease, must the Jew open up the last dike he possesses to the influx of the world? Must his impression of security—illusory as it may be but nonetheless valuable—be destroyed? In his attempt at reconciliation with the non-Jews, he runs the risk of self-disintegration and self-destruction.

In the final analysis, the success of a mixed marriage depends on the amount of dislocation which each partner can withstand. One cannot know in advance how greatly such apparently trivial details as cooking or bed-making methods may disrupt domestic life. And the newness of the situation is certainly more disturbing when the distance is increased by differences in such important and unavoidable institutions as religion or language. While adolescent strength is still intact, one can joyously brave everything for long periods and then one day suddenly weaken and sigh with nostalgia. I must admit that I have sometimes dreamed of a Passover evening, of Purim, if for no other reason than their picturesque qualities: waiting for the prophet Elijah, the door open to the night; the story of the traitor Haman, hanging on the gallows; the rustling of silk handkerchiefs, overflowing from the paschal basket, like the caress of warm and soothing flames. . . . Childish pleasures, perhaps, but why deny oneself forever all recourse to childhood? Why weigh all one's anchors? For a mixed marriage is that, also, a voyage without return. Does a person have to remain a hero all his life, functioning tirelessly at his highest pitch?

Am I dramatizing again? Couldn't I have solicited my wife's help from time to time in satisfying my nostalgia? Or, failing that, I might have set out alone to quench my thirst at some source outside our home; or, better still, taken my wife with me to friends or relatives. Wouldn't she have agreed, if only out of love for me? Of course, and especially in the beginning of our marriage she went along with the best will in the world. It was I who quickly came to feel it was an imposition and a lack of human respect towards her. Why should I have insisted that she mimic my ghosts? I also sensed that it was a danger for our union. Wasn't I emphasizing our cultural differences, insisting on the fact that we did not share the same memories, the same inner universe? In seeking reassurance for myself, wasn't I running the risk of wounding her?

As victims ourselves, we too often forget that as individuals we can hurt as well as be hurt. I must say here that the anger of the Jew or the colonized toward mixed marriage is too often placed in an exclusively egotistical context. The vast majority of non-Jews who marry Jews deliberately accept a difficult future. Most of the young European women who marry Moslems return to their husbands' country with their hearts on their sleeves, ready to understand and adapt to everything. Even more, taking a critical view of their own past, they are often distrustful and reserved toward their own compatriots in North Africa. But human beings are made of more than good intentions and a concerted desire to do the right things. Sooner or later they learn that though one can give a great deal, one cannot and must not be completely submerged in others. And as they learn about themselves by comparison, how could they fail to realize—even if the thought had never occurred before—that they belonged to a more powerful and dynamic civilization? Although they might not hold their own people in great esteem, they had not totally disowned them, though they might have thought this to be the case. And I hasten to add: why ask them alone to pay the price of a common enthusiasm? Isn't suffering reciprocal? In short, their attitude stiffens and, if they do not retreat, they at least begin to exist for themselves, with a kind of painful shock. In general they are not even able to go back. Beset, since their marriage, by the suspicion of their own group, mortified by their own failure after so much defiance, feeling guilty themselves, they no longer even try to confide in anyone. Many young women, having abandoned any hopes of integrating themselves into their husbands' group, end up by withdrawing into a final and complete solitude.

"He feels more deserted with a second person than when alone. If he is together with someone, this second person reaches out for him and he is helplessly delivered into his hand." (Franz Kafka, *Diaries,* May 19, 1922.)

Mixed marriage, seemingly an ideal ground for synthesis and harmony, for an opening and for reciprocal generosity, more often turns out to be a dangerous crossroad, open to currents from every direction and offering every opportunity for all kinds of collision. The mixed couple, instead of becoming an ideal oasis, a neutral zone between mutually devouring groups, is often transformed into an arena in which the whole world erupts. How can the partner help representing and constantly bringing to mind the others? How can the partner help bringing the viewpoint of others into the intimacy of their daily lives?

Even into the abandon of sleep? And conversely, how can he not awaken somnolent suspicions of others, nor bring to life old ties and hidden guilt feelings?

It is paradoxical, but I have seen it many times: mixed marriage revives Jewishness, makes one more aware of the Jewish fate and awakens solidarity in people who have never before felt it. As in the case of conversion, it is after a mixed marriage that many Jews become the most sensitive about their Jewishness. These men, who so badly wanted to open their arms to others, suddenly turn violently against them. This is, of course, because they feel guilty towards their own people. Thus these Jews feel they must furnish their people with proof, march in the front line of combat and be among the most orthodox or at least the most obedient. This may also be an angry reaction against the majority group which has succeeded in surrounding them. Although it may seem paradoxical, it is not an accident that so many national leaders of ex-colonial countries (the Tunisian Bourguiba, the Algerian Ferhat Abbas, the Senegalese Senghor, etc.) had also contracted a mixed marriage before becoming the nationalist leaders of their people.

Inversely, I have noticed that the husband is often outdone by the wife who, not content with merely embracing the cause of her husband's people, reproaches everyone for lack of vigor and combative zeal. One of my Zionist friends married a Parisian who literally dragged him to Israel. Another, a woman whose husband was a very active F.L.N. militant, finally accused her husband of weakness and ended up participating alone in some very dangerous missions. In short, it was not enough for them to stop being adversaries; they had to become accomplices, alter egos; they had to identify totally with their new role. Saints, in short; but I must admit that I mistrust saints and situations which give rise to them.

In any case, the result is too often an unhealthy, confused situation in which each difficulty becomes complex, filled with every kind of malaise, without anyone knowing clearly what caused what (if, for example, the partner is fought through the intermediary of the group or the group is fought through the intermediary of the partner); a situation in which almost everything is blown up, aggravated by so many diverse problems, weighted down by the historical and social conjuncture. I remember the somber period of the Franco-Tunisian conflict, during which each event fell like a stone on the water, creating ripples and undercurrents among the young mixed couples we knew. I can still remember the sardonic joy of one of my Moslem friends at the announcement of each catastrophe, even the most atrocious—a slaughter, swimmers machine-gunned on the beach, a grenade tossed into a crowd of children. When the Dutch dikes gave way and Holland lived her night of terror, he danced with glee; to him the Dutch were nothing but the colonizers of the Netherlands East Indies. Certainly justice was on the side of the colonized, and in this awful confrontation almost any means were permissible; but aside from the principles of the battle, there was the concrete suffering and death of individuals. One may become accustomed to it, but how is it possible to rejoice so uninhibitedly? But since then, I have asked myself if it really weren't his wife that he wanted to injure. . . .

Fortunately, such paroxysms were rare, but a little saintliness was needed to emerge from such situations without scars. And, without being absolutely certain, I am convinced that mixed marriages break up far more frequently than do others.

Strangers was not our story, that of my wife and myself, nor even a true story. It was a condensation of hundreds of stories, reduced to their essentials and dramatized to make a single, coherent work which would command the reader's attention. But we had at least a presentiment of all these fluctuations of the heart and mind, and we had anticipated all these upheavals and to some extent lived through them. Only a steady, positive desire for happiness and intelligence, a determination to maintain self-control and health allowed us to forestall, disarm and exorcise them. In short, if we have, as I hope, been successful in this important venture of our life, our marriage, it is *in spite* of its mixture.

THREE

This conclusion embarrasses me all the more since I refuse, in spite of everything, to despair of mixed marriages and persevere in one myself. I feel that a totally negative attitude regarding it would be absurd. How is it even possible? It has been said that every marriage is mixed, and the saying is profoundly true. All marriages are necessarily a form of exogamy; otherwise they would be restricted to incest, to marriage between brothers and sisters. Marriage is the traditional, the simplest way of opening up groups without damaging them; of uniting them, causing mutual participation without offending.

That is why those generous people who have faith in humanity and wish for a unification of peoples are in favor of mixed marriage. The most rigid people, the traditionalists, the chauvinists and the xenophobes distrust and reject it as a peril to their group. And I seem at this point to be on the side of those insensitive guardians of tradition. But what can I do? Unfortunately, distrust often uncovers more truths than the well-intentioned sympathy of the generous. When the colonized began to agitate a few years ago, the colonialists understood far better than our friends on the Left that it was the end, their end, and because of this they fought. All this time our friends kept saying that no one would be forced to leave. . . . Since each human group today tends towards

isolation and has its own prejudices, it is unfortunately
the traditionalists who make the most exact prognostica-
tions on the future of mixed marriages. It is also true that
these traditionalists contribute to the best of their ability
to make this future as bleak as possible. . . .

In addition, both sides think in terms of the group. As
soon as mixed marriage is mentioned, most people immediately bring up general ideas of politics and morality,
philosophy and religion. And mixed marriage does have
this extra significance which deserves careful thought. It
is not enough for me to hope that mixed marriage might
hold the key to so many difficult problems; I want to
know if I myself can find in it the solution to my problems of integration in a difficult world. It is not enough
for me to think that mixed marriage is socially moral or
historically desirable. I want to know what it will cost me
and if this price does not exceed my strength.

I have learned that mixed marriage is above all a personal, individual and intimately experienced drama. I
have very often noticed that, apart from their philosophical or political opinions, the majority of people around
me do not approve of it. Even in the so-called civilized
countries, marriage between Jews and non-Jews remains
suspect, and marriage between Negroes and Whites is
positively scandalous. How many times have I indirectly
learned that a woman who has nothing against the Jews
has nevertheless said that she could never have sexual relations with them? That certain liberals or even revolutionaries who loudly, and even sincerely, affirm their anti-
racist positions declare that they would never let their
daughters marry a Jew. And I might add that in a sense I
almost understand these parents who want to protect
their children from these unnecessary difficulties, because
it is objectively true that these marriages may complicate
their lives, and that they are therefore a priori less desirable than others. It is not an accident that the literature

of mixed marriage is generally a black literature, which almost always describes the unalterable mistrust of the foreign partner. Even a queen continues to be called "the foreigner," and Marie-Antoinette, Queen of France, remained "the Austrian" to the end.

"And then there are the children." Here we come to one of the most common objections of the man in the street. But this is justified, and even if the interpretation is often debatable, the objection is well-founded. Generally children strengthen the couple whose fate is often sealed with this common responsibility. But, at the same time, the children bring to light the problems inherent in the situation and make the parents more aware of the importance of their acts, for they demand immediate and decisive choices which are pregnant with serious consequences. Suddenly all theoretical options which had been relegated to the background and left in a convenient and equivocal shadow require urgent attention and threaten to materialize by themselves and at random. Should the boy be circumcised? According to religious law, there are only eight days to decide after which the boy will remain uncircumcised. Should the girl be baptized? It must be done within a year or it will never be done. What upbringing should they be given? A religious upbringing or not? How do you present them with the fact of being Jewish? I still don't know what I should tell my children about Jewish history. Besides, is it exactly *their* history? Should I decide that it is and that they will be Jews? After all, their mother is not Jewish; they are thus only half-Jewish, and I no longer believe in the privilege of the male!

Once started down this path a little voice whispers: "And if you decide to make them into non-Jews? Why push them in one direction rather than another?" The little voice becomes more insidious: "Why not spare them a dangerous destiny? Why deny them a salvation to which they are already half entitled . . . ?" But immediately my heart begins to beat more quickly. In answer to the little voice comes this loud cry which I have so often heard uttered by so many partners of mixed marriages: "I do not want to become a stranger to my children." Of course this is valid for both partners. Of course it is a question of irrational fears, an often unfounded anxiety to which time will fortunately give the lie. But there is, at the heart of most mixed marriages, a real obsession with exclusion.

In the abundant literature on mixed marriage, there often comes a melodramatic moment when one of the partners, generally the one belonging to the stronger group, rises up theatrically and, under one guise or another, declaims: "Go! Go back to your own people! You are nothing but a Jew!"

And if things almost never really happen in this tragicomic way, a pale specter does float between the partners which could at some point murmur something quite similar. This fear of having the division revealed and enlarged poisons even the silences. The most awful possibility would be that one of the children should pronounce the curse. A non-Jewish professor told me that when the Germans came to arrest his Jewish wife, their twelve-year-old son suddenly and violently reproached his father: "Why did you marry a Jew?" It is a fact that some half-Jewish children hate their mother or father for this reason, as if one part of oneself began to persecute the other. I suppose it is like a form of insanity. . . .

So what do you do? Do you do nothing, so that the child is drawn toward neither side? This would seem to be the most honest solution, the one to which the least prejudiced mixed couples most often turn. But let's not pull the wool over our eyes: in this case, to do nothing is a decision with the probable consequence that the children will become part of the majority. There is in the so-called neutrality of the non-Jewish partner a not always unconscious hypocrisy, "Let's not influence the child, neither of us. Let him choose for himself and decide when he can." This also means: Let society have its way —the school, the neighborhood, the surrounding culture. This is really playing it safe; the entire society will do the job. The reader may answer that many, perhaps the majority of Jewish couples today contribute nothing to the Jewish upbringing of their children either, but this is absolutely not the same thing. A young Jew of Jewish parents, even if these parents are indifferent to Judaism, will be Jewish because it will never occur to him to be anything else. I have already stated that a cultural milieu is not only a religious milieu. Jewish parents feel this and can envisage the future of their children, and their common future with them, without affective anguish, in spite of the uncertainty of this future.

Paradoxically, the Jew who makes a mixed marriage feels a greater anxiety concerning his children. He shoulders a supplementary anxiety and complicates further an already complex future. In most cases, an unnamed apprehension gnaws away at the partners of a mixed marriage, its presence manifested by small compromises, petty bickering and little tricks which would be distasteful if they weren't so laughable.

"I insisted on calling my son Emmanuel," I was told by a Jewish friend who had married a Catholic. "On thinking it over, I sincerely believe that I wouldn't have done so if I had married a Jew. I don't particularly like the name, but I spontaneously felt that in this way the child would somehow be more mine."

In Tunisia, the French wives of Moslems picked ingenious Moslem names which might one day be adaptable if the child were to live in France: Saphia (Sophie), Hedi (Eddy), or Nèdié (Nadia), etc. . . .

Sometimes all this degenerates into an open struggle,

and in this more or less artful wrestling for the children, the grandparents are not the least tenacious or the least ferocious. Approaching death, more concerned about the species than about the individual, they will use the most unfair methods if necessary—clandestine baptism, masses and catechisms for each occasion, or secret visits to temples. My own mother fought as hard as she could, alternating tragic sighs with enticing smiles, offering her services to organize the ceremonies, etc. I can't even hold it against her; it was her world and she thought it was ours, that of my childhood. She could not agree to let a child, born in part from herself, be torn from her.

In short, the children, far from being a bond, might well become the prize. And when you think of the fragility of these little creatures, and how badly they need this unique being called Papa-Mama! How dismayed they are when faced with dissension between their parents and how extraordinarily they can sense the slightest discord. Certainly a healthy stomach can digest anything, and stable children can in the end overcome anything. But why place an extra obstacle in the already long and arduous road to adulthood? Isn't it better for them to start out on a solid ground, leaving difficult adventures for later on, should they discover in themselves the desire and courage for them? I don't know what the statistics are, but I would not be surprised if a greater percentage of troubles, failures and defeats are not to be found in children of mixed marriages than in children of other marriages.

I would like to remind the reader here that we have not been discussing all possible mixed marriages; my purpose was not that all-inclusive. I simply wanted to know if mixed marriage was an answer to a particular situation: that of the Jew. I must honestly say that it is not. Nor have I been trying to moralize or be political. It is difficult enough even to live when one is Jewish. Why exclude any possible way out of the many difficulties if one can thereby find happiness, or simply peace? Had I discovered that mixed marriage was a passable or even partial solution to the Jewish problem, I would have considered it favorably. But I have been convinced, by my own experience, by all that I have seen and heard, that a Jew who marries a non-Jew resolves nothing either for himself or for his children. As a Jew, that is. Obviously a mixed marriage can be a good marriage, but only to the extent that it can be separated from the quality of being mixed and to the extent that the Jewish fate can be disregarded. A Jew who makes a success of his marriage to a non-Jew has succeeded in his marriage, but he has in no way alleviated his Jewishness.

The day will perhaps come when mixed marriage will be one of the most helpful and beautiful contributions to the great communion of peoples of a single humanity. But first, or at least at the same time, these peoples must cease being hostile to one another. The tempting oppression by the strong of the weak must find other outlets. To sum up, far from being able to resolve the present, brutally unjust relationships of groups among themselves, mixed marriage requires a relative equality among groups and an end to oppression. The scorn of the oppressor and the resentment of the oppressed must end before we can hope for the majority of mixed marriages to succeed. For the moment, far from resolving the conflicts between Jews and non-Jews, far from smoothing out the differences, far from eliminating the misfortune of being a Jew or a Negro, mixed marriage forces individuals to bear the weight of the differences and the burden of a more intimate barrier, even more obsessional and guilt-ridden. Moreover, this is not very astonishing: mixed marriage is an effort towards individual salvation within a conflict of groups. Instead of avoiding this conflict, partners in a mixed marriage are obliged to live as part of the dramatic laceration of these opposing groups which invade their union and the very individual. In short, instead of hoping that mixed marriages might solve the problems of the Jewish fate, we must solve the problems of this fate before encouraging such marriages.

Self-hatred

7

ONE

I was not far from a horrible feeling which we had better call by its name, self-hatred. I still have anguished memories of this short paroxysmal period. Luckily this state of mind is practically unlivable, and one cannot remain in it for long. This sort of self-destructive fury is, at least with most oppressed people, far more frequent than one might suppose. In this light it would be interesting to reread the autobiographical novels of colonized North Africans or the cruel tales of Negro novelists. As astonishing as it may seem, you will discover that the mechanism of self-rejection is once again at work. There is no absolute rupture between the first harmless verbal camouflage, as in name-changing for example, and the furious fight against the self, or even suicide. They are gradations of the same impulse, easily recognizable in the diverse and multiple aggressions which the oppressed inflicts upon himself.

The other day I found a bundle of notes which I had entitled no less than "Anti-Jewish Writings." In them I pointed out, stigmatized, or ridiculed the weaknesses, faults, and errors of my coreligionists in Tunis. Of course, I also proposed a vast program of psychological, moral and social reforms. We were to have a more precise political program, abandon commercial careers, be more discreet in public, speak more softly, etc. . . . Oh! I had the best intentions. I have been able to compare dates: I wasn't even in a period of breaking away; on the contrary, I was an active militant in the Jewish cause. But desiring the good of my people, I demanded that they first change their ways. They all had to be noble and unselfish and courageous. They all had to be paragons of virtue; otherwise they fell under the gavel of my condemnation.

Why not exact the same purity from others? From the Tunisian Moslems who lived almost the same life that we did, or from the French Christians whom I nonetheless admired? Was there still in my attitude a sort of reverse pride? Surely a little, since I wished my people to be the best. But above all, this perfectionism, so frequently found in Jews, was based on a confused irritation against them, and of course against myself who belonged to them and shared responsibility with them. The behavior of non-Jews did not seem to necessitate my criticism. The colonial solidarity of the French, for example, who excluded us all, did not yet call for a declared revolt on my part. Despite their age-old slumber, the customs of my Moslem cocitizens appeared perfectly natural to me. But the life and the conduct, the habits and the customs of the Jews were not perfectly natural and, basically, I rejected them under the pretext of improving them.

Doubtless this anxious self-examination was linked to the objective threat, to the distrust of others. If the Jew accuses and protects himself, it is because he knows he is accused, and he protects himself in advance. Without doubt, the Jew's irritation with himself was only an echo of the foul accusation. The result was nonetheless a kind of steady drilling, boring right into the wound of the Jew's own self-doubt. When I went back to Tunisia a few years ago I had already done a lot of traveling and I had somewhat forgotten how a compact Jewry, in which the humiliation of each individual had repercussions on all, lived and reacted. One day, in the suburban village where I lived, after an argument over some small matter with my neighbor, he cried, "You are nothing but a Jew like the rest of us. Don't forget it!"

He was telling me in his way, I suppose, that they found me too aloof. I had suspected as much. Preoccupied by our moving in, by a book I had to finish, and also by shyness, I had been unable to establish easy contact with the villagers. But in tones which hurt me he also cried out the little esteem in which he held us and himself. We were nothing but Jews in this country where the French Christians were the upper crust, where the Tunisian Moslems were in the majority. However, he was warning me that no aloofness, no affectation would be enough to make me pass for a member of one or the other of the dominant groups; I knew this too. This self-contempt was also to be found in the Moslems, another group oppressed by colonization. But ours was not a uniquely colonial phenomenon. How many times in Europe have I not heard this same bitter accent of wounded modesty? "We are too noisy! We show off too much! We ought to . . . ! We shouldn't . . . !" Has some offense been committed? "Ah! A Jew again!" Just three or four years ago a great collective embarrassment overcame us during the tribulations of a swindler named Joseph Joanovici. Its effect was similar to that of the Staviski affair on the preceding generation. We were obviously angry at our offenders for replenishing the arsenals of the anti-

Semites; we imagined the probable sneers of our waiting enemies. And the result was that we viewed our delinquent coreligionist with increased severity, and more violent anger. Having escaped the French police net, Joanovici found asylum in Israel. There was no extradition convention between the two countries. For most non-Jews the affair was juridically closed. Most of the Jews, on the other hand, thought that Israel should have given up Joanovici. The crime committed by a Jew is always more severely judged by the Jews themselves and calls for a more severe punishment. The reader is perhaps familiar with Pierre Daninos's bitter joke: "The Irish don't like the English, the English don't like the French, the French don't like the Germans, but nobody likes the Jews, not even the Jews!"

TWO

Assuredly there is a certain Judeophobia of the Jew, as there is a Negrophobia of the Negro and an anti-feminism of women which are the logical end results of self-rejection. Fortunately this Judeophobia is never total for it would lead to death, which does sometimes happen. It is almost always attenuated and combatted by the Jew himself. The same interlocutor who severely criticized our "faults, which we have to admit," explained a minute later that "we are more intelligent and more humane." Be that as it may, these manifestations of self-hatred could be carried to an atrocious degree.

The reader will again protest, "What hyper-sensitivity!" I have written elsewhere, for example, that I was at one time absurdly troubled about my own body. I asked myself if the shock of circumcision might not have contributed to the Jew's anxiety or even his collective defeat. To reassure myself I had to find an example of another circumcised people, the Arabs, who had all the same con-

quered half of the Mediterranean world. Now, such notions, barely disguised, abound in the works of Jewish
writers. On a trip to Israel I could not help thinking,
"Here is the crucial occasion to verify if the Jews on the
whole are biologically identifiable." I recently discovered
in reading Arthur Koestler that he had at least asked
himself the same question. Here is how one of his heroes
sees an assemblage of Israeli pioneers:

"Joseph was struck by the ugliness of the faces around
him as they were lit up in the intermittent ghastly flash
of the searchlight. It was not the first time that he had
noticed it, but tonight his revulsion against this assembly
of thick, curved noses, fleshy lips and liquid eyes was particularly strong. At moments it seemed to him that he was
surrounded by masks of archaic reptiles. Perhaps he was
over-tired and the one cup of sweet wine had gone
straight to his head. But it was no good denying to himself that he disliked them, and that he hated even more
the streak of the over-ripe race in himself." (*Thieves in
the Night.*)

I am well aware that Koestler is suspect to many people, unjustly in my opinion. Here then is an American
writer, a member of one of the largest Jewish groups in
history. Isn't this basically the same anguish and doubt?

"A long time he stood staring at himself, at his fore-
head, his chin, his nose. It took many moments of de-
tailed inspection of his parts before he could see himself
whole. And he felt as though rising off the floor. The
beating of his heart caused his head to nod slightly in
rhythm. Saliva filled a little pool in his throat and he
coughed. In the mirror in his bathroom, the bathroom he
had used for nearly seven years, he was looking at what
might very properly be called the face of a Jew. A Jew, in

effect, had gotten into his bathroom. The glasses did just what he had feared they would do to his face. . . . Now with the lenses magnifying his eyeballs, the bags, being colorless, lost prominence and the eyes fairly popped, glared. The frames seemed to draw his flat, shiny-haired skull lower and set off his nose so that where it had once appeared a trifle sharp it now beaked forth from the nosepiece." (Arthur Miller, *Focus*.)

These are, I repeat, extreme sentiments, frightening and paroxysmal. Moreover, neither Koestler nor Miller dared make the ultimate confession: Koestler's hero is only half-Jewish, and Miller's is a false Jew accused of being a Jew who almost ends up by accepting the accusation. The cause of these disguises and half-measures is obvious. It is difficult to admit to the malaise; one can hardly take pride in one's self-rejection. The Negroes who spend millions of dollars each year on illusory products such as hair straighteners and skin bleachers carefully conceal this activity. In an almost unbearable scene Richard Wright describes the reactions of shame and hatred of a young Negro woman, surprised during a hair treatment session. The number of Jews who shorten their noses do not all decide on this measure for purely aesthetic reasons, but they don't acknowledge this fact. All this points to an absurd and cruel truth; these measures are the poisoned fruit of a too-long oppression. What inner anxiety and destructive forces have invaded these people to make them disfigure their faces so! The oppression must have been most effective if the oppressed tries so furiously to respond by delirium to the delirium of the oppressor!

For self-rejection has far-reaching and corrosive effects on a human being; it attacks his body, language, traditions, religion and culture. I remember the notices posted in the courtyard of the Alliance Israelite school: "Speak

French!" It was, of course, in part a colonial rejection of the Arab tongue. But it was more than that, for we added with great seriousness, "We mustn't speak Arabic; it sounds Jewish!" For over and above the Arab language we were aiming at our Jewishness. Elsewhere it was Yiddish or Ladino which had Jewish connotations. And, as what was Jewish varied so from place to place, this rejection was objectively really absurd. To dress in bright colors was Jewish. To speak too loudly, to call out, to gather in the streets, was Jewish. On the days of Yom Kippur the stampeding of the Jewish crowds in front of the synagogues, too small to hold everyone, threw many of us, especially the youngest, into agonies of embarrassment. Few believing Jews would visibly display the star of David on their chests as the young Christians did their cross. In reality we all acted as if it were just a little indecent to be a Jew, while at the same time we felt obliged to drive back this shame. When I decided to entitle my last book *Portrait of a Jew* I tried the title out on some of my friends; the result was overwhelming. While most of the non-Jews encouraged me to keep it, most of the Jews were against it. Some of them tried honestly to explain their malaise. "I would certainly not want to have to ask out loud in a book store, 'Give me *Portrait of a Jew!*'"

What is more serious, however, is that this indecency is not reserved for others; the Jew is often embarrassed with himself, like some adolescents before a mirror. As soon as I left the rather restricted circle of Jewish activists, I discovered the immense ignorance of Jewish intellectuals concerning everything regarding Judaism and themselves. I remember my astonished consternation at the first Israeli propagandist whom we saw.

"Ah! If you only knew," he kept saying, "if the Jews knew what riches they possess! How proud they would be!"

It certainly was a matter of pride; not only were they

unfamiliar with these riches, but they didn't want to know about them. After this period of militancy, I myself suddenly lost all interest in them, as if I wanted to dig a ditch between Judaism and myself. I studied everything, including the Chinese and the Indians, who were not yet fashionable—but the different Jewish, Hebraic, Yiddish, Biblical and Talmudic literatures . . . no. I would willingly have cited an Arab proverb, but not one of the Judeo-Tunisian sayings, which were, however, numerous and racy. And yet, having been long fascinated by our common problem, I at least knew what I was giving up almost willingly. Most of my new friends did not disguise their contempt for these texts (what rubbish!) which they had never even glanced at.

It is true that an equivocal aura of religious significance surrounded these works and made them suspect to liberal Jews. But would the idea of rejecting a priori all of Descartes, all Pascal, or even all Kierkegaard and all Malebranche because they are authentically Christian philosophers have occurred to us? On the contrary, certain Jewish university students carefully studied all the Christian Middle Ages, but deliberately ignored Maimonides who was an important author of the period. Another juggled with moral doctrines, but abstained from considering Jewish morality other than through the detour of the Judeo-Christian context. My first week at the Sorbonne I succeeded, in spite of myself, in acutely embarrassing one of our professors, a sociologist and a Jew, by asking him if we ought to study the relationship between Spinoza's thought and that of the rabbis of the period with whom he strongly quarreled during a good deal of his short life. By a paradox which we failed to perceive, and fearing to recognize our own culture, we coldly sacrificed an aspect of this universal culture which we so cherished, and on the point which should have concerned us the most.

Let me state clearly that I do not revere these texts, nor am I seized with wonder each time I read a page of the Talmud or the Cabala. I do not in any way affirm that this specifically Jewish tradition is the best in the world nor that it can totally satisfy any Jew today. I will take this matter up again later and state its exact significance for me. But I do not believe that our problem is posed in terms of absolute pre-eminence or unprecedented discoveries. I continue to find all cultural chauvinism ridiculous. But I must admit that in a still largely particularist world it is not useless for me that this tradition should exist. For it does exist, and the fact is that in some ways it is more important to me than are others. The collection of the *Pirke Abot* ("Sayings of the Fathers") is as good a collection as any people possess; Jewish wisdom has its own originality among the wisdoms of the world. And, since I continue to recognize myself as a Jew, since I no longer wish to disappear, then I will simply no longer consent to this systematic mutilation.

In short, like all the oppressed, the contemporary Jew finds all his own culture progressively amputated. While in the ghetto he was content to be a parasite of his own past, he now decides to forget it. For the face of the oppression has changed; to survive today, it is better to resemble the oppressor. And so we had to tear out our souls and scour our features; shorten our noses and get rid of our vain nostalgia. We judged the old heritage as undeserving of our attention, for it contained no usable truth, no beauty, perhaps, other than mystic. And if one day we needed to talk of mysticism, or theology, it was no longer necessary to call upon Bar Yohai, Ibn Paquda, or Ibn Gabirol since we were familiar with Saint John of the Cross or Saint Theresa of Avila, or the very admirable Thomas. Ask a cultivated Jew point-blank what he understands by theology or mysticism and I am certain that he will cite *The Dark Night of the Soul* or the *Imitation of Christ*.

Of course, we must add in his favor that that is what he was taught. But on the whole, even in this domain, his point of reference is Christian.

THREE

Am I giving the impression that I condemn any and all self-rejection? I repeat, not exactly. Every oppressed person rejects himself, at least at first when he sees no other way out of his despair. And I maintain that every Jew has more or less rejected himself. This impossible self-directed anger, this awful malaise in which I have lived, I have observed too often in those around me. It is, in fact, this tension and the way each Jew handles it which gives him his special characteristics and the originality of his Jewishness.

However, I could also see the implacable logic of this rejection. Either it resolved nothing or you always had to go one step further, to destruction, to death. For you cannot tear yourself apart without cruel and continual psychic destruction. The oppressed almost always becomes ashamed of what he was and what remains as a vivid reminder of his defeat. What's more, he still is, to some extent, what he was, since his existence remains differentiated and separated from others. His past subsists at least in his religion, even when poorly practiced; the old ancestral language still smolders on the grandparents' hearth; his history continues to pursue him no matter how clever his flights and his defenses. And so his impatience increases; he becomes furious with all the resisting elements within himself which prevent him from completely resembling the others and passing unnoticed. If he could he would pitilessly tear off his cumbersome old skin with no regard for the grave wounds he would thus inflict upon himself! Self-rejection sours and turns into hatred.

Today I still have to make an effort to extirpate such memories from myself and put them down in black and white. (And I have the feeling that few people will want to recognize such feelings.) But what does the anti-Jewish Jew wish for, if not that self-rejection? How can the determination, the despair, and finally the death of Simone Weil be otherwise explained than by this impossible fight against herself, through her people? Without going to such extremes, how can we describe some notorious Jewish behavior? Dr. Zola, son of the famous writer, told me that at the time of the Dreyfus Affair the Jewish bourgeoisie laughingly affirmed that the two Jews who had done them the greatest damage were Jesus and Dreyfus. It was a joke. But, added Dr. Zola, had it depended on them they would surely have hushed up the affair and left Dreyfus alone in his cell.

Let there be no mistake, this feeling against the Jew who calls attention to himself and to other Jews is already a kind of self-hatred. We have not yet forgotten the bitter discussions which raged during the affair of the Russian Jewish doctors stigmatized by Stalin as the "White-coated Assassins." The most violent, the most ready to justify the death penalty of these unfortunates, were uncontestably the Jewish Communists, and moreover, the Jewish Communist doctors. Baruch Hagani tells that the great Trotsky, who was asked to help put an end to a pogrom, refused. He did not want to take sides in a question of nationality or religion. He had his reasons. Refusing to consider himself as a Jew, considering the Russian Jews solely as Russians, why should he intervene as a Jew in favor of Jews? But the end result of this false neutrality was the continued assassination of his own people. And would he have refused to help an Uzbeck or Tcherkesse community in peril?

I have even known some Jews who were frankly anti-Semitic. I was amazed to see some of my school friends from good middle-class Jewish families join a political organization which had an avowed anti-Semitic program. Was this an egotistical wish to save their own necks by joining, in advance, the camp of the probable conquerors? Or more foolishly, did they think their good will would disarm the future asssassins? History has witnessed some of these political simpletons who, in hopes of attracting the good graces of the incendiaries, have procured them their kindling. And hasn't it been said that numerous Jews were among the first donors to the Nazi coffers? But I do not think that my friends were capable of such calculations. We were of an age when cold Machiavellianism had no place in our political conduct. I followed the career of one of these madmen quite closely. He lacked neither courage nor generosity, but he stupidly suffered from thwarted snobbism and a social ambition which he thought was unattainable because he was a Jew. He thought he had found a way out by joining the *Jeunesses Croix de Feu* and working fanatically with them. Later on he volunteered for the notorious paratroopers. The last time I spoke to him he explained that his party was not against all Jews, only some of them, and that in fighting against those few Jews he was doing us all a favor. He obviously did not convince me. On the contrary, I was certain that my poor friend now hated the Jewishness which stuck to his skin and prevented him from living among the people of his choice. He had a frenzied need to battle this Jewishness and himself, and one day I heard that he had attempted suicide.

At the extreme of self-rejection there is a sort of death-fascination and a morbid interest in whoever wishes our death. A relative of Gobineau's revealed to me his astonishment at the number of Jews who were passionately interested in the personality of the racist writer and who came to glean souvenirs from his family. Moreover, it is a Jew who first thought of publishing his complete works.

After the war an American Jewish professor, Milton Hindus, made another racist writer fashionable—Louis-Ferdinand Céline who is, unfortunately, excellent. The hatred directed towards themselves which attracts many Jews cannot be solely explained by their apprehension; it is probably because it reflects their own self-hatred. I can no longer judge these unfortunates as severely as I used to, for I have understood how one can wish to get rid of an implacable destiny. Only I learned at the same time that self-rejection can never be a real answer to an oppressive condition. Actually, it leads to this paradoxical result: the Jew rejects himself to ward off the rejection of others, and in so doing he confirms their rejection and consents to the condemnation and the sanctions which they exact. The internalization and passing on by the oppressed himself is one of the most dramatic aspects of the oppression.

"To the point where at one moment I found myself, without wanting to put myself there, in the state of mind of an anti-Semite," a young and overly sincere Jewish writer recently wrote. (Raoul Eskenazi, *Elie le Malrenv.*)

Not long ago the Larousse dictionary printed that the French Socialist leader Léon Blum was in reality named Fulkenstein. The indignation of family and friends was very great. They threatened Larousse with a suit and had the edition confiscated. They were right. I do not know whether Larousse did it intentionally, but to state, in France, that a politial figure is in reality nothing but a foreign Jew disguised as a Frenchman is to disqualify him objectively in the eyes of the majority of Frenchmen. But in their over-emotional reaction to this accusation, by taking it to court, the Blum family recognized in fact that it was insulting to be called Fulkenstein. In their own way they ratified the opprobrium; they agreed to play the game according to the rules imposed by the anti-Semites. To be a foreign Jew in France is a sort of defect; therefore one must protest violently if one is accused of being one.

But what should they have done, the reader will ask? Frankly, I don't know. Perhaps they should have simply shrugged their shoulders? "You claim that my name is Fulkenstein? So? There are lots of French Catholics of Russian or Italian or German origin who have had fine political careers! Isn't the head of General de Gaulle's cabinet called Palewski? And aren't some other French statesmen called Bodanowski, Schuman, etc. . . ? I suppose that in designating me as Fulkenstein you wanted to insult me? Well, you're wasting your time because I recognize no injury in the fact of being named Fulkenstein."

But actually, this shrugging of the shoulders, this superb indifference, would only have been possible if we had not accepted the language and the rules of the insulter; in other words, had we not already become the accomplices of our own misery. Certainly I do not see how, living among others, we could have avoided adopting their values, the values which irrevocably judge and condemn us. Self-rejection had to become part of the Jewishness of the contemporary Jew. But the absurd logic remains; the oppressed can only reject himself and self-rejection can never resolve anything.

Worse still, having set out to save the oppressed, self-rejection ends up by destroying him. And the more successful the oppressed is at it, the more he destroys himself. In the same way many women—and some of the most lucid, and the most dedicated to winning their freedom —have been led to an absurd condemnation of their maternity. Who has not been struck by the little importance Simone de Beauvoir accords in her works to this beautiful and great feminine state? How can these courageous women not see that this shame and hatred of maternity are nothing but the veiled rejection of their femininity? In other words, one of the most insidious masks of their oppression?

Would it be too much to say now, in concluding this part on self-rejection, that far from liberating the oppressed, it contributes to his oppression? For it helps to shape this figure of the oppressed which I am trying to trace throughout my different books.

part two

SELF-ACCEPTANCE

"God was not made for man, but man for God."

PAUL CLAUDEL, Correspondance

"The rabbi, an uncle of his, sent an emissary to ask if he had repented.

'Tell the rabbi,' Varady cried, 'that I remain a Jew. At no time did I deny my religion or my people. But I still hold, and more than ever, that man is more important than God. . . .'"

ELIE WIESEL, The Town Beyond the Wall

The Encystment

8

Nonetheless, I did not begin my Jewish itinerary by rejection or indifference. My young
life at home and at school was regulated by
daily ritual and religious holidays which
were never questioned; Saturday was our
holy day of rest. The Jewish community of
Tunis was sufficiently large and self-suffi-
cient so that, for a time, I was able to believe that it would form the background of
my whole existence. Unlike many European
Jews, I needed no particular deliberation or
historical impetus to *return* to the Jewish
world. I knew from the start, and without
regrets, that I was part of it.

Chance, or my temperament, even led me
to be militantly involved. One day a young
scout leader came to wait for his troop at
the lycée; many of them were friends of
mine at school. At first I made fun of their
uniforms and cowboy hats, but then I agreed
to accompany them on one of their outings;
this was the beginning of my entire political

life. As it happened, these scouts were innocent only in their appearance. Youth organizations in Tunis provided an excellent front for all kinds of subversive activities. We learned more about tossing grenades and marching than about the three-finger salute. Twice a week, for some years, I learned all that the regular school could not teach me: the doctrines and precepts of revolutionary action, plus a very good Jewish education, ranging from the Bible to the most modern Hebrew poets. On Sundays, we would set out for the country, pretending to be Israeli pioneers. We didn't even forget to imitate the internal bickering of the distant, young national movement. This is how I broke my first pair of glasses, in a fight with an opposing group, the Betarim, whom we pompously called our "Fascists."

Thus, whatever my subsequent doubts and the violence of my rebellion, they took place over and above a very basic allegiance. I have never, even during the most serious crisis, evaded my responsibilities to the vanquished that bore me. And I have always in some way believed that peace with myself would ultimately depend on rediscoveries, the exact nature of which I was simply not yet aware.

However, the nature of the question soon changed. I was trying to live by standards which required something more severe than this spontaneous bond made up of family memories and adolescent enthusiasms. I had to know the meaning of a resolute attachment to Jewry, a serious adhesion to Judaism and, finally, a deliberate acquiescence to my fate as a Jew.

I know very well that most Jews have never tracked down their Jewishness in this way. And many of those who loudly proclaim themselves Jews-and-proud-of-it today would beat a quick retreat if they could measure the consequences of their verbal boldness. Neither yesterday's lethargy nor today's foolish insolence have helped solve

our common problem in the least. I wanted to understand myself completely and to find my exact place in the
midst of others. Wasn't it essential to ask myself first of
all where such an inquiry would lead me? If one accepts
oneself as a Jew, just what does one accept? What logical
conclusions and what acts? What resources, too, were at
my disposal? Of what did this well-known Jewish culture,
of which we were so proud, consist? What was the value
of this celebrated religion, a religion defended up to the
funeral pyre? Only by answering these questions would I
know if this radical self-affirmation, severe and coherent,
could in the end furnish a definitive way out of the misfortune of being a Jew.

TWO

I am not writing a novel, and I am not trying to sustain
the curiosity of the reader, so I will at once state that I
did not find the solution to my problem as a Jew in an
acquiescence to my fate. I tried it, honestly, I believe, for
a long time. Acceptance did not eliminate the suffocating
ties of the Jewish fate; it pulled them even tighter. Worse
still, in order to avoid the new difficulties created this
time by an affirmed Jewishness, I had to cheat myself and
give up my most cherished conquests as a free man. To be
a Jew, I needed to commit an offense against my dignity
as a man.

Today I am ashamed of what I supported and heard
without protest. It is as if we were all seized with a selec-
tive and accessory foolishness as soon as we approached
our common problem.

During one of my recent visits to Tunis, once again
overwhelmed by the misery of the ghetto, I wrote an arti-
cle which was, perhaps, too full of pathos. In it I described the extraordinary overcrowding, the promiscuity,
the undernourishment and the mental stress of the peo-

ple. I concluded by advocating the disappearance of the
ghetto. Carried away by pity and indignation, I was certainly radical and Utopian in my approach. It was necessary, I felt, to tear down the ghetto walls and disperse the
people throughout the modern and airy sections of the
city. I expected to be vaguely laughed at for my economic
naïveté, but commended all the same. To my astonishment, I brought down on my head the most violent protests in the name of "Jewish spirituality." I underestimated, it would seem, the "immense wealth" of the
ghetto, the "intensity of its inner life."

Actually, I had underestimated nothing at all. Concentration had certainly more effectively maintained our
family and religious traditions. How could I have failed
to realize that we felt more at ease within the ghetto than
without? I myself had often described the pleasant sensa-
tion of warmth, relaxation and security which I found
here and there during my walks along the cluttered
streets, safe from the ironic and hostile eyes of the outside world. However, I was beginning to think that we
paid too high a price for this illusory peace.

The integrity, quite relative furthermore, of our traditional ceremonies and customs did not seem worth the
decay of bodies and even of spirits any longer. (Imagine
my childish consternation when I learned, apart from the
number of cases of tuberculosis and syphilis, the figures
for mental illnesses: contrary to what was thought, these
were far more frequent than in other sections of the
city.) Other Western communities could well afford to
envy our "intense spirituality." I told myself angrily that
they didn't have to pay the bill. If this famous spirituality could only flourish on the dungheap of misery and
sickness, I would not be inconsolable at its transformation—which is what happens, after all, to all Jewries as
soon as they have access to Western civilization.

Nevertheless, I could see by the uproar that I had

touched on a very sensitive point. Obviously, they preferred this collective intimacy, however morbid or hunger-
ridden, to the dangers of fresh air among others. I came to
discover at the same time a fundamental truth: the
ghetto was also inside the Jew. It was more than a stone
wall and wooden doors, more than a collective prison imposed by others; it was an inner wall, real and symbolic,
which the Jew had built. This fortress which the Jew had
slowly prepared against the hostility of the world was one
which he would be horrified to see crumble, leaving him
naked and vulnerable before a potential enemy. Since
then, each time that I have dared touch upon this barrier, visible or invisible, or dared question its advantages,
I have aroused the same distress and unleashed the same
anger.

It is true that only the ghetto permitted the intense
communal life of the Jew and defended him against erosion without and within. In this sense, it is understandable that the Hara of Tunis or the Mellah of Casablanca
should be enviously admired by some Western communities. "We are no longer worthy of the ghetto," a Parisian
Jewish intellectual told me seriously. I had trouble understanding him until I had observed Western Jewries. I
am convinced that they were almost all inhabited by the
same vague dreams. Every Jewry, however wealthy, opu-
lent and self-confident, is the conscience of a ghetto; its
nostalgia for a more homogeneous and warmer community is the nostalgia for a lost ghetto. There is no doubt
that a Jew who wished to affirm and fully live his Jewishness had to strengthen or reconstruct a kind of ghetto and
carefully guard its walls, whether real or symbolic.

Unfortunately, this stronghold, built up by the tides of
the others, will always remain besieged. A stroll down a
heavily populated Jewish street such as the rue des Ro-
siers in Paris vividly gives this impression; it is a closed
world, living painfully and disastrously within itself.

The Jew who accepts himself in the non-Jewish world to some degree adopts a psychology of the besieged; he is always on the alert, with constant rumination, an inner armor and an always-ready riposte.

In the space of a few months I visited the Mea Shearim section of Jerusalem and the Hassidic community near Spring Valley, outside New York. I was struck by the similarity of their collective attitudes. One wondered, in both cases, if the meat had not been raised and butchered on the spot; if the hats and clothing, so perfectly unsuited to the climate, had not been manufactured from designs produced in the dreams of somnambulistic artisans. I have described at length in *The Colonizer and the Colonized* and *Portrait of a Jew* what must be *encystment* of the oppressed. Spring Valley and Mea Shearim are extraordinarily concrete incarnations of this. Mea Shearim especially, with its life rigorously enclosed within walls blind to the outside, its crowding of a community on top of itself, its continuous growth towards the center in successive layers, forms a strange and disturbing little abstract city.

These are, of course, extreme cases which give an almost physical impression of a falling back on the self and a kind of collective schizophrenia. But every ghetto is to some extent a world outside space and time, and each man of the ghetto places himself more or less outside the space and time of the majority among whom he lives. I have been to a few gatherings of orthodox Jews in cafés in Paris. The most disturbing moment is when they pull their yarmelkehs out of their pockets and, under the inquiring eyes of the waiter and the other customers, place these small circles of cloth quickly on the tops of their heads. I was not sure, each time, that I did not notice their eyes roll imperceptibly, stealthily observing the other customers until they had become accustomed to the spectacle. And it was a spectacle. Such an assemblage of beards topped by these curious hats produced quite an effect. It was clear that my companions were trying to cut out, to some degree consciously, in this Parisian café, a special area for us. To reunite us, even in the midst of strangers—this elevated the symbolic pillars of a Jewish community. Instead of living in a ghetto, these devout Parisians took their ghetto with them. "The Jews of the Diaspora," writes an Israeli humorist, "recite in their morning prayers, 'My God, give us this day our daily ghetto.' "

In the extreme, the Jew who accepts himself as a Jew tends to construct a small but complete world, mental as well as material, inside the world of others. He takes all kinds of Jewish newspapers and magazines, builds a library of Jewish works, lines his walls with Jewish objects, sees almost no one but other Jews, introduces Hebrew or Yiddish words into his conversations, often grows a beard and puts a yarmelkeh on his head. He decides, in effect, to lead an exclusively Jewish life. Ideally, he would even construct the future with the same stones and from the same blueprint. He would open purely Jewish schools where his children could grow up in an enclosed milieu, protected throughout their formative years.

I do not ridicule or condemn this abnormal rejection of the world, just as I did not completely condemn the temptations of self-rejection. I cannot forget the origins of these serious perversions of Jewish behavior. What discomfort and fear can force a man to this desperate act: to withdraw his child from the world of other children and put him back into the educational system of the Middle Ages! I know how unbearable it must be for the already-wounded Jew to see his son returning home from school dressed as one of the three wise men or to hear him accuse the cowardly Jews of crucifying Jesus.

But I well know that one can live in that state of sleep-walking. I spent some of the strangest years of my life in that way. It was only with great effort that I woke up to what was going on around us, to the things that would greatly influence our destiny, the next war for example. I was better informed of the Lilliputian problems of the Jewish community of Tunis than I was of the deep and decisive currents which were disrupting the world and the country in which I lived. In one sense, it is fortunate that history always knocks at the door, that life necessitates exchanges with non-Jews and that a collective good sense finally puts an end to this flight from reality. If not, just how far might the Jew, in his encystment, have gone in his panic? The ultimate consequences of that attitude were described some years ago by one of its chief proponents, a serious thinker:

"We ask you to look for a solution neither in history nor sociology, nor in existence, science or philosophy, but in the Bible alone. . . . We propose as a method neither hermeneutics nor introspection nor speculation but the Scriptures alone. . . . (André Neher.)

What madness! Very few Christians, no matter how devout, would have dared write such a sentence. It was madness, but it was also, like all madness, an excellent proof by enlargement. It was absolute mistrust of the present, of all life and of every event. It was a radical condemnation of every effort at elucidation—all for an exclusive tête-à-tête with the past, with one book and one method. Another sage derives the necessity for the following conduct:

"In the lycées, practicing Jews demand—and obtain—permission not to write on Saturdays. My daughter, who is a doctor, has always been able to adjust herself to this. Some choose a career which coincides with their customs. One of my friends gave up all competitive examinations because they fell on Saturdays. He had to content himself with a marginal job." (E. Levinas.)

I could not have said it so well: the Jew who rigorously accepts his Jewishness must lead a marginal life, separate from the life and thoughts of the rest of humanity—and not only if he is devout. Judaism is not only a religion. It is a mental attitude and a total conduct, individual and collective, which includes a religious dimension. If I want to be faithful to Judaism and to Jewishness, I must accept the logical consequences of this fidelity: that is, not only a spiritual heritage, but also the institutional implications and group customs. My daily life, my marriage, the burial of my friends—all these must be conducted in a special way. Who will fail to see that in doing this I make a point of my differences and multiply the extent of my separation? I retreat more and more from the world. I choose to retire without a fight in order to protect myself from a world which rejects me.

THREE

Imagine what eating exclusively kosher food would really mean! A limited choice, purchased in a few prescribed places, specially prepared and cooked in special pots. It would be infinitely less difficult to have acute liver trouble or be a total vegetarian than to be completely Jewish in one's eating habits. What self-imposed exclusion from the world and its riches, from so many human relationships and even most trips! Such an ancient and extraordinary taboo, perpetrated on human beings. Strictly speaking, no meal should be eaten with just anyone at all; the Jew must forgo the important and symbolic bread-breaking communion with the entire universe, except other Jews—Jews with the same degree of orthodoxy at that. I have already described the serious drawbacks of self-rejection. All considered, however, the life of the Jew who accepts is probably more troubled than that of the Jew who rejects his Jewishness, since the former adds to the difficulties created by others those difficulties he inflicts on himself. His social, professional and civic life as well as his body and his spirit must bear the marks of this basic decision. The hats and warm clothing of the inhabitants of the Hassidic community in Spring Valley are obviously not suitable for the torrid heat of the New York summer. But the modern, pious Jews of European capitals should not smile too broadly; their furtive hair styles and assembly of beards are certainly more out of place in a Paris café than the clothes of those inspired Jews in their countryside. They are only a more symbolic manifestation of the same behavior.

The effort to alleviate Jewish misfortune by self-affirmation, far from saving the Jew, in the end precipitates other disorders; it imposes one type of alienation in place of another. I have already shown how this encystment also ends by creating a veritable network of *protective institutions* for the oppressed. This process is not completely disastrous, and these protective institutions are both havens and swamps which shelter and engulf the oppressed. If it were really necessary for the Jew to restrict his eating habits and to wear a hat in all climates and not to work on Saturday, so what? The sick must avoid certain foods and there are many people who don't dare cross a bridge or enter a tunnel, people who refuse good jobs because of claustrophobia. Encystment and protective institutions are, in this sense, one of the solutions to oppression. They are possible adjustments to a hostile or reputedly hostile universe; the price paid for not having to face it and be wounded by it every day. The encystment was still a *defense,* an answer to the all too difficult problem posed to the Jew. But what a laughable response! How paltry and above all misleading to-day!

Far from resolving the conflict with the non-Jew, abolishing the threat, it substantiates it and makes it seem insoluble and final. To form a little Jewry in the midst of a non-Jewish world is to *separate one's life from the life of others*. To confine oneself to a tradition, no matter how illustrious, is to separate one's thought from the mainstream of universal thought. It serves no purpose to maintain stubbornly that all things can be found in a few books—that argument is really too pitiful. "To live among Jews," "to live a Jewish life" in non-Jewish surroundings, like it or not, is to confirm and reinforce our limitations and mutilations. To solve my problems, serious ones, must I a priori retire from the human arena? Must I avoid all competition, true and healthy, with other men? Must I renounce most of the spiritual fruits of the earth? If only salvation could be bought at that price! If this removal, this retreat to a closed universe had opened up to me a kind of inner paradise, a private garden whose cultivation would bring me happiness . . . Actually I found out that salvation was to be found neither inside nor outside that pathetic dominion. As with any place deprived of air and sunshine, there was a mustiness and decrepitude on the inside; while on the outside the threat did not change in the least and could at any moment force the old stones of this illusory fortress to crumble. At best, Jewish communal life reminded me of the poor synagogues of my childhood, of the pale green light, falling from a high grated window, which blended with the flickering fires of the death vigils. I loved this atmosphere of mysterious meditation and the odor of warm oil, yellowed paper and rotting wood, but I could never have developed my full potential in this humid, collective intimacy.

We have seen what psychological disasters are bred by

the Jewish family, which is otherwise so admirable in its warmth and solidarity. I have tried two or three times to participate actively in the life of a Jewish community, but I found nothing but mediocrity, fear and Machiavellianism, on a small scale, all around me. I was, moreover, one of the very few who even attempted some sort of involvement. The troubling and humiliating fact is that no young man of any worth ever devoted his energies and enthusiasm to Jewish community affairs for a very long time. The best of them quickly became either Zionists or révolutionaries, as if they instinctively guessed that they would not be able to give their best in any other way, that the leaders of a vanquished group could only express fatigue and resignation. This is probably the reason for the pallor of our community and spiritual leaders and, conversely, the reason why most of the great Jews of modern times have been men of revolt and rejection and not of faith. Freud hit hardest at Jewish mythology, Marx was almost malignant and Einstein was interested in Judaism only out of solidarity and a kind of politeness. The dramatic, sword-point relations between Spinoza and the Jewish group of the times is well known. On the other hand, who remembers the assailants of that great philosopher?

Finally, encystment has not helped to protect the Jew against any slightly pressing danger from the outside. A fragile shell in a very difficult world, it sometimes enabled him to avoid humiliation, to soften lesser shocks and to alleviate minor wounds. It had permitted him to withstand better the constant anguish of the threat, and this, I repeat, is appreciable. The oppressed who encysts himself plays dead like certain animals, so that he might better pass through the shadows of history, like the celebrated rabbi who thus succeeded in saving the Torah by placing himself live in a coffin in order to cross the Roman lines. But more often than not a more attentive sentry or a slightly sadistic rider is enough to destroy the snail with its meager armor. Encystment has never prevented the world from periodically crushing the Jew who was encysted in his institutions, rites and laughable exorcisms; it did not stop the Nazis unleashed against the Warsaw ghetto.

On the contrary, encystment blinds and disarms the oppressed in his state of artificial sleep. Participating as little as possible in affairs of state, he no longer understands them nor can he any longer predict the reactions of his fellow citizens. At the beginning of the Algerian war, cruelly forewarned by our Tunisian experience, we tried in vain to alert the leaders and the French Jewish intellectuals to the meaning of these events, the very probable exodus of North African Jews and the inevitable upheavals in their own Jewish communities. This was really in vain, and they didn't even feel the urgency of a common perusal of the problem. Our history abounds in these political or spiritual leaders, often marvelous rabbis, who, in the face of an imminent assault, advise against action, counciling instead meditation and contraction of the community, leaving the faithful to be slaughtered. I have been told, with an admiration I suspect, of two or three episodes of the same type which occurred during the battles for the foundation of the state of Israel.

Often, I know, they could hardly do otherwise. The disproportion of forces was such that they could only invent mystical consolations. However, if the slightest chance of salvation existed, it would not have come from these living-dead who believed themselves safe in their dreams and who were even more vulnerable than the others. The only resistance in the Warsaw ghetto came from the sons of Hashomer Hatzair, who were revolutionaries and atheists. In any case, I understood, for myself, that you cannot save a people by putting it in a catalepsy.

Sanctuary-values

9

Can Judaism mean nothing more to you than this misery and this mockery? The irresponsible ghetto, the suffocating family, the mean rabbis of your youth! . . . Judaism is made up of those eternal values which the Jews have offered the world and which the world has generally adopted! Even those rites whose significance you pretend you cannot grasp are but an imperfect means of materializing those values and of venerating them.

After the publication of my two novels and particularly my last book, *Portrait of a Jew*, this was the objection I often heard. Fine; these famous values are indisputable; they are the essence of Judaism. As long as I didn't touch them, nothing had really been broached. So I must now discuss the undiscussable: when I examined the Jewish fate what meaning did these basic principles, to which one must come sooner or

later, have for me? What did Jewish tradition teach me
when I attempted to decipher it?

Before delving into this difficult question there is one
point I want to make very clear: Judaism is a monument
of moral and religious values, it is true, but it is not only
that. Certainly Judaism is more than the ghetto of Hara
whose memory revolts and fascinates me, more than those
ignorant and good-natured rabbis for whom I can now
feel indulgence; and more than our devoted and intrud-
ing families, overheated and emotionally secure. Of
course, Judaism is not merely the Jewish community of
Tunis, the thought of which awakens in me an ambiguous nostalgia. But it is *also* that. Judaism is more than a
garland of pure values, sublime stars perched at the ze-
nith of humanity, which only the clairvoyance of the
Jewish doctors can perceive. It is also the manner in
which these values are lived, or even rejected, by the mass
of Jews—the rabbis and the faithful, the learned, and the
man in the street. It is both dogma and ritual, institutions and beliefs, mental attitudes and collective behavior. Judaism is all of these at once, because to be a Jew is
to take all these into account.

Furthermore, whenever I, clothed in my philosopher's
robes and armed with instruments of logic, too closely
scrutinized these famous values and demanded clarity,
conciseness and coherence, people cried: "Stop, unfortunate one. Judaism cannot be measured by such modest
criteria; the Jewish religion is not a religion in the Western sense. It is not even a religion like other
religions. . . ."

That is true too. Judaism is above all a way of life, a
concept of existence in its relationship to a divinity and
to other men. Theory and practice, ethics and religion
form an indissoluble whole.

What am I getting at? The touchstone of my argument, still of greatest importance to me: to understand Judaism, you must of necessity refer to the concrete existence of the Jew. I tried to show this in my last book. But I must repeat myself as this is one of the cornerstones of my entire edifice. To understand the Jew you must of course take Judaism into account, but to understand Judaism you must refer to daily life as lived by the Jew.

To be a Jew, I have been told time and time again, is to "live a Jewish life." Now what is a Jewish life if not the aggregate of the Jew's positive and negative relationships with other Jews and with non-Jews, according to the will of God if he is a believer? To be a Jew is *to live* in a certain way, to marry and bury one's dead as do the mass of Jews. It is also *not to live* like the majority, not to attend the same church, not to celebrate the same holidays. Finally, it is the misfortune of living in a hostile world with all the ensuing psychological, cultural and historical consequences. To be a Jew is, briefly, to share a communal destiny, both positive and negative, which unites Jews among themselves and separates them from everyone else.

To accept oneself as a Jew then is to accept the solidarity and the threat, as well as the prestigious values which are the symbol of this destiny. And to understand Judaism and be able to make a completely lucid decision concerning it, it would be insufficient, even fallacious, to examine the values themselves like precious gems, perfect and inalterable since their creation. On the contrary, it is necessary to explain how and why they have taken on their present and apparently definitive form. It is necessary, finally, to examine them in relation to Jewish destiny as a whole.

Obviously, I had no intention of making an exhaustive study of Jewish rituals and values. Whether you arrive at a total of 613 commandments, or whether the charming holiday of the Rabbi Chem'oune has any scriptural value, seemed to me, perhaps unjustly, of little interest. On the other hand, it did seem essential to discover at least the meaning and the dynamics of the construction, and in what perspective it had most consolidated. Under a pile of tangential or baroque details, I felt I had to discover the structural principles of the edifice and the intentions of the collective architect.

Today I can see what false modesty there was in my apparent prudence which aspired to reach the heart of the system with a single thrust. But without this youthful presumption, would I have even dared to undertake such a bewildering struggle, one which shook the very foundations of the life I had formerly led? From my long apprenticeship in philosophy I had gained the impression that a doctrine, no matter how complex or diffused, exudes a particular atmosphere, that there are at least some salient points, crests which, taken together, characterize the mountains. At the time I thought it possible to place the whole Jewish tradition into a relatively simple mold, the better to grasp it at a glance. Its complexity seemed to me to revolve around three main axes: monotheism, election and Messianism. Or, more explicitly: a belief in one Supreme and Moral *God*, the *Election* of the Jewish people to receive the Law, and *Messianism*, which will recompense and save the chosen people. Let me say right away that in this trinity monotheism did not appear essential to me.

Let me explain myself: it is not that a single universal and moral God is not one of the greatest discoveries of mankind. It is precisely because of this that it has been adopted by so many peoples and is now indisputably common property. The success of the Bible, which has become *The Book*, has caused it to be so well absorbed into the substance of humanity that humanity has almost forgotten to be grateful. So, paradoxically, monothe-

ism and moralism can no longer distinguish the Jewish
religion from other religions, nor the Jew from the non-
Jew.

It is not that monotheistic morality has ceased to be
one of the cornerstones of the Jewish edifice. But it no
longer assures its originality. Was I going to become more
moral merely by affirming that I was a Jew? Moral scruples were no longer uniquely Jewish. By accepting the
famous Ten Commandments I could not see in what way
I was distinguishable from non-Jews; they respected them
as much as I. To steal, to kill, to covet another's wife,
what man would do so today without any remorse? I recall the heavy-handed efforts of many of my friends to
deride Christian charity. It avoided, they claimed, simple
and dignified Jewish justice. That seemed grotesque to
me. I had never particularly noticed that the Jews were
more just and the Christians more charitable. And anyway, if charity was a morally good concept, and if it was
another acquisition of humanity, I saw no reason to exclude it under the pretext that it was not explicitly found
in the Jewish heritage. The truth is that rules of morality, the search for the best conduct, was something Jews
had in common with the rest of mankind and, I might
add, this is how it should be.

In the same way neither the uniqueness of the divinity
nor any of the ideas associated with this—the concept of
the Almighty, omniscience, the creation of the world
from nothingness, the revelation to man, center of the
creation and interlocutor almost worthy of God—are
today indisputably Jewish property. Better still, the
Christians have played a trick on the Jews! By considerably developing meditation on the nature of God, they
have transformed the old Jewish foundation into a flourishing Christian enterprise. Theology and theodicy, the
largest part of religious philosophy, are today Christian.
And like all Jewish intellectuals, I became seriously

aware of them at first only through the intermediary of Christianity.

It even seems that Jews have become progressively less willing to talk of their God and to make him speak. The familiar divinity who argued with Abraham in the first pages of the Bible, who arranged audiences with Moses, becomes increasingly silent and distant. The desperate call of Christ, agonizing on the Mount of Olives, is but an episode, after that of Job, in the growing absence of the Jewish God. May I suggest in passing that this remoteness and this increasing deafness of the Jewish God to the despair of his people probably correspond to the growing implacability of the Jewish fate? The result, in any case, is that nothing very special can be said about the Jewish God to the point where certain perspicacious souls of courageous honesty have wondered if we couldn't eliminate him.

"Surely it would be rash to represent Judaism without the name of God, but the discretion used in its pronunciation, the silence which enshrouds it in so many important texts, authorizes the commentator to leave it out if he can possibly dispense with it." (Maurice Blanchot.)

I don't believe that we can go quite that far. The divinity, even abstract and obstinately silent, is too important in the Judeo-Christian and Judeo-Islamic schemes. But I have been convinced that the life line of the doctrine was no longer to be found in that direction. Moral monotheism has not, for some time, been sufficient to assure Jewish singularity. It no longer symbolizes, except perhaps negatively, the historical drama of the Jewish people. One has only to look honestly at this limited but decisive proof: it is no longer a belief in God which might hinder the Jews from conversion to Islam or Christianity, for in either case they would find this belief intact. Had the Jews made use of monotheism alone, they might have disappeared. This unique belief, which separated as much as it protected them from other peoples, has ceased to be original.

I am convinced that the faithful who are courageous enough to be lucid and sincere would admit that in Judaism today the divinity has been de-emphasized in favor of man, or more precisely, in favor of the double relation of man to God: Election and Messianism. Thus the insistence of numerous and intelligent commentators (Buber, for example) on the importance of the Dialogue between the Jew and his God. In any case, even if one does take issue with this interpretation, the countenance of a divinity is still shaped within a context. Thus Christ is the God who sacrifices himself to redeem the sinner. The Jewish God is today certainly he who chose the Jewish people, he who ordained a *mission* and who will send the *Messiah*. From this point on, significance stems only from this double relationship.

It is, therefore, an analysis of this context which will best reveal the profound attitude of the modern Jew towards his fate. It is through the intermediary of the myths contained in this doctrine that the Jew can express the drama of his existence.

TWO

Whether mythological or sacred, there is a complex which has resisted the erosion of centuries: the Election. It is easy to follow its reverberations throughout the entire system. The Election elicits and confirms most of the other Jewish themes. The Jew was chosen by *God* to carry out a *mission*. Already the reminder of a divine partner and the idea of mission appear. Then, immediately following, the notion of *exception* and choice. The Jew has been preferred among all peoples for an extraordinary mission. Then comes the idea of *oneness*: that of a people and a responsibility which find nourishment in the oneness of God. Again monotheism is strengthened: only one Supreme God could confide such a task and choose one people in his own image, etc.

It would be simple to develop the myth for page after page, and specialists in this relatively simple genre have not missed the opportunity to do so. But as tempting as it may be, it is a sterile game if its significance is not questioned. What does it *presuppose*? What is the meaning of this cascade of myths in relation to the *actual* destiny of this people? What is this people trying to say about itself? It is clear that it is trying to translate the feeling of an exceptional destiny. All these ideas confirm one another and express with an obsessed insistence the astonishment of these people in the face of their own fate. Happy or unhappy may be a matter of opinion, but the fate of that people appears unreasonable in their own eyes.

I do not have to remind you that Jewish history has been an essentially tragic one. Not always, of course, but it became progressively more so. It is enough to read a true historian, a Graetz or a Dubrow, to see it clearly. Jewish history is punctuated by catastrophes. All nations know the taste of defeat, from which they may recover to a greater or lesser extent, and into which they sometimes sink. But these are accidents, forgotten or isolated in their memory as dreadful exceptions. The cataclysm which threatens the very existence of the Jewish group is so often repeated that it renders this existence a constant menace, an endless near-disaster, a rescue which is never final. The entire Jewish populace is continually and literally saved from the waters of a monstrous tempest in which only the calm comes as a surprise.

I was made aware one day of the extraordinary importance of the exile theme in Jewish thought. It is enough to look at a synopsis of its real history! Exile is certainly one of the most frequent and familiar events in Jewish existence. Indeed, one might even divide Jewish history into periods from exile to exile, from conquest to conquest: Assyria, Babylonia, Greece, Rome, Byzantium, Islam, Christianity. . . . It is as if Jewish health were but an intermission between two illnesses. And this has continued to this day when the Jew still contributes a majority of all emigrants and displaced persons. Have we not just gone through a bitter experience in North Africa where we thought ourselves safe from such upheavals by virtue of our deep roots in these countries where we were contemporaries of the Phoenicians? It is then easy to understand the repercussions on Jewish thought of this periodical and inevitable uprooting from a soil, a climate, from the heart of a nation and finally from himself.

There lies the sinister originality of Jewish history. Tragedy, once having entered the life of this people, has almost never left them, to the point where it has definitively invaded their consciousness.

And here is the originality of their traditional culture: Jewish tradition is a continuous meditation on a collective tragedy. All this the Jew knows and continually repeats in all his great works and in every manifestation of his collective genius. He knows he is weak, isolated, and permanently threatened, periodically crushed and without possible human recourse. This, in any case, is the first lesson of the Jewish myths.

The relative importance of the various elements which constitute this culture has certainly varied, and it would be useful to reconstruct its socio-historical evolution. But it is obvious that the cultural themes which express this tragedy have been progressively strengthened and accentuated to make up the whole which we now know. All Jewish tradition thus appears to be the long and painfully elaborated response of a people at grips with a crushing fate. The idea of exile, which has become mythical, as a punishment for the strayings of the people very probably makes its appearance with Amos. It might have remained secondary as have so many suggestions contained in the Bible. What then gives this theme its obsessional character, this extraordinary Talmudic and Cabalistic development, if not the insistence of history, if not the unmitigated fear, and soon the definitive burden of *real* exile?

In Roman mythology the city of Rome was born of a plow and a mythical fratricide, probably a real agricultural foundation and a real inter-tribal war of secession. Jewish mythology situates the mythical birth of the people of Israel at the end of an oppression: "Remember the time when you were a slave in Egypt!" is one of the most haunting refrains of our collective memory. Moses, the first great man with whom the people identify, is first a liberator. All Jewish history, written and oral—that is to say, the image Jews have forged of themselves—is constructed or reconstructed in this perspective: oppression-liberation. In this regard the passage from Biblical to Talmudic culture is singularly enlightening. The Bible is the literature of a relatively free people, still fighting for its threatened freedom; the Talmud is the literature of an oppressed people who have almost given up, without ceasing to hope.

It is from the incredible persistence of historical misfortune that Jewish myths were elaborated, or at least refined and given their full scope. How do you bear an unbearable fate if not by transposing it, correcting it and interpreting it through fiction? All the power of dreams, all the inventiveness of the Jewish people were thus mobilized to explain the tragedy and alleviate the despair. Thanks to this antithetic inversion, which we now know to be quite common in the genesis of all creation, a cycle of marvelous stories, the mysterious election of a small people from among all the others, the sublime mission confided to them alone, the pact of eternal alliance with God—these mold for the Jew a glorious, superb and exacting destiny. But this myth barely hides the other side, which is the misery, the luminous projection of the shadow, the historical twilight in which the Jew struggles. The Election is the other side, which is the curse, the sublime distinction of the sad fate of the exiled. Never does the Jewish narrator not deny that this exceptional fate is at the same time too heavy to bear. But, from now on, the suffering becomes the result of the glory, the evil an episode in a triumphal march.

One more example: the theme of solitude. In one breath the Jewish narrator frequently confesses the terrible solitude of his people and magnifies it. It gives him the hues and dimensions of the sublime, which is appropriate to this momentous fear. Abraham, the first patriarch to have the honor of signing the alliance, was he not already, and for that very reason, a solitary man? Moses, the hero *par excellence,* the interlocutor of God and legislator of the people, did he not complain bitterly of his solitude, caught between God and man? The meaning of this twofold trait regularly imputed to the great men of Jewish history and legend is clear: isolation is the corollary of Election; it is the price of this glorious destiny. Who would not courageously accept the inevitable accidents of such a high destiny? To play the role which the divinity proposed, Abraham had consented to circumcision, exile and even the sacrifice of his own son. How could the Jew, the entire Jewish people, not in their turn endure the uprooting, the assassination and the pogrom if God exacted it, if their Election is bought at that price?

The proof was not, however, quite complete. It needed one last touch, the brilliant discovery of the inventors of Judaism: the Jewish fate is not only metaphysically explainable, it is also morally *just.* It was not enough to explain it to be convinced; they had to legitimize it. The historical weakness of the Jews, their abandonment, catastrophes, oppression, are the consequences of their Election. But couldn't the Jew resist this divine choice and refuse this awful distinction? He does! Judaism is full of these protests. Abraham, Jacob, Moses, Job, the Prophets, major and minor, all complain, groan and sometimes revolt. But they always submit in the end, recognizing their mistake. Why? Because they discover that they were *morally* wrong, not merely metaphysically wrong. They are bound to humanity. Their mandate is more than divine, it is a mandate from all mankind.

"Abraham stood alone for humanity . . . for humanity Judaism *must* continue through time its lonely march." (Samson Raphael Hirsch.)

Thus Election is not only the choice of God, a terrible duty, but it is also proof of the *worth* of the Jew. His honor requires him henceforth to contribute of his own accord to his sublime destiny. That is the meaning of all Jewish morality. The pact was proposed by God, yes, but it was ratified by the great ancestors, definitive examples of the tradition. If he does not exclude himself from the Jewish community, whoever accepts his Jewishness confirms the conditions of the alliance. Is it not *right* then that every failure be sanctioned by a just punishment? And then, through thoughtlessness and weakness, the Jew frequently sins! Thus the misfortune is morally explained.

One might reconstruct and follow step by step this astonishing dialectic in which the catastrophes of history and the periodic strengthening of moral values are so closely related. So closely related are they that it is hard to tell whether the Jew chose this God-Judge, so rigidly moral, to explain the punishment which periodically falls to his lot, or whether he is periodically punished for hav-

ing failed in this assignment. In any case, the cycle is now
complete. A painful need to understand consumes the
Jew: why this cruel fate? Why is he thrown into this terrible history which crushes him, punishes him permanently? The Election explains it all, is consolation for
everything; it reassures and flatters him, it demands and
attracts. It is at the same time the glory and the duty of
the Jew, and the burden, privilege and protection. It is
the classic example of the sanctuary-value.

THREE

The other aspect of this fundamental relationship of man
to God is Messianism, probably the second cardinal idea
of Judaism. Now the meaning of this myth seems to me
equally obvious. Again everything becomes clear if one
places it in the context of the concrete and unhappy fate
of this people. I am once more convinced that I am inventing nothing; it will suffice to examine Jewish tradition from the point of view of an historian and not of a
believer. Messianism first appears as the hope of an *effective* liberation of an oppressed people. It is almost possible to follow the progressive transformation of this historical wish into a fabulous myth, as liberation became more
and more improbable.

As far back as I can remember I find the *Messiah,* half-
man, half-event, familiar and mysterious, his features im-
precise, but capable of extraordinary words and actions.
"When the Messiah [literally the Savior, the Anointed
of God] comes," he will load us with favors, resurrect the
dead, avenge us from our enemies, and lead us back to
Jerusalem . . . in short, totally transform our condition.
The change seemed so desirable to us, and yet so extraordinary that we spoke of it with bitter and audacious
irony, "When the Mashiah comes," as if we hoped without daring to believe. Certainly the Messiah was sur-

rounded by a mystic aura, but not so much more so
than Moses or Abraham. We expected him to fulfill the
Law, but also to throw off the yoke of nations which
weighed down our lives. It was the latter aspect which
was clearest in our minds, while the Messianic constella-
tion as a whole remained quite nebulous.

And for good reason. In most of the ritual texts themselves the personality of the Messiah varied considerably.
People are not aware of it, or it is not said enough, but
the Messiah is very often pictured as a real and relatively
commonplace person. He is sometimes a civilian, sometimes a soldier, a layman or a priest, and even once a non-
Jew! Cyrus, King of Persia, who allowed the exiled Jews
to return to their homes, was also called Messiah by the
Prophet Isaiah, to the horror, it is true, of the Jewish
community. So it would seem that there isn't even one
Messiah, but several:

"In the Midrash the number of Messiahs is discussed.
One held that there were seven or even eight, while another maintained that there were but five. But if you
study the history of the Jewish people for the last twenty
centuries, you will find more than ten Messiahs, without
counting those described in the historical books of the
Bible. . . ." (André Zaoui, Chief Rabbi, a liberal.)

In short, Jewish history has continuously generated
Messiahs. Sociologists have yet to give an exact picture of
the circumstances of each particular Messiah, but the important thing, once again, is that the basic mechanics are
the same: every time the collective misery worsens, the
need of the Messiah springs to life. Often the recipient of
the awesome title arises and tries to liberate his people.
Bar Kochba, the last Jewish military leader who fought
the Romans, and in our time, Theodor Herzl, the Vi-
ennese journalist who undertook to found the new Jew-

ish state, were thus acclaimed; not to mention the seventeenth century Sabbatai Zevi or the eighteenth century
Jacob Frank, who were unjustly called false Messiahs
after their failures. Actually, why false? Which Messiah
has been completely true to date? Have they not all been
relatively false since the Diaspora remains and the people
have not yet been completely liberated? *If Jewish history has never stopped giving birth to Messiahs it is because it could keep none.*

It is because the Jewish historical misfortune continues
and the Jewish condition has not fundamentally
changed. Only once, perhaps, has a Jewish Messiah succeeded: it was Christ. But he proposed an unacceptable
solution: accept the human condition, which was recognized as a state of worldly defeat. However, the counter-
attack was electrifying. Jesus was irremediably banished
from the Jewish community, more violently, more radically than all the false Messiahs who still retain advocates
among Jews and are periodically rehabilitated. There is
nothing shocking in the affirmation that the Messiah has
already come, nor is it inconsistent with the rest of the
doctrine. Why would the Messiah, so eagerly awaited, not
come one day? But here again the quarrel was not
purely ideological; or, more exactly, the ideological conflict was only the expression of a real and infinitely more
serious drama: so long as the Jewish condition remained
the same, the Jewish Messiah could not already be there!
Or then one would have to despair! Await nothing more?
How could the Jew resign himself to life as it was? How
could the Jew cease hoping for an end to his historical
misfortune?

That is what Jewish tradition taught me when I en-
deavored to decipher it. Far from advising me to resign
myself to the Jewish condition, it convinced me that the
Jew has never consented to it. Perhaps even more than
the Jew who rejects his Jewishness, the Jew who accepts it

is condemned to eternal protests. That is why Messianism has become the life line of Jewish ideology. Judaism is the reflection of the Jew on himself, mournful meditation on his isolation and his fragility and on his hope of finding a way out. What is Messianism if not this obstinate, frenzied expectation of the end of a misfortune which is almost without exit? The Messiah, first a human liberator with the help of God, was transformed into a myth and another great sanctuary-value.

But this miraculous solution of the Jewish drama has never stopped being necessary. It must have an end, the Jew must continue hoping in order to continue living. One day, thanks to the Messiah, the Jew, Cinderella of history, separated, despised and beaten down, will shed his rags and his cloak of ashes, to appear at last to the dazzled eyes of humanity, as what he has, mysteriously, never ceased to be: the chosen, the predestined, the prince of peoples. In a word, the Jew will again become a free man. Yes, that is what Jewish tradition suggested to me: if I accept myself as a Jew, it is only the beginning of a new conquest and the confirmation of the oppression. That is my true mission, and that is how I might one day obtain the equivalent of the coming of the Messiah on earth: freedom.

The Counter-Myth

10

ONE

Meanwhile, these were the two sides of the picture: the suffering and the glory, the slavery and the triumph. The hues were so finely blended that one hesitated; the Jew himself could no longer recognize his own likeness. Yet how could one fail to notice that the misery was real while the glory was only a promise? That the oppression was actual and the triumph a hope? That the one made the other bearable? What despair but for this continuing dream of a vanquished people: the day will come when they will be free, happy and proud among nations! Better still: they are already so, secretly and mysteriously. The Election precedes the future coronation, the Messianic hope is deposited in the cradle of every Jewish infant.

I admit that for a long time I had not clearly seen the necessary correlation between the two themes. The Election, for example, might have been sufficient: why would a chosen people need further recompense? Was it not enough to have been chosen by God? Why this premium, this radical transformation, spiritual but also worldly, promised with the Messiah? The fact is that one link in the chain was missing: misery. To throw light on a great deal of Jewish behavior, I have since learned, you must always have recourse to misery. The Election is both glory and duty; for how long and to what extent? There must be an end to this perilous honor! That will be the role of the Messiah: one day he will bring peace to this overburdened people. In a word, the Election explains the sufferings of the past while Messianism promises a future without suffering. The two complement each other and transmute the actual misery of the Jew into a perfect future happiness.

For what can the oppressed do, as long as he eschews revolt, but be patient and take reassurance from more or less precariously constructed alibis and shelters? The traditions of the synagogue are the culmination of this slow conditioning of the Jew to servitude. To the smothering coherence of oppression, the Jew will progressively oppose the invulnerable solidity of his inner dignity and the perfect hope of a sublime future. To a destructive accusation and an unbearable fate he will oppose a sovereign image of himself and a universal order in which justice will necessarily triumph in the end. Every wound becomes a special glory, a battle scar. Every negative aspect of his life is but the negligible counterpart of an enviable happiness. Every lack is but the sign of a nobility which cannot descend to vulgarity. A complicated machinery of survival, an assemblage of defense institutions and sanctuary-values, a veritable counter-myth, are thus tirelessly built up, perfected, until they now constitute the Judaism of oppression with which we are familiar.

I do not hold all myths in systematic contempt. As a

writer how could I have contempt for fiction? I must even admit that I have often been tempted to espouse these fabulous metaphors and experience their voluptuous fecundity. But one must not take them literally. Myths are the daydreams of a nation, and Judaism is the old, infinitely repeated dream of the Jewish people. Myths are a precious source of information about the people who invented them, but they must be deciphered and interpreted. For this I know of only one serious method, which is to situate them in the real life of that people. Otherwise it is merely adding fiction to fiction, delirium to delirium. And the work of many so-called Jewish intellectuals is nothing but that: embroidery on a collective dream.

I add, for anyone who cares to listen, that this undeniable correlation of their myths with the life of a people does not in any way exhaust the possibilities of the works in which they are expressed. When I say that to understand the growing silence of God you must look to the growing despair of the Jew, I know that I have not exhausted the meaning of the divine myth, nor even that of the progressive veiling of God. Every great creation of the human mind has a life of its own and attains a relative autonomy. The glorious success of the Jewish tradition lies just there; it was able to weigh anchor and leave the little port where it was born for the great ocean of universal culture. Its themes, its symbols, its images have imposed themselves so victoriously on so many peoples that they recognize in them their own torments. What remains, however, is that myths, born of the anxiety of certain men, will appease the anxiety of other men, being transformed and enriched along the way. What remains is that humanity retains only those fables which match its obsessions. Whatever their fecundity, their astonishing survival, their apparent freedom, myths are only understood in the context of the sufferings and the hopes of the men who invented or adopted them.

All of this is to say again that, confronted with Judaism, I wanted to be neither complaisant nor unjust. It is true that I was no longer paralyzed with sacred fear, but I didn't shrug my shoulders like many young men of my generation. I must admit that at times when I was particularly impatient, these discussions seemed to me unbearably futile and gratuitous. If the Jewish people were or were not the chosen? If the Messiah would or would not come? . . . I wanted to scream with rage: "For heaven's sake wake up from these absurd dreams! Grasp your real destiny!" And to myself: "Give up the whole thing and go on to something else! You can't argue with sleepwalkers!" But then I told myself that I wanted to make this inventory methodically; therefore I must experience the whole road and even, perhaps, those paths which lead nowhere. I must also examine these collective fantasies. If they have counted for so much in the life of my people, perhaps they hold some useful information. What can they teach me about them and about myself? What happened, what is still happening to the Jews to make them conceive of Judaism? And to continue to cherish it so ardently? To make them so patiently and painstakingly carve out this representation of themselves until they obtained this apparently definitive shape?

TWO

I believe I have understood this much: illuminated by the sinister glow of Jewish history, all these values reveal what they owe to the tormented destiny of this people. By more or less complicated detours, they appear to be almost always a desperate façade behind which lurks an implacable fate. To this intolerable condition, to the obstinacy of a monstrous persecution, the Jew can but constantly oppose a glorious past and a triumphal future, which reassures him and intimidates his assailants. To the persistence of an incomprehensible accusation, he can only tirelessly repeat his defense, to the point of delirium and the shriveling of body and thought.

I would like to show one day the astonishing relationship, the more or less unconscious osmosis, between the traditional sanctuary-values and the more modern ideology of many Jewish intellectuals, often resolutely secular in their outlook. It is as if Jewry always needed to manufacture the same counter-myths, as if the old myths were content to mold themselves into fashionable language. Messianism became revolutionary, and divine justice was transformed into socialist justice. Universalism is the prolongation and extension of prophetism. I would also show how the modern Jew has never stopped perfecting new defense institutions, without abandoning the old ones. It is no mere accident that we are so impressed by two types of success, money and knowledge: they are the most effective in the world which surrounds us. It is in this perspective that you must understand the prestige of certain professions such as medicine. It is because the same compensatory mechanisms come into play; it is because the Jew today continues, in order to survive, to forge arms, which are seemingly new but which bear an astonishing resemblance in their origin and in their functioning to the ancestral arms.

There, in any case, is the probable key to all the so-called *mysteries* of Israel: Jewish myths have survived because they are still *usable*. Because, even today, the Jew still needs these same myths.

We have continued to celebrate Passover because we have always been in the desert and we have always awaited our liberation. One can understand, at the same time, why Judaism has survived and why, for so long, it has kept relatively the same characteristics. This absolute expression, at once admirable and terrifying, this sublime severity was assuredly born of the inhuman severity of our destiny. And as long as the oppression lasts, the Jew will probably enclose himself in the same limited dream, this fabulous fairy tale in which he cuts a marvelous figure, all the more superb and consoling, as he is the more crushed, humiliated and hopeless.

Why did I too not resign myself to this obsessive collective fabrication? Or simply to its paler secular counterparts, which flourished under my eyes in the most unexpected places? In this way my friends—socialists and revolutionaries, apparently completely liberated—betook themselves to defend, with a new kind of subtlety, the Jewish revolutionary germ, or the duty of testimony of the Jew. As though they, in turn, had been stricken by the common, anxious thirst for anything that could reassure us.

I did not consent to it out of dignity. (I will not take up again the argument from my chapter on conversion. The proposal of conversion to Judaism is as grotesque as that of conversion to Christianty, even if it is affectively less shocking. How can one propose a faith as a *rational* solution? Isn't this a mockery of reason and belief?) Above all, too, because the counter-myth, on the whole, seemed even more onerous than an exact picture of my condition.

Just because my people perhaps had need of it, did I have to ignore all the weaknesses and misery in this marvelous story they told themselves? Had I fought so hard against the myths which crushed us only to maintain others which exalted us? In opposition to the awful Jew, monstrous, incarnate evil, should I defend the sublime Jew, as false, as unreal as the other? I was not very sure, to tell the truth, whether a people could live without myths. I was convinced, however, that lucidity, courage, dignity of thought and self-control exacted from me a straightforward confrontation with our real condition. Even today I feel that all spiritual inquiry is a hazardous journey through the continually rising mists of our minds, forcing on us a constant exorcism of mirages and imaginary monsters, born of our fears and weaknesses.

In the final analysis the only serious, effective approach to my self-imposed itinerary was to throw away the crutches and rip off the convenient and reassuring blindfold that my countrymen had spent so many centuries weaving. How, from this moment, could I consent to the slightest laxity of thought? I will admit to having searched out with ferocious joy and without a care for the disquieting consequences all those whom I suspected of such accommodations, which I called frauds and which were nothing but piteous little deceits practiced to establish an equivocal peace with themselves and others.

In the middle of a discussion I would ask point-blank: "What do you call God and the Messiah? Give me a definition of the Election, of the Mission." I verified with rage and, I must admit, some delight, to what extent excellent minds could, in these matters, accept confusion and shadowy changes of meaning. When I demanded clear concepts, concrete descriptions, they played at hide-and-seek, became indignant or solicited from me an amused connivance:

"The Messiah! Now, you know perfectly well that I am not awaiting the arrival of a supernatural being! Who still believes in such dreams? Not even the Bible, perhaps! Don't you see that it is a question of the arrival of a better world? That yes, I hope so! Is not the glory of every Jew to continue to hope for more and more justice?"

Isn't God, the divinity, they explained to me, still the best symbol of harmony and justice? In the same way, Messianism signified revolution, humanism, the best of all possible worlds, the golden age. God: a value, an ideal, a moral principle, the collective spirit of humanity, a mysterious force, nature. . . . The Election: destiny, historical fatality, moral conduct, civic courage. . . .

The Mission: the duty of every man and of every citizen.
. . . etc. . . . etc. . . . Is this definition, no matter how
good, of religion really worthy of a philosopher?

"We must understand by the word religion . . . adherence to an uncomfortable destiny, and, even in the
state of Israel, a dangerous destiny . . . the destiny to
which one adheres surpasses the natural fact of a people."
(E. Lévinas.)

This is what a socialist revolutionary writes: "That
which defines the Jew would be . . . a manner, peculiar
to him, of accommodation with the 'world of values,' with
the absolute or, why not say it, to simplify matters, God.
. . . The term religion does not necessarily imply the
belief in God." (F. Fejto.)

(One wonders then what is left of the Jewish religion
and the Jewish God, and why they insist on using these
terms which are so manifestly perverted.)

"Modern Judaism concentrates more on the Messianic
era than on the personality of the Messiah . . . it is from
the inner development of man and human societies that,
whether orthodox or liberal, the Jews await the distant
accomplishment of the ancient prophecies." (Edmond
Fleg.)

(What is left of orthodoxy, even in this way cor-
rected, in sociological Messianism?)

Obviously I could not content myself with this fruitless
labor, this mystic-coated laity. Words were my most precious tool, and I refused to play with them in that fashion.
I would have been loyal neither to myself nor to our tradition. Religion presupposes faith and, in the Jewish religion particularly, faith in an only God; the Election

signifies a truly theological event in the history of the Jewish people; Messianism announces a new divine intervention in this history and a new supernatural upheaval of its course; the Mission, entrusted by God to the Jewish people, is as mystical as it is earthly.

We don't believe in all that any more? The modern Jew, even with his televised rabbis, does not seriously hope for a marvelous savior who will lead him out of his wretchedness? No longer claims his Election by God for an exceptional destiny? No longer claims a glorious mission, other than that of remaining faithful to a vague kind of morality? So be it; then let us dare to draw the proper conclusion: *Judaism, as a doctrine, survives as a series of ambiguities.*

THREE

Even so, I might have been more cautious in my approach to these myths and counter-myths because they helped my people to live. I might have kept quiet, had I not discovered that the counter-myth exacts an equally high price from the entire oppressed collectivity. In the end the cure was almost as harmful as the sickness. I was present one day at an extraordinary public discussion which I will not soon forget between one of those unconditional defenders of tradition and a leader, respectful but all the same amazed by the absolute, the opaque, almost schizophrenic obstinacy of his interlocutor. Our devotee quite simply sanctioned the slaughter of all Jews if this were necessary to save tradition. I invent nothing.

André Neher (Professor at the University of Strasbourg): "The biological survival of our community . . . is nothing compared to Jewish morality. Let the Jewish community perish, let the state of Israel perish, if this community, if this state, becomes unjust! . . ."

Louis Kahn (President of the Consistory): "I have heard Mr. Neher's words with great emotion . . . I am obliged to say that I do not agree with him because, after all, there are other beings, the children, whom you commit . . . when you say, 'Let the entire race perish!' I can concede that the adults should perish, but we have lost 1,800,000 little children. . . . I have no right to send them to their death. They will choose when they are of age and responsible. . . . This solution of absolute morality leads to the negation of justice."

For a moment, like all those present, I wondered of what "injustice" it could be a question, for what terrible crime one had to punish with death the entire Jewish people, children included. But our devotee, with an unquestionable sincerity and particularly well-chosen language, The wished to clarify his thought: crime is the lack of faith.

Neher: "I will be very brief. In André Schwarz-Bart's novel *The Last of the Just,* you will remember the famous episode in which the rabbi of York, seeing that the enemy was approaching and that the danger of forced conversion existed (a greater danger for the children than for the adults since the latter could refuse), slaughtered the Jewish children. . . ."

Kahn: "Would you do it?"

Neher: "Let me develop my idea. . . . Slaughtered the children one after another. The rabbi of York did it because he was obeying the law of Jewish teaching which is typologically presented in an eternal fashion in the twenty-second chapter of Genesis: the sacrifice of Isaac. . . . If I were sure, Mr. Louis Kahn, that we, and our spiritual children—afloat in the same vessel, tossed by the waves—that we could not save ourselves, or that I could not save the others, that I could not save my children, that I could save my own people only by committing an injustice, by committing a crime, only by stepping over that limit which it is not possible for me to step over, for then, neither I nor my children would be men any longer, then I would let myself perish with my children, then I would open the hole in this vessel which would allow the waters to enter and cause us all to perish." (Third Gathering of Jewish Intellectuals, in *The Jewish Conscience,* Paris, 1960.)

After that the devout gentleman remained quiet; it was too horrible, at least in the eyes of any but the most fanatical, in whom the reversal of values leads to a veritable perversion of feeling and intelligence. This man, totally devoted to the Jewish community, preferred to see it destroyed rather than have its religion tainted. I have also been told with a sort of foolish pride that even in Israel there are cases where religious agricultural colonies have allowed themselves to be massacred rather than bear arms on a Saturday.

I have explained myself enough: there can be no doubt that for centuries it was the same for the Jew to fight or to let himself be massacred; he was too downtrodden to hope for any other way out of his oppression. The counter-myth had at least the virtue of giving a meaning to his death and helping him to bear his life. Without a doubt these institutions and these values help the oppressed to exist. Tradition (their sole retreat, their sole consolation) had to be defended at all costs. And from this fact stem the famous fences around the Law, and the fences around the fences. But the means finally triumphed over the end. The reversal was complete. Invented by man to ease his fate, the counter-myth became more important than man. The Jew dies in defense of the Law which ought to have defended him, and the devout ardently proclaim: "Let the Jew perish rather than Judaism."

Today historians of Zionism pass prudently over an eminently significant episode. When, with Zionism burgeoning, the effective liberation of the Jew dawned on the horizon, who opposed it most violently if not certain traditionalist leaders? They who ought to have welcomed it more gladly than anyone, because they were the ones who had repeated tirelessly, "Next year we will be free in Jerusalem!" and "If I forget Thee, oh Jerusalem, let my right hand wither!" But it was logical; more or less consciously, they remained faithful to themselves. The liquidation of the oppression might put an end to the utility of Jewish mythology. If the Jewish people became a people like the rest, what need would they have of an ideology almost completely constructed to explain an exceptionally unhappy fate? They foresaw that the Jewish people, once liberated, would no longer need to be a chosen people and a holy people or even to believe themselves the salt of the earth or the revolutionary germ of nations. "Those fellows want to be happy!" said the philosopher Hermann Cohen, who became a believer towards the end of his life. And Franz Rosenzweig, the last great representative of traditionalist Jewish thought, never believed in this terrestrial happiness.

I began to wonder at the time if it was not necessary to effectuate another reversal of values; if it was not necessary to save the Jew in spite of Judaism, or even if the liberation of the Jew was not contingent on his simultaneous liberation from traditional Judaism. For the counter-myth, conceived to console the Jew for the impossibility of any real liberating action, had become one of the obstacles to this liberation. Far from answering my question—what is the way out of oppression?—Judaism sent me right back into it. Far from revealing the hidden glory of the Jew, Judaism, once deciphered, told me of his immense weariness. The sanctuary-values and defense institutions were too obviously the eloquent children of his

continuing misery. And since Judaism expressed in mythical terms the misery of the Jew, was it not now necessary
to retranslate it and start some action against the real misery? Far from accepting myself as a Jew in the end, the
examination of Judaism finally confirmed what I had
suspected: the Jewish fate is fundamentally unacceptable.

The Literature of
the Jew

II

I never wanted to become a Jewish writer,
nor for that matter a North African novel-
ist. Although I could not put my finger on
the reason for my repugnance, the idea
seemed ridiculous to me. In the beginning,
I wanted to write in French and tell stories;
why become preoccupied in my books with
Jewish martyrology and with colonization?
It is true that fate seemed to decide otherwise. I have told how, at a crucial period in
my life, I felt compelled to come to grips
with these problems, and I set myself to this
enormous and urgent task. And so, although
at first I had no intention of doing so, I described in succession the life of a North African, the story of a mixed marriage, the portrait of the colonized, then that of the Jew.
And perhaps I will never get to the end of
this inexhaustible inventory. But I have always saved for later my dreams of, let us say,
a less necessary literature; I have obstinately
accumulated manuscripts, and continue to

believe that I have not yet produced my real work.

Why this hesitation? I suppose that I sensed that Jewishness was a further obstacle to the realization of a project so dear to my heart and already sufficiently hazardous. But I must admit that it is only in endeavoring to explain myself here that I understand the real cause. I would certainly have preferred not to use the same word endlessly and discover the same major difficulty: today I am also convinced that in the condition of the Jewish writer there has been a dilemma which was but one more variant of the common impasse and anxiety.

No Jew, for example, was to be found among my literary models, and undoubtedly these key figures are explicitly or implicitly important for the beginner. The artists I admired and dreamed of equaling were Montaigne, Rousseau or Stendhal. From time to time I discovered quite by accident that some important writer was of Jewish origin, but he himself had never mentioned it, nor was any Jewish character to be found in his work. In what way does the alleged half-Jewish parentage of Montaigne throw light on the *Essays* or the Jewish fate? I did not see any connection. On the surface, at least apparently, Jewry played no part in the creation or the destiny of literature. I have since discovered that the matter is far more complex. Nevertheless, it cannot be denied that, for reasons of which I was unaware, the best writers of Jewish origin were at the very least careful to mask their affiliation. Kafka, whose posthumously published diary and letters revealed to the world a sensitivity, preoccupations, family relationships and friendships which were so typically Jewish, never wrote, to my knowledge, the word Jew in a single work published during his lifetime. On the other hand, by a paradox which I found most distressing, the majority of avowedly Jewish writers seemed pretty mediocre. Perhaps I shared every Jewish reader's ambiguous attitude towards a Jewish work. But it was more than a personal impression. I had only to leaf through a Jewish anthology of the period, that of Edmond Fleg for example, to note the aesthetic weakness, the provincialism, the inability to make themselves heard, in the very great majority of the texts collected. Even Yiddish literature, certainly the most abundant of the contemporary Jewish literatures, produced no "masterpiece before the end of the nineteenth century," according to one of its important specialists, Arnold Mandel. In Hebrew we had to wait for Bialik and the renaissance of the Hebrew language to have at last a first-rate poet. It is another Jewish critic who noted:

"It is a fact that for various important reasons the Jewish world has always remained quite poor in the domain of pure literature." (Rabi, *La terre retrouvée*.)

This deficiency is all the more surprising as the Jews have always written a great deal, and this activity has not been confined to the middle class, as is the case with most other peoples. Thousands of manuscripts probably still lie dormant, buried in family caches throughout the world; other thousands surely disappeared in the last tribulations of the unfortunate Jewries before the war. The Jews were, one knows, a people of voracious readers and, therefore, commentators. My father, a humble artisan who had no pretensions to any particular learning, read fluently in Hebrew and Aramaic and understood French, Italian and Maltese, not to mention his native language. The Jews of Djerba lived in a distant Middle Age but corresponded in Judeo-Arabic. Such a tradition, though scholastic and self-enclosed, might nevertheless have been an excellent breeding ground for literary development—had it been possible. Yet nothing came of it. The plants which grew there remained desperately stunted. I recognize this all the more calmly as we are perhaps on the threshold of a new era. Signs of this are already detectable in many Jewries. I am thinking, for example, of the astonishing and simultaneous emergence of many young American talents and the promise of the flowering of the Israeli branch. But until now, very few avowedly Jewish writers would have deserved to enter into the pantheon of humanity. And that troubled me considerably.

Here, as usual, the anti-Semitic explanation is, of course, aberrant. It is obviously not a question of natural deficiencies since the contribution of the Jews to the sciences and philosophy has been tremendous. I do not wish to answer fatuity with fatuity and go through the usual inventory of Jewish glories, but it is true that to date eleven per cent of the Nobel prizes for science have been awarded to Jews. To mention only those areas with which I am familiar: the French school of sociology was founded by a Jew, Durkheim, and has always included since then an imposing number of Jewish scholars; psychoanalysis was created by a Jew, and Jewish psychoanalysts are still among the best in the world; the French philosophical scene was largely dominated, until the appearance of existentialism, by two Jews, Bergson and Brunschvicg; Husserl, one of the fathers of contemporary philosophy, was also a Jew. Better still, in the other arts, the deficiency at first seemed less serious. But I recognize immediately that one does not compensate for the other, and that the problem remains in its entirety. In fact, my very admiration for the thinkers and perhaps the painters made me all the more confused; why should there be this particular shortcoming in the field of literature? I now believe that the explanation was to be found both in the nature of literature and in the nature of the Jew, in other words, in the Jewish fate: if we set aside the absurd racist suggestion—that the Jews are by definition less gifted than the other peoples—then we are once again up against the specific difficulties of their collective existence. Once again we are made aware of what this existence was and to a great extent still is: that of an oppressed people. I wish to restate here that the characteristic of literature is the manipulation of language, that is to say words; words have a meaning and are always revealing. All the arts reveal, of course, even colors and sounds; but only after long and debatable deciphering. In one way or another words are always immediately and shockingly revealing, often contrary to the wishes of their author. Should an avowedly Jewish author decide to expose himself as such, he could hardly avoid telling us of his special condition, that is to say, his oppression. This fundamental aspect of the Jewish fate could never have been dodged by an explicitly Jewish literature.

Perhaps I am mistaken about the nature of the literary act, but a specifically Jewish literary response should be a confrontation, direct or fictional, with the actual drama of Jewish life. A clearly Jewish literary domain can not be defined by this hodgepodge in which we place anyone and everyone who has a Jewish name, even if he is totally indifferent to his Jewishness or if he rejects it or is ashamed of it. Nor can we include just any fabricator of wisecracks or light humor—in other words, all the fugitives of futility or idealistic gossips. A Jewish literature should consist of the aggregate of adequate answers to questions raised by the Jewish destiny.

TWO   /

When I published my first novel, *The Pillar of Salt,* which described, among other things, the life of my coreligionists in Tunisia, they raised such a storm that I abandoned publication of the second half which still lies tucked away in my storage boxes. I was wrong, of course; the reader's emotion is often the surest indication that the work has hit its mark. But the writer lies who pretends he cares nothing for any public. My Jewish readers could not stand these images of themselves and their destiny which I proposed. I still maintain after twelve years that these images were perfectly exact, and events, alas, have confirmed this. I, in turn, found it hard to bear people's dismay at this perhaps premature unveiling. So under one pretext or another, helped by historical urgency, I moved to other areas and applied myself for many years to the problems of colonial oppression.

These agitated relations with the Jewish public were in no way peculiar to me. Paradoxically, it is with the Jewish public that the dialogue of the Jewish writer has always been most difficult. One of the causes of the sterility, or semi-paralysis, of a properly Jewish literary expression has certainly been the Jewish readers' extreme susceptibility. As soon as the Jewish writer heedlessly, for the most part, and in a youthful work approaches Jewish themes in a manner which is not purely apologetic or argumentative, the Jewish readers become suspicious, bitter and sarcastic.

Worst of all are the *professional Jews,* those who believe they must staunchly defend the institutions and values of the group; who live off it. They read with red pencil poised. They rummage, consider and always end up by discovering the inexact detail: the hero has confused two ritual details, has read such and such a chapter of the Scripture on the wrong day, has worn the *tefillin* on a Saturday! Horror, sacrilege and derision! That certainly proves that the author is an ignoramus, that his book is false, harmful and, worse still, perverse! The reader will recall the hue and cry raised by *The Last of the Just* before its success finally sealed the lips of its detractors. Now this relative ignorance is the lot of ninety per cent of living Jews. The typical Jew is made up of a mixture of dogmatic ignorance and sentimental fidelity, of impatience with tradition and of submission to collective solidarity. And above all, this exact erudition, although desirable, really has only a very relative importance in a work of art. But even the professional Jewish critics seem to forget what literature is all about as soon as they have to speak of an explicitly Jewish book, and they transform themselves into implacable guardians of the temple. One of them thoughtlessly admitted one day with savage innocence: "We await the author with the susceptibility of a man who has just been skinned alive. Let him be forewarned that *whatever his conclusions,* they will never satisfy me. The machine-guns are ready." (Rabi.)

The author could hardly be more openly warned that, whatever the case, the judgment will lack benevolence, and his execution is most probable. Fortunately the career of the Jewish writer does not solely depend on Jewish critics! Luckily their claws are quite short and their scratches superficial! Nor does Jewish criticism grasp the fact that it is in this way contributing to the deficiency which it deplores and adding to its impotence. And here is the dilemma of Jewish criticism: it obviously exists only through these already precarious attempts and it works with determination for its own destruction.

Having said this much, however, the suspicion and extreme sensitivity of the Jews are, as always, alas, only too understandable. When one feels threatened by the ever-possible catastrophe from without, one tolerates little questioning from within. The Jewish writer in questioning himself questions his Jewish reader and the entire group and so can only provoke its anxiety and its anger. Only, what can the writer do? Jewish reality is hardly joyful and true literature is revelation. Examine what Wasserman suggests, what Heine says when he takes up Jewish themes; or even Zangwill and the humorists, over and above their wit. Where are the great Jewish writers of tranquil happiness? When you demand that the Jew-

ish writer not express the shadows, the anxieties, the ugliness of the Jewish fate, and even the weaknesses of the
Jew, you literally ask him to abandon the idea of being a
Jewish writer. Unless he veers into apologetics—but is
that even literature?—the truly Jewish writer is obliged
to translate this painful complexity of the Jew and his
destiny.

"One of the worst temptations which awaits the novel-
ist when it is a question of the Jewish tragedy, is Maniche-
anism, with the good, the persecuted on one side and
the bad on the other. . . . Such an attitude inevitably
arouses the incredulity of the reader. A man who suffers
is not necessarily a saint. He is a man who suffers, that is
all." (Anna Langfus.)

In any case the result is disastrous. Caught between the
demands of his creation and those of his people, dumb-
founded, heartbroken by the uproar of those he thought
he was serving, troubled by this accusation of quasi
treachery, the Jewish writer is torn, sometimes totally
broken. In effect, the author who has an absolute need to
express his Jewishness, yet does not have the strength to
resolve these preliminaries, is a tragic case. If he goes
ahead anyway, the Jewish writer generally swears he will
never again expose himself. A good plot will protect him
in his next book; he will dress his heroes in exotic cos-
tumes, change their names and move them in non-Jewish
circles—in other words, carefully cover up his tracks.

Nor does he get off the hook so easily: in this feint the
same censors find the proof that he had never been really
interested in his own people. Isn't his too easy abandonment the confirmation of his treachery and of his selfish-
ness? Whatever the case, the immediate result is that he
ceases writing directly for the Jewish public, and above
all he disappears as an explicitly Jewish writer.

Of course he might try to address himself, still as a Jewish writer, to the general public. If he succeeds on this level he could hope at the same time to convince his Jewish readers, who are generally flattered by the approbation of others. In opposition to what the professional Jews suggest, it is my firm opinion that this attempt is not an easy way or a pitiable ruse. On the contrary, to sum up my feelings on this subject, the man who, at the start, decides to be merely the artist of one school appears more suspect and timorous, and I have greater instinctive esteem for the writer who, without ceasing to be himself, wishes to address himself to the world at large. For a Jewish writer, true courage, true success, is surely to be able to speak, as a Jew, to all men. And in fact it is rare that a good writer—as I have shown in the case of statesmen—could be content with writing for the Jewish public alone; if he does, it is often, alas, that he has got off on the wrong track.

But here is the second and not the least serious aspect of this dilemma: the avowedly Jewish writer discovers that it is no easier to make himself heard as a Jew by the non-Jews. For, in effect, what is he going to speak to them about if not his wounded, crushed and demanding Jewishness? What can he offer them if not a literature of difference which accuses them and makes them ill at ease; in which they do not and obstinately refuse to recognize themselves; for they would have to recognize their crimes and justify this long oppression? All writers certainly offer a particular story, often their own, to some extent disguised. But their success depends on this fleeting miracle: that they be listened to, understood and justified beyond these specific characters, in their clothing, institutions and local customs. Now this miracle is too difficult for the Jewish writer to achieve if he insists on presenting himself openly as a Jew.

To be a Jewish writer is, of necessity, to express the

Jewish fate, set it before others, and to a certain extent even make them accept it. And, in order to make the identification, the non-Jewish reader cannot be too repulsed by this gloomy, personal destiny! The reader finds it difficult to identify with a slave, and it is hard to relate to the story of an oppressed person unless he is a temporary slave, a captive king, a disguised prince; this protects the dignity and the future of the hero, in other words, that of the reader. The non-Jewish reader cannot bring himself to believe in the dignity of the Jew. He does not even hope for the triumph of the Jewish hero.

Not only was the birth of a Jewish literature difficult, but the offspring always ran the risk of a poor reception, of finding little love. His existence almost seemed a provocation, an indecency; and this did little to encourage procreation. Certainly few avowedly Jewish writers have deserved universal acclaim, but I must add that, had they legitimately deserved it, it would only have been accorded with reservations. Jewish cultural works have always been systematically ignored, mocked and despised by triumphant Christianity and by its heir—our so-called lay society. Even today I cannot see that an avowedly Jewish writer can easily become part of the French literary Areopagus; become a member of the Académie Française for example; a Maurois who has changed his name, yes; a Kessel, perhaps—in other words, not avowedly Jewish writers; but a Jewish writer, clearly known as such—no. (I am thinking for example of Edmond Fleg, who was quite as worthy as most of the members of the so-called illustrious company, and who well represented "one of the spiritual families of France." Since the Académie has always counted several bishops among its members, why has it never included a great rabbi?) It is true that we had to wait until 1963 to see a Protestant minister (Marc Boegner) enter the Académie Française, but, let there be no mistake, that was not an accident either. In short, for an explicitly Jewish writer there was no public, either Jewish or non-Jewish.

THREE

Was a great Jewish literature therefore impossible? Not in the absolute, of course, since a few attained these heights all the same. It is my belief that almost everything can be surmounted by a great passion. But the effort was exhausting and success problematical. I do not want to reopen the eternal discussion of whether or not one writes for someone. However, to speak to someone, one must at least entertain the hope of being heard. The Jewish writer did not even dare to speak of himself as a Jew, for he knew in advance that he would be shown the door. He did not dare advance his claims since the world was his oppressor, and his own people did not wish to be reminded of their common misery. What was the use of addressing the deaf? The worst factor was certainly this preliminary discouragement, this sterilization, which sapped the strength of the young Jewish writer. Unless he quickly pulled himself together, understood the danger and decided that in the future he would proceed under cover.

Thus, there remained for the writer, when he was a Jew, only a mask, or silence, or futility, or apologetics—in other words, all the degrees of self-rejection as a Jewish author. If he nevertheless insisted on expressing himself, if he wanted absolutely to become a writer, he had to suppress, mutilate or camouflage a Jewishness which was too embarrassing for everyone. Wasn't this what Kafka, a man so overcome by being a Jew that he speaks of nothing else while never admitting it, instinctively understood? Just imagine: would he have been so universally accepted if, instead of relating the adventures of Joseph K., the anonymous hero accused of an imaginary crime, he had overtly expressed his own tormented appraisal of the extraordinary trials for ritual murder which actually flourished at that time in the Austro-Hungarian Empire? The fame of Kafka is paradoxically related to the fact that he was not exactly understood. (The Jews would not have listened any more than the non-Jews had the Jews understood what he thought of the Jewish fate, of the extraordinary abandonment of the Jew faced with his permanent historical misfortune; how he judged the suffocating sclerosis of the communal institutions, the formalism of the tradition, the crushing of the Jewish son by his father; undoubtedly they too would have abhorred him.)

Such was the further dilemma of all Jewish literature: *either it was explicit, therefore ineffective because it was without echo; or it was masked and disappeared as such.*

I know that all literature is more or less veiled, that every artist maintains difficult relations with his art and his readers. But the struggles of the Jewish writer were further complicated by the ambiguities, the demands and the impasse of the Jewish fate. A Jewish writer, if he was to be a Jewish writer, had to reveal his own people's anxiety and the injustice of others. A true Jewish literature could only be a literature of explicit accusation and revolt. How could the Jewish writer, that is to say a Jew even more attentive and anxious that the rest, fail to discover in himself and in his people his resentment at these shadows and the acute antagonism which the world offered? How could his silence have been anything but self-mutilation and a lie, and the abandonment of his liberation through writing? The truth of the matter is that I do not believe in a great literature of avoided or accepted oppression. And this speech, condemned to have no audience, generally stuck in the throat of the author. Worse still, the oppression had lasted so long that the Jews were not even able to give birth to such spokes-men.

That is why Marx, Einstein, even Freud were Jewish, but there has never been a Jewish Dante or Shakespeare. It is always easier to rationalize one's anxieties and des-tiny than to come to grips with them out in the open; for this reason the Jews are more successful in philosophy or the sciences. In literature, the writer would have had to speak of himself, his childhood, his father and mother—their Jewishness in short, and of the particular circum-stances of every Jewish life. Literature is born of a singu-lar affectivity and is addressed to other affectivities which it must touch, move and conquer. Now the affectivity of the Jew had been perturbed for too long, its expression too shackled and too unsure of itself when it came to communication with others.

This is why each time the oppression seemed to recede, become less unbearable, a Jewish literature tended to blossom. Every time the Jew has believed, rightly or wrongly, in the possibility of his liberation, his audacity rose with his hopes, and he dared stammer once more. It was so with the German Jewish writers around 1925; in the eighteenth and nineteenth centuries the Haskalah movement was a sort of Renaissance for Eastern and Cen-tral European Jewries; before that was the golden age of the Sephardic communities in Moslem countries; and it is perhaps so in our time in America. In all these privi-leged periods the Jew believed that the barriers between men were beginning to fall, that the great dialogue had at last begun. But it was never anything but the other side of the coin, equally illusory.

In effect, when the threat subsides, Jewishness is less painful, and its expression becomes less necessary. Why introduce oneself as a Jewish writer when to be a Jew seems so undramatic? Wasn't it in bad taste to remind

Jews and non-Jews alike of a disagreeable difference when by a common accord everyone seemed to want to forget it? This explains the paradox of why, rather than finding more freedom of expression, the Jewish community no longer produced explicitly Jewish writers when it had at last found a relative equilibrium and thought itself definitively installed. It is for this reason that old established French Jews ceased producing any representative writers a long time ago, that the few notable Jewish works in the French language are now authored by newcomers.

In short, for the Jew, literature could never be the royal road to liberation, self-liberation if nothing else, that it has been for so many other peoples. Contemporary Jewish culture has not known this compact flourishing of works which sustain and complement each other, thus forming the continuously growing field which we call a tradition, so indispensable in all the arts to assure the continuous passing from master to disciple that we call a literature. For the Jew has never been able to completely forget his fate. The Jew of modern times, constantly overcome by sudden catastrophes, is trapped even in periods of short-lived relaxation.

Today we are in what appears to be a favorable period. A few successful publications after the war, and the number of young writers just about everywhere in the world who dare attack Jewish topics prove it. Perhaps we have at last inaugurated a new era in the history of Jewish literature as we have in that of the ex-colonized. For the oppressors have at last begun listening to their ex-victims, and, above all, because their victims have at last dared to speak. From this point of view there can be no doubt that the last collective crime of the non-Jews was too atrocious; their remorse is still too acutely painful for it to be easy for them to plug their ears. The conscience of the world seems almost in need of these Jewish works which accuse it, for in them they find some relief and help to bear the guilty remembrance of so much horror. More than any other single factor, the existence of the state of Israel has given some courage to the Jews, even those dispersed throughout the world and, like all the oppressed, the Jew is respected in the exact measure that he respects himself. It is possible, and we must ardently hope that we have at last entered a definitive Renaissance: that the liberation of the contemporary Jew, and of the colonized, has really begun. And perhaps it will be one of the great new marvels of our time. But up to now, we have to admit, Jewish literature has lived only between eclipses; until recently true Jewish literature, that of the free Jew, had not yet begun.

The Language of the Jew

12

ONE

And then there was this terrible language problem which, curiously enough, is rarely mentioned. I collided into and struggled with it long before I thought of writing. I believe I have impressed upon the reader the fact that I am telling a particular story —my own. However, I think that the linguistic difficulties of the Jew are infinitely more frequent and more serious than is generally believed and than the Jew admits. They have certainly dictated the cultural life of the majority of Jews and largely influenced their daily life.

My mother tongue was the Judeo-Arabic dialect of Tunis, a crippled language reinforced by Hebrew, Italian and French words. Hardly understood by the Moslems and completely ignored by everyone else, it became inadequate as soon as I left the narrow streets of the ghetto. Apart from simple emotions, notions of eating and drinking, it was completely inadequate in the political, technical and intellectual universe which I was yearning to conquer. Fortunately the primary school presented me with the gift of French. It was an intimidating present, exacting and difficult to handle; it was also the language of the colonizer. But this superbly sophisticated instrument could express everything and opened every door. One's cultural attainments, intellectual prestige and social success were all measured by one's assurance in the use of the conqueror's language. Joyously I took the bet and played for the stakes. With my mother, who did not understand French, I spoke the language of my childhood; in public, in my profession, I was an Occidental. It was a question of inner organization. After all, I was not the only man on earth not to know a perfect unity.

But man proposes and history disposes. With the liberation of Tunisia this fragile edifice crumbled: we would soon be obliged to express ourselves in Arabic. I have told how I applauded this turn of events, whatever difficulties I feared for my own people. But I felt it was beyond my strength to go through another linguistic apprenticeship. If necessary, with the help of my native dialect, I could have learned to speak properly in Arabic; but I had never learned to write it. For a time I forced myself to attend adult classes and even took some private lessons but I quickly had to admit that I was beaten. Excessive discouragement? Sclerosis? Was I fundamentally ill-disposed? I do not think so. But I could see perfectly well that official Arabic would have been, once again, nothing but a *learned language*. In any case, I would have been handicapped, mutilated in my social and professional life. In the acquisition of French I had already expended too much effort to attain a barely sufficient mastery for me to undertake such a task again.

It is true that the ordeal was almost as dreadful for my Moslem friends who had been educated in the French

schools. Many cabinet ministers and important government officials thought and wrote in French, then had
their notes translated into Arabic. But for the Moslems
the return to Arabic was an absolute necessity; the restoration of their language was part and parcel of the reconstruction of their national personality which had been
crushed and dismantled by colonization. For us, no; it
was only a new acrobatic exercise exacted by history.

At the beginning of each school year, faced with the
imminent and final choice imposed on the children, a
contingent of emigrants left the country. The day the
first circulars written in Arabic were placed on his desk,
my own brother left the administration where he had
worked with enthusiasm; he had suddenly become a linguistic cripple. Today the majority of Tunisian and Algerian Jews are in France where they have again found
the French language. And perhaps it is better this way:
they have rejoined a way of life, a universe they admired
and of which they approved, to which they were already
adapted.

Here a pause is necessary for anyone who cares to reflect on this pitiless Jewish destiny; a question arises.
When, for the second time in my life, I found myself
obliged to change my language, I was seized with an old
and never-forgotten anxiety: that which gripped me on
my first day of school at the terrifying idea of confronting
a teacher who would speak a different language from that
of my mother. For what was my language? What was the
Jewish language? I know perfectly well that the question
may be judged fruitless, insoluble or badly stated. But
once again I remind the reader that it is not the Jew who
asks these questions of history and imposes his choice; it
is history which asks them again and again of the Jew. I
firmly believed that my linguistic choice was final. History cruelly demonstrated that my parents' language was

but a poor, laughable, ineffectual tool, then sought to tear from my lips the wonderful instrument which I had taken such pains to master. It is history which periodically reminds the Jew that his language is only borrowed, since at any moment and without notice it can be taken from him.

An exhaustive enumeration of languages used by the Jews would be interminable. To start with there are all those of the non-Jews among whom they have lived: English, German, French, Italian, Spanish, Russian, Polish, Turkish, etc., etc. . . . Not to mention all the truly mixed languages: Judeo-Spanish, Judeo-Arabic, Judeo-Persian, Judeo-German, etc., almost original creations compounded of an astonishingly unyielding past and a new present. As one Israeli humorist observed, the result is: ". . . Such chaos that in comparison the tower of Babel looks like a flat-roofed mud hut. The number of languages spoken in Israel surpasses those known to humanity." (Ephraim Kishon.)

And even worse than this extraordinary *diversity* which separated the Jewries into scattered, alienated and estranged fragments, preventing two Jews from understanding each other despite their identical concerns and their interdependent destiny, was the incessant *variability* of the Jew's linguistic situation. This agitated destiny, these multiple upheavals, moves, transplantations, all this furious commotion which history has improved, have made the Jews a people of a faltering, provisional tongue which is rarely the same for very long; in short, they are deprived of a language, without a legitimate language.

For it is no use deluding ourselves: the absence of a unique and stable language is the absence of communication, with all the catastrophic consequences such a deficiency entails. Perpetually displaced persons, the Jews have spent a great part of their collective existence in relearning; in leaving behind what they knew, painfully initiating themselves into new habits; in discarding what they were, in order to survive. Does anyone ever think of what an exhausting price has always been paid for this, what disorder has resulted in the life of this poor people?

In any case, if I wanted to affirm myself as a Jew, I had to base my activities on this absence and dispersion, on these poor unfinished monuments scattered throughout the world which were impossible to collect together. Had I merely wished to familiarize myself with the culture and the past of my people, with their multiple personalities, I had to know every civilization, learn every language: Hebrew and Aramaic to really understand the Bible, the Talmud and the Zohar; Greek for Philo and the Alexandrians; Arabic for Maimonides, the philosophers and theologians of the Middle Ages; Yiddish for that late flowering in Russia, Germany and Central Europe and even America where just recently I was made cruelly aware of my lack of knowledge. Did I have to learn every modern language before I could approach with intimacy this curious and dismembered culture scattered about the entire globe? Or to gain an understanding of my people did I have to see them through the veils and deformations of translations?

TWO

It is true that the Jew possesses the "gift of language." The gift! This diversity has been interpreted as a sort of wealth, a secret weapon which permits the Jew to understand everything and find his way everywhere. A poor defense, in fact; one which sometimes helps him on a multiple and changing front. In effect it is the weak, exposed nations which need several languages; and it is they who happen to have the famous gift. Does the Frenchman learn several languages? What for? French interests are everywhere defended; everywhere he will be understood and helped. The Englishman knows no language other than his own: it is universal. The Greek, besides Greek, speaks French, English and German—because he studied in French, his land was occupied by the Germans and his country situated in the English zone of influence. So this arm, this strength is merely an indispensable defense, an imposed dispersion. And who is more dispersed, more vulnerable than the Jew?

In Tunisia we were at least bilingual, often trilingual, sometimes more, depending on our origins or the neighborhood. It is true that Tunisia, a little country of successive colonizations, presented the phenomenon in a particularly magnified light. However, far from a feeling of accrued strength in the free use of several keyboards, we were never completely at ease in any of them. Except for a few middle-class Jews who succeeded in an almost perfect imitation, generally speaking we had a specific accent, vocabulary and even syntax. The Arabs laughed at our Arabic, the French at our French. And we ourselves justified this mockery by carefully avoiding the use of our native language in public or even by making fun of our own gaucheries. Later on in Paris I found the same whispering discretion, the same ambiguous jokes about Yiddish, a nostalgic domain reserved for our collective intimacy, but separated to some extent and slightly shameful.

Here again I know perfectly well that we were not the only ones to live through such linguistic troubles. I remember one of my old professors, a remarkable scholar, who made desperate and laughable efforts to disguise an undefinable accent. But to the same objection we must give the same answer: why should the misfortunes of some justify the misfortunes of others? This simply means that the difficulties of the bilingual Jew belong to a larger category, that of linguistic and cultural deficiencies in

every oppressed person. I have already noted the catastrophic importance of bilingualism for the colonized;
and the same answer was forthcoming: wealth, variety,
accrued effectiveness. And inevitably the happy example
of some English child or some little French boy whose
parents systematically speak two languages is trotted out.
This only proves that I was not very successful in making
myself clearly understood. I never claimed that all bilingualism was disastrous. (Although I am not certain that
too early a start at this double apprenticeship is not without disadvantages.) Bilingualism is dangerous, seriously
disturbing, when it is *conflictual*. Now, in the case of the
Jew, as in that of the colonized, the two languages are
generally in a relationship which is, at best, unhealthy.

The bilingualism of the oppressed is not a simple technical matter, in which he who can command two tools is
more favored than he who possesses only one. A double
inner-kingdom literally imperils the unity, the psychic
harmony of the oppressed. His second language, far from
complementing his solidly acquired, self-confident mother
tongue, dethrones and crushes it. And worst of all, the
oppressed finally consents to this defeat and accelerates the decadence. The rejection of one's native language and the embarrassment which it henceforth creates
is certainly one of the most cruel manifestations of self-
rejection: what is the profoundest, the most affective, the
most intimate is repressed, made inferior, despised to the
advantage of the most recent and the most artificial.

In my opinion the oppressed person does not maintain
easy relations with his new language. It is too often forgotten that the victorious language is usually the language of the oppressor. The resentment of the colonized
was found to extend to the language of the colonizer.
And why not admit that the only explanation of our resistance to Arabic was not merely our admiration for
French; it was also nourished by still-living memories of

several centuries of terror. Even without going to such extremes, the learned language is disturbing; its most ordinary details have a strange quality about them, for it is not naturally adapted to the sensibility or the unconscious.

I am amazed that more people have not noticed that most of the recent works on language destruction are the product of foreign writers who have had to take up residence in France in spite of themselves and have been obliged to use a language other than their own. Nor to my knowledge has anyone remarked on the large percentage of Jews among these bizarre artists. It is probably not an accident that the father of Dadaism, Tzara, was a Rumanian Jew. Nor do I think that they deliberately set out to destroy language, but that they were profoundly uprooted, overcome by a feeling of strangeness vis-à-vis the language of others. Dada so doubts the usual value of words that it simultaneously affirms and denies the same meaning. Kafka's attitude towards language, although diametrically opposed on the surface, stems from the same uneasiness. Treating German as a foreign domain which he must respect, he denies himself, whether voluntarily or not, all excessive liberty. This explains his rigid, meticulous precision, his way of tightening his words which paradoxically results in making them so strange, revealing the same anguish. And that brilliant writer was certainly conscious of the close relationship between his Jewishness and his tortured attitude toward language:

"They [Jewish writers] lived among three impossibilities (which I find simpler to call the impossibilities of language, but one might give them another name): the impossibility of not writing, the impossibility of writing in German, the impossibility of writing in another language, to which one might almost add a fourth impossibility: the impossibility of writing." (Franz Kafka, *Letters to Max Brod*.)

In short I believe that linguistic duality is more often than not the source of a double disturbance—in the native language as well as in the new language. In any event that was my own experience: an increasing rejection of Judeo-Arabic, unbearable and hardly admitted, coupled with an exaggerated, stilted and paralyzing respect for French. It is perhaps one of the reasons why I became a writer; and I willingly admit that this estrangement with words can be at the root of a fruitful experience. But not everyone can overcome his anxiety by fighting, more or less successfully, to express it. All Jews do not become writers and are not recompensed for their miseries by their work. Far more frequently the young Jewish writer is exhausted by this preliminary conquest of a perpetually new tool, by this constant effort at readaptation to a new society. Where some see a gain— multiple wealth, a clever trick—I see an additional crack, one of the symptoms of the forced rejection of the self which affects practically all Jews.

THREE

The double language of the Jew is one of the signs of his oppression. This linguistic confusion, never completely healed, has been one of a whole string of unjust confusions in my life. Certainly the language of every oppressed person is more or less affected. Women are the great silent partners of history. Even the proletarian, although he lives among his own people, is faced with the dominant language of the middle class which in no way coincides with his natural way of speaking and which he suspects, which he has not quite mastered, and from which he is more or less excluded—with the inevitable

corollary of his exclusion from the reigning culture. Mezz
Mezzrow, author of *Really the Blues,* devotes some astonishing pages to the language of the American Negro. And
I have said that for the most part I shared the linguistic
drama of my North African friends. In the common misfortune, however, my own always retained a special hue.

Kafka despairingly concluded: "I am the guest of the
German language." I was, myself, the guest of the French
language. Worse still, I was a perpetual guest for although I was never completely at ease with others, I
could never dream of going home. I foresaw that sooner
or later the Tunisians and the Algerians would return to
their language and their home. And I gave them my support. But where, I asked myself, would I ever find a definitive home? On what hearth might I sit down for good?
(At times I told myself that it was perhaps not necessary to
ever settle down. But at least it should be possible for me
since it is for all free men.) But I could not even dream of
it; had it been possible I hardly knew what I would have
wished.

In *Portrait of a Jew* I remarked on the *distance,* never
completely overcome, which separates the Jew from himself and from others. I am convinced that these odd relationships with language were partly responsible for this.
The language of the Jew differed from one Jewry to another, vacillated from one generation to another, hesitated inside the Jew himself. Too often it was another's
language which echoed in his head; a tool he admired
and willingly adopted; but it was still borrowed and contributed to his unease. Too often, though he might seem
perfectly adapted, the hiatus subsisted, discreet yet tenacious, in some unexpected form. The Belgian Jews speak
excellent French, but they insist on speaking it in the
Flemish sector where French is condemned; Canadian
Jews use English in French Canada; the Jews in Prague
speak German and the Jews in Cairo speak French. Of

course, it can all be explained: at times they try to resemble the majority; at others, the protector. They endeavor to reassure themselves, try to subsist without too much self-destruction. The motive is not, you may well imagine, to obtain the good will of others, and it increases the separation. Is it normal and healthy that Jewish children should speak a language different from their parents? My daughter, ten years old, is still not sure of my exact identity, and therefore her own: "You are an Arab, Papa? Since your mother speaks Arabic . . . and, then, what am I, Arab, or French, or Jewish?"

I have often discovered the usual trouble at some turn of the conversation: some of my friends in fact speak another language with their family, Turkish or Spanish, Italian or Yiddish. The Jew too often harbored this backlog of nostalgia, moving and annoying like a laughable family secret: this language of our parents and of our grandparents which we no longer wished to hear and which we vaguely regretted that our children already heard no more. It was all that remained, along with a few culinary customs, a few ritual details, of a strange past lived under other skies, among other peoples.

"Strictly speaking I did not spend my childhood in the world of Yiddish culture, but on the fence between Yiddish and French. Among my near relations—with my uncles, aunts, and cousins, small artisans, small workers, small shopkeepers, countless times I have heard Yiddish take the place of French, the better to translate some shade of meaning, some subtle joke whose flavor was lost in French." (Roger Ikor.)

Here a word concerning Hebrew. Of course, there was Hebrew, and the mere mention of it attracted me and from time to time I obstinately returned to it. But why not admit the facts? As long as we lived in the midst of another people, I felt too deeply the superficiality and above all the ineffectiveness of this return. For, aside from terms of ritual, how much Hebrew did we have left? The first exile had already entailed the loss of Hebrew as a spoken language. Babylon's displaced persons used Aramaic, and the Scripture, their own literature, henceforth had to be translated for them! In fact, the oppression also raised a linguistic barrier between the oppressed and his culture. I will not dwell on the efforts which my Hebrew apprenticeship cost me. What with evening classes, seminaries and enforced readings I almost ended up by learning it: yet what a paradox for a Jew! It was further from me, stranger, infinitely less malleable than Italian or English which I heard in the street or at the movies, and which evoked familiar civilizations. Hebrew led nowhere. Strain as I might in my stubborn insistence on building up my Hebraic culture, I was well aware that it was a perfectly useless luxury. What good did it do us to insist, with somewhat foolish pride, on calling the Bible, *Tanakh,* if we were understood by no one—not even the Jews? At best it could never be anything but a small supplementary culture. In fact, *outside of a Jewish nation,* Hebrew was nothing but the mythical language of the Jew. To live among others and to choose seriously and completely a language and a culture other than theirs would have been an aberration.

In short, the ambiguity of my linguistic situation mirrored and maintained the ambiguity of my relations with others and with myself. It was one of the most illuminating symbols and one of the most concrete manifestations of my Jewish fate. And, in affirming myself as a Jew, did I also have to accept the always-open wound which split me inwardly, the ditch which they never tired of digging which separated me from others? In this case even revolt would have been of no avail: this dispersion was perhaps a necessity. The truth of my linguistic existence was that unless I was successful in this obligatory mimicry of others, I paid the penalty of still further augmenting my exclusion. Each time history demanded it I had to apply myself humbly to this extraordinary apprenticeship, just to survive. I had to consent to this paradoxical and sterilizing multiplicity.

Again let me say that perhaps it was not absolutely necessary that the Jew possess a particular language. Perhaps it was better for him to forget where he came from and what he was, so that as rapidly as possible he would become indistinguishable from his new fellow citizens. Perhaps, after all, it is in the interest of the oppressed to lose his memory, the better to blend in with his oppressors. But *what was legitimate when I decided to reject my Jewishness was no longer so as soon as I wanted to affirm it.* To accept myself as a Jew, without defining what I was accepting, would have been empty chatter. To affirm my Jewishness without giving it a specific content would have been an empty proposition and in the final analysis contradictory. Now what is a specific Jewishness without a specific culture? And what is a culture without a specific language? When you think how much literature depends on language, what is a Jewish literature without a Jewish language! Even a borrowed language would do if necessary, but it must be finally adopted at the very least, until it runs in the blood of the people! That was the singular chance for Yiddish literature: Yiddish, that awkward, strange, bastardized mixture, was nevertheless, for quite a long time, a Jewish tongue. But even Yiddish was never anything but the partial and threatened language of a partial and finally assassinated Jewry.

In the final analysis, to accept being a Jew is to consent to the whole drama, including the cultural drama. And the source of the cultural drama was to be found in language, but the language of the Jew was in bits and pieces, as all his culture was in bits and pieces if there was a culture.

The Art of the Jew

13

ONE

I was not able to discover any plastic or musical art which was *specifically* and *openly* and, above all, *continuously* Jewish, unless it was minor—another disagreeable truth I had to admit. Not that I did not search them out in the exhibitions and retrospectives; discuss the subject ad nauseam with painters and musicians. But to what end? My aim was to set the record straight, not to produce apologetics or to reassure myself at any price. I had to conclude that with the possible exception of a few synagogues here and there, which I avidly visited during my travels, and a few questionable ritual objects, no important Jewish plastic current has ever existed in the past.

At last the twentieth century brings with it the advent of the marvelous participation of so many Jewish artists in the pictorial school of Paris. But there again the significance is open to question: is it really a Jewish art? Rumor has it that contemporary abstract art was of Jewish origin and essence. This is unfounded. It is more of an international art, rooted in remotest times, which came to fruition particularly after the arrival of cosmopolitanism, and perhaps the industrial civilization. Undoubtedly the Jews found it easier to become a part of this movement; but neither abstract nor any other modern plastic art possesses a particularly Jewish characteristic. The Jewish artists themselves refuse to make such equations. Soutine, who is presented as *the* great Jewish painter, became furious when it was suggested to him; Modigliani always firmly denied this qualification; Zadkine refuses to refer to Judaism. Even the case of Chagall (Chagall too refuses to be called a Jewish painter: "I am a painter. That's all.") is open to discussion: is he a Jewish painter or a Russian painter in Paris? Is he expressing a particular Jewishness or his nostalgia of a lost world whose Jewish aspect is noteworthy mostly for its exoticism? And who is unaware that Chagall will have no posterity? His descendants, living in Paris, will paint Parisian paintings and will lose even the remembrance of this exoticism.

But I hasten to shield myself behind the experts, before I can be accused once again of pessimism! In 1961 in Paris a seminar brought together museum curators, art critics, a professor, an architect, an appraiser, a sociologist, an archeologist and a gallery owner: not one of them claimed the existence of an important Jewish plastic art, either in the past or in the present:

"There has never been a great Jewish art" (G. Francastel, Director of Studies). "In my opinion there has not been a Jewish art in the course of history" (M. Rheims, appraiser). "There is no specifically Jewish painting" (R. Cogniat, Chief Inspector of the Beaux-Arts). "I do not believe that there is a Jewish art" (Berr de Turique, art critic). "It is only in the twentieth century that there have at last been some important Jewish sculptors" (E. Roditi, art critic).

And despite his good intentions, the keynoter had to regretfully conclude: "What emerges from this seminar is that the role of the Jews in the history of art appears, after all, quite marginal." (M. Salomon, director of the Jewish review, *L'Arche.*)

What is the explanation of this deficiency? Of course for some time, like everyone else, I was satisfied with the traditional answer: there has been no great Jewish plastic art because the Jewish religion forbade it. Absolute monotheism opposed any figuration of the divinity, and, by extension, his creatures. Everyone is familiar with the rigorous and insistent Biblical condemnation of all "graven images," of any "representation whatsoever." The only trouble with this most useful explanation is that it is also most mediocre. Undoubtedly the secular prohibition was very consequential—less so than was at first claimed; more so than people have begun to affirm as a reaction to the earlier opinion. But I decided that it was not a sufficient explanation for such an enduring paralysis when I discovered comparable deficiencies in the majority of oppressed peoples. Had it only been a question of the sacrilege of reproducing divine, human or animal figures, the artists would probably have circumvented the prohibition by finding other outlets for their expression, in spite of everything—in geometrizing, for example, abstracting or, since writing has such importance in Jewish culture, in lettering. And they did make an attempt; some interesting illumination was done by some Jews and others have perhaps made a contribution to stucco work in Moslem countries. But under a religious law which was no less severe, Moslem lettering and arabesques of the great period were incomparably superior.

Better still, today we have certain knowledge that this terrible law was often violated. In the last fifty years a better interpretation of Biblical texts, important archeological discoveries such as those of Beth Alpha or Doura Europos, have clearly shown us that if the sum of Jewish art remains meager, mostly of interest to the historian, it is not totally without value. Even some synagogues were decorated with animated figures. Suddenly the intangibility of the religious prohibition as an argument no longer holds good.

Moreover, the ancient Hebrews made a distinction between idols and images which were not destined for adoration, the signs of the Zodiac, for example. The Talmud even suggested that sculpture should not be confused with painting, the latter being less dangerous: the painters might have escaped through this loophole. If they did so at all, it was with excessive timidity. It appears as if the Jewish artisans did not know how, or were not able to circumvent *to a greater extent* an equivocal obstacle. So that even if there is a history of Jewish art, there are no great Jewish artists. Or if there have been great artists of Jewish origin, their art was no longer specifically Jewish. The exact letter of the law was apparently maintained with almost complete success. The pertinent question is: why did this law survive? Why did the Jewish artists not dare, or why were they not more successful in defying it? Why was the synagogue able to gain this Pyrrhic victory? Why, *in spite of their law,* did the Jews not produce a great plastic art?

TWO

I am now convinced that the Jews did not produce a great plastic art because they could not produce one. This is not a self-evident truth. By that I mean that beyond the religious prohibition there was a more serious, a more radical prevention. Here again the explanation perhaps ought to be reversed: the Biblical veto did not deprive the Jews of an important plastic art; the actual conditions of Jewish life since Biblical times perpetuated the law. The Jewish condition did not permit the creation of a major plastic art and in this way seemed to confirm the triumph of the tradition. The proof is that the general religious decline did not give birth to a Jewish painting or sculpture, and when at last the Jews set themselves to paint and to sculpt, they no longer produced Jewish works.

If further proof were needed it could easily be discovered in the field of music. Not only was music not denounced but the tradition seemed well disposed towards it. For example, the image of David, the singing king and lute player, was a type they were pleased to promote. Song and dance had a secure place in the life of the Biblical people and, later on, the rabbis never objected to it. It is true that the synagogue quickly ceased to take an active interest in it; the orthodox even seem to have professed a certain scorn for those who practiced music, and it is non-Jewish scholars who were the first to note Hebraic music. But the source was never completely exhausted, and it trickles obscurely down to the Hassidim, ecstatic singers and dancers of the eighteenth century. What was the result? How did this relatively free branch develop when it was at last able to benefit from the fresh air and sunlight of the emancipation of the European Jews? Did the Jewish musicians consider themselves more as Jewish artists? One journalist went straight to the man who passes for the most Jewish of the modern musicians and asked him. His denial is as energetic and as significant as that of the painters.

"I never composed Jewish music! . . . Actually the only Jewish music is liturgical. For there was no folkloric

Jewish music. The folkloric music of the Diaspora is closely related to that of each country in which it was worked on." (Darius Milhaud.)

The revolt of the musicians moreover defines another impossiblity of an authentically Jewish art: that of a specific style and form. Up till now I have only spoken of the content of the works, of their anecdotal significance, because it is more understandable and makes the biggest impression. If it is said that Chagall or Mané Katz are Jewish painters, it is because they often paint Jewish subjects and because you believe you recognize Jewish characters on their canvases. But has a painter created a Jewish work if he has sketched a few rabbis? In that case Rembrandt would be the greatest Jewish painter of them all. If the treatment of Biblical themes sufficed, Jewish painters of adoption would be innumerable. *Subjects* of Jewish inspiration will not by themselves enable us to isolate an original Jewish art; we would need a recognizable *technique*. Jewish artists would have to have a formal method of operation peculiar to themselves, particularly in music where the anecdote is so subordinate. However, this requirement is valid for all the arts. But for this, a continuous *tradition,* a style transmitted from Jewish artist to artist, was necessary. Here is the conclusion of a study on contemporary Jewish composers by an excellent Jewish conductor, René Leibovitz:

"In the history of music there is no example of a Jewish composer working within the repertory of occidental forms, composing a sonorous idiom which was explicitly Jewish. . . . The occidental Jewish composer is above all an occidental composer. Purely Jewish musical elements are rare in his work; their influence is always exercised on unimportant details; even their action is always subject to more general laws. . . ."

In other words, technically speaking, there is no original modern Jewish music. And it becomes apparent that
it was hardly possible for there to be. How could the Jewish musicians, scattered throughout the world, assimilated by so many different cultures, have had a common
originality? An artist develops on a certain soil, takes his
subject matter from his surroundings, imitates the mas-
ters which surround him, even if he surpasses them. The
Jewish artist had no choice but to borrow habits of feeling and working from the men among whom they lived.
How could he have done otherwise without shutting
himself off, sterilizing himself from the start? Mané Katz
has been nicely described as a Jewish painter "of French
expression," and yet, over and above his Russian imagery, "he paints in French." The same could be said of
the majority of Jewish artists living in France. Conversely, should a Jewish artist innovate or make some
technical discovery, it is immediately put to the account
of the country that shelters him and will henceforth become part of the national heritage of that country. And
so it should be; the flower must embellish the garden in
which it is planted, though its origins be distant.

Thus we are faced with the same difficulties which
sapped the vigor of literature. Everything pointed to the
fact that *there could be no great Jewish art other than
secular; now, when a secular art is at last possible, it cannot be Jewish.* Either the Jewish artist respects his tradition and then resigns himself to the role of a minor artist, or he liberates himself from it to become a true artist,
but to do so he must renounce being a Jewish artist. The
Jewish artist must rise above the Jewish condition to develop as a free man. But his revolt begins with self-rejection. Once again the rejection of the Jewish context is the
first toll on the path of liberation. Modigliani, who absolutely denied that he was a Jewish painter, slapped a

client in a café who was making anti-Semitic remarks. This gesture sums up the difficult dialectic of the Jewish artist in the process of self-liberation: at the same time he spurns his Jewishness and the oppression.

This is easy to understand. They were intermingled for so long, and they still are so strongly intermingled, that it seems necessary to reject both at once.

THREE

Either the situation is paradoxical or I seem to be contradicting myself. I have insisted on the fact that Jewishness was too often pregnant with meaning; and here are the artists, in other words the men most attuned to inner fluctuations, who deny or seemingly do not wish to express it. But I have also shown how the rejection of Jewishness seemed a constant temptation, to a greater or lesser extent avowed, for every Jew. In producing a work of art the Jewish artist spontaneously rejects being a Jewish artist: because he rejects himself and because he knows that he is even more rejected by others. But neither silence nor subterfuge signify that Jewishness does not exist, or that it does not manifest its existence to some degree in a musician's or a painter's work. On the contrary, I can easily conceive of a series of studies on the Jewishness of numerous Jewish artists. I take the precaution to say that in some cases such a study might produce no results; in others, I am convinced that they could be astonishing.

Chaplin made seventy-eight films; only one is devoted to the specific description of a defenseless little Jew in the grips of the terrible Nazi machine. Only because of exceptional circumstances which compelled the pity of the world and largely prepared the spectators, did Chaplin feel it possible to present them with such a film. Is it believable that this great artist never before considered the

Jewish aspect of life? Had Chaplin—born in poverty —never been aware of it? Too many fleeting moments provide ample proof of the contrary: his eminently social humor, even the frail little character he invented, constantly battling brutes and the establishment, finding his only salvation in stratagems and the versatility of his intelligence. Can we believe that so many directors, so many Jewish film people whose childhood, family and friends were Jewish, have never felt the need to translate these Jewish characters and surroundings into film? The conflicts of Jewish life were too great not to be aesthetically fruitful. The number of Jewish artists, or more precisely the number of Jews attracted to artistic expression, are ample proof of this.

But these were the aspects of the problem: Jewishness was often too heavy to bear and for that reason could not be openly expressed. Truly a paradoxical situation, but in our existence, what wasn't? How could the Jew's art not have been a paradox? Wasn't his place as a citizen, his religious life and his language ceaselessly threatened and overturned by history? Such were the conditions imposed on every Jewish artist: unless he is able to avoid the subject entirely, he has to translate his Jewishness, and the real difficulties and anxiety it inspires. This he hopes to achieve without expressly unveiling himself as a Jew. I can submit only the same hypothesis here: like Jewish literature, Jewish art could only be a masked art. It was probably the only possible way out. I know perfectly well that all art is more or less disguised; every artist temporizes with his public. But the Jewish artist disguised precisely that which would have revealed him as a Jewish artist. A condition which is refused is still a condition if only disguised.

I have left aside any mention of the calculations, the strategies on the part of the artist. How can we fail to understand his hesitations and denials, at times his fury, when he is labelled a Jewish artist? Every painter would like to see his canvases on every museum wall and in every exhibition; every musician dreams of being the bard of his time and having his praises sung by multitudes. As long as the Jew remained society's outcast it was certainly better that he not present himself as a Jewish painter or musician. Let there be no mistake: as for the writer, it was not simply a matter of glamour or financial success. The discovery of his Jewishness could impede the artist in the completion of his task—his communication with the others. In any case, whether it was profound self-rejection or necessary camouflage, an instinctive repugnance to expose himself or a concerted decision, the modern Jewish artist has generally preferred, as a Jew, to remain incognito or transparent. Rightly or wrongly, he believed his salvation was in maintaining the greatest possible distance between his creation and his people and his Jewishness. Such is the paradoxical explanation of why Jewish characters were infinitely rarer in books by Jewish authors than in those of non-Jews. In describing Jewish heroes non-Jewish writers were introducing an exotic element; Jewish writers in doing so would have exposed themselves completely.

That is why humor was the modern Jew's only relative and collective success: it satisfied a double need—to speak and to dissimulate, to reveal the difficulties of the Jew and to make that revelation bearable. That is why the modern Jew's first success was in painting, even if it was not explicitly Jewish, while he still hesitates in literature. It is so much easier to cover up your tracks with form than with words—all the more so with abstraction: hence the triumph of Jews in these recent trends.

To sum up, as long as we remained a separated and threatened minority, two series of difficulties—internal and external—prevented the development of a specifically Jewish art. Jewishness was too difficult to live, to express and to communicate. From every point of view it was better to feign ignorance, to forget it and make others forget it. If the Jewish artist wished to be heard by a majority of men, it was better for him not to present himself as a Jewish artist. How, under these conditions, could an openly and firmly Jewish tradition of themes and techniques be formed? The Jewish artist was too often perturbed in his very being, affected by all these necessary subterfuges.

Better still, universality soon became a prerequisite for the attainment of a great art. The Jewish artists, painters, sculptors and writers, like their colleagues, could only become great artists to the extent that they were capable of universal culture. In this they were often fortunate. But for the Jewish artist who turns his back on the Jewish folklore and particularity, what remains that is Jewish? How can we recognize him as such? Here again we are faced with a dilemma: as soon as the Jew accedes to universal society he disappears as a Jew because his Jewishness is not embodied in a particular political society. Whatever a French, English or German author writes, he remains a French, English or German writer. Were he to describe leaves or insects he still enriches the French or English domain. The Jewish writer who extolled the trees or the birds did not exist as a Jewish writer. A French artist does not have to affirm that he is French: he is so through his automatic inclusion in French society. When a Jewish artist hides the Jew in himself, or simply does not insist on it (and he can hardly do so), he disappears in the dominant society. Such is the usual drama of all literature, of all art of the oppressed who do not possess an autonomous language or a free political society.

Even today, I admit that, as long as the relative condition of the Jew remains unchanged, I do not see what can be the solution to these difficulties. In any case, at present, it is clear that we can hardly speak of a Jewish art, except by hypothesis or unraveling. A history of Jewish art could only be conjectural and spectral. And, in this case, does the concept of a Jewish art have a well-defined meaning?

Is There a
Jewish Culture?

14

ONE

I had to conclude by asking myself: was
there even a Jewish culture? Would a Jewish culture today even be possible? Words
cannot express the drama of this debate.
For culture was our undisputed birthright,
our originality in relation to other peoples,
our title of nobility and our visa for the
future. We were weak, without a country,
without a flag, permanently humiliated, periodically crushed . . . but we were Princes
of the Spirit. Culture was our last trump
card, but it was the ace: it enabled us to
smile condescendingly even on our executioners.

Yet when we put our cards on the table
were we to discover that it was cruelly insufficient? Had we nothing to oppose all the
evil of the world? It is as a consequence of
such suspicions that many of my friends,
who had been devoted militants for years,
ceased all activity to become simple money-
makers, disabused and ironical. They were

wrong. One does not fight for ideas, but for men, though their values may be doubtful. But I must admit that the drop from such heights was too great and, at first, I was as disturbed as they were. Exactly what did this famous culture consist of, if it excluded practically every activity of importance in the world, including that of the Jews themselves? Since the masterpieces of Jewish painters were not Jewish, nor the great music of the Jewish composers, nor the literature . . .

I almost wanted to turn back then and there, stop this disastrous investigation. But how could I forget that most of our so-called riches did not hold up under even slightly critical examination? I have told how my first ambition was to become a philosopher; and I willingly prided myself on the idea of uninterrupted Jewish philosophy and, in particular, a specific moral philosophy. I even found among my student papers an outline of a "Panorama of Jewish Philosophy" in which I planned to reveal to the world a host of little-known treasures. The same pride which motivated the endeavor rapidly forced me to abandon it. Ever since, from time to time when someone gets excited about some Jewish philosophy which is ignored or unfairly treated, it brings a bitter smile to my lips. Just what is the philosophy? And more importantly, how much of it is left today? How do you distinguish it from Christianity and the secular humanism with which our lives and all our intellectual efforts are saturated? I have often confirmed the extraordinary mediation of Christian thought and sensibility in my own self. Many Jewish intellectuals understand their own Jewishness only through the intermediary of Christianity.

At times I told myself that I was too quickly discouraged because of too much pride. Still, the advent of a great Jewish philosophy almost became a reality in the Middle Ages. And much might be gleaned from the interminable and obsessive Talmudic meditations, or the fascinating delirium of the Cabala. But on the whole I was still convinced that the historians' severity was justified. At best the Bible might have served as an inspiration to a philosophy; no one can seriously hope to discover in it complete, coherent and methodical thought. With the best will in the world the Talmud cannot be considered a philosophical structure either in intention or in fact. "Nothing in all that seems very original to me," noted one of my professors, the historian and philosopher E. Brehier, in speaking of the Cabala. "It denotes less a particular doctrine than the Jewish form of neoplatonic mysticism." All the efforts of the Jewish thinkers of the Middle Ages, Maimonides included, were not so much directed towards the construction of new methods of thought, or towards the construction of a new system, as they were towards the reconciliation of their faith with already existing philosophies. In the recent history of Jewish thought, J. B. Agus, a university professor but also a rabbi, concluded that it is not possible to discover any coherence between the different aspects of this religious philosophy, if it can be called a philosophy. Let us admit that mysteries are rare and no amount of effort will ever give us back the great philosophical tradition which we have not had. Past Jewish philosophy has never been anything more than one long rumination on the law. The interest of our traditional texts lies elsewhere. They contain, more than a philosophy, a continuous telling of our collective life. But that is something else, and another book. . . .

But, again, let's leave the past alone. I will leave the inventories and the precise measurements to the specialists. Let us simply say that we were not one of those rare peoples who created an original philosophy and that we had other claims to glory. There is no point in making an issue out of long-past deficiencies. On the other hand, it was of prime importance for me to know what we had become today; on what I, a living Jew, might count. Did we really have a philosophy at our disposal? Now, this inquiry seemed even more disappointing. Not that the modern Jew has not taken to philosophy as he has to painting, to the point where philosophy seems to have become one of his most frequent temptations. However, he has not founded his own philosophy. On the contrary, this time there is not even any mention of a specifically Jewish thought. Even the promising embryo engendered during the Middle Ages seemed quite dead. From Bergson to Husserl, including Brunschvicg, the much esteemed Wahl, Jankélvitch, Schuhl, or even Lévinas who came nearest to these preoccupations, can anyone seriously affirm that their thought is a continuation of Judaism or even stems from it? Did they themselves desire it? Had they done so, nothing assures us that they would have been acknowledged for it. Spinoza, the greatest of them all, was violently rejected; it is a fact that he did philosophize outside the tradition and often against it.

"If since then [the end of the fifteenth century] philosophers have appeared among the Jews, they belong to the history of world civilization and had no influence, as philosophers, on their coreligionists in particular. . . . In reality the Jews as a nation or as a religious society play but a secondary role in the history of philosophy: such was not their mission." (S. Munk, *Mélange de Philosophie juive et arabe*.)

Thus attempts at suggesting a Jewish point of view, gleaning anything and everything having any relationship to Jewish science, Jewish chemistry or medicine, seemed at best an exercise for collectors, museum curators or minor historians. How do you define Jewish medicine if not by theories and practices peculiar to Jewish doctors? Yet how could such theories exist when the Jews had for so long learned from others and quite naturally given them the gift of their discoveries? In effect, when an original portrait of Jewish medicine is drawn, the best among the Jewish discoveries of all times and all countries are not generally chosen for they have obscurely passed into the universal heritage. The most curious, the most unusual, those things most closely related to the intransmittable peculiarities of the life of a group—the picturesque—are singled out. (How could I blind myself to the humiliation of such concerns!—a typical reaction of the oppressed who needs to reassure himself, to show others that he has given his share, that he, therefore, deserves to live. These efforts are explicable in a period when so many nations are searching for an historical past in order to justify their new-found liberty, as if the mere fact of living does not give them the right to live! As if the past had ever legitimized anything!) In any case, if we had no great artistic, philosophical or scientific past, was it necessary to invent one?

In the last few decades more prudent and more honest thinkers such as the French philosopher Brunschvicg have proposed a more ingenious formula which has had some success. "The Jewish contribution to civilization" has been much discussed. But what exactly does it mean? The nature of this contribution becomes equivocal as soon as you try to define it. If this influence is limited to the religious and moral tradition, then it is limited to a past which no longer acts directly on us since Christianity has largely taken it over. Or if we are alluding to the actual cultural contributions of the great men of Jewish origin, in what way are they Jewish? At best it is "the contribution of certain Jews to civilization," and, above all, not necessarily as Jews. So we can paradoxically affirm that at the moment Jews can at last contribute effectively to the common culture, their culture ceases to be Jewish.

The former rector of the University of Jerusalem, Leon Roth, clearly stated:

"A distinction must be made. In a sense the most important contribution made by Jews in this period was not Jewish at all. . . . Their contributions are contributions made by Jews, but neither in scope nor intention are they Jewish contributions."

TWO

"So what!" you will perhaps say. "Isn't it enough for you to finally become artists, philosophers and scholars! Why do you insist on creating a *Jewish* art! A *Jewish* philosophy! . . ."

But at the time I insisted on nothing! I didn't know what I wanted most. I no longer knew if a Jewish culture really existed. I wasn't even sure that I wanted it to. I was only sure of this: I wanted to get to the bottom of the Jewish fate as it was imposed on me. I was looking for a decisive answer to my problem—that of a Jewish man living among other men. I had provisionally decided that the answer lay in accepting myself as a Jew, in claiming my Jewishness, if necessary. This led me to look at exactly what I was accepting, what I should lay claim to. Now what is Jewish affirmation without a Jewish culture—without art, without philosophy, without religion, without Jewish values, without Judaism? . . . Was it perhaps impossible or absurd to accept my Jewishness in the midst of others, since this acceptance was condemned to remain empty? Perhaps the only possible attitude toward this oppressive condition was to reject it. . . .

I was unable to use the usual escape hatch, piously maintained by many of my friends: the Jew does not need a particular culture. They stated that it is even necessary to combat such an eventuality, for modern Jewish thought coincides with and must in the future coincide with universal culture. At a time when the trend of all culture is towards universality, when art, philosophy and science seek immediate international acceptance, shouldn't the Jew accept one of the rare advantages which history has at last conceded him? Contrary to most peoples, no great effort is necessary for him to produce a vision cleared of all prejudice, personal interest, ethnic or national peculiarities. Nietzsche had already said that the Jew was the true modern man, the closest to his superman. To seek out a specifically Jewish culture would be a regression, an intentional delusion and the abandonment of enviable progress.

At times this reasoning seemed more seductive, more flattering and generous than my painful and myopic self-searching. Unfortunately, I also saw that once again it saw false liberty and false greatness. The construction was too beautiful; as soon as I tried to approach it, I discovered that it was a mirage. It is perfectly all right to think that the true realization of culture is the suppression of all particularities in favor of only those problems common to all men. Yet these summits are rare, accessible only to great mountain climbers and, most important, borne by an entire mountain.

With all my heart I wished the Jew might rapidly reach these heights. I didn't have to be pressed very hard to admit that I hoped the Jewish intellectual would become more rapidly acclimatized than the others. But where was the mountain which bore the Jewish mountain climber? A purely rational definition of the Jew, made in complete justice and absolute liberty, would deny him all attachments, amputate all that constitutes the collective body of every other people. Effectively, this definition, splendid and proud on the surface, was just another formulation of Jewish negativity. In saying that the Jew's only culture was universal culture, or that it belonged to some other people, was once again stating that there was no Jewish culture.

At that time, I repeat, I would not have fought for the promotion of a Jewish culture. I would do so today because I believe a culture is essential to the health of a nation's attitudes, the common dreams on which each member embellishes. But having decided to accept myself and my people, I failed to see what there was in them and in myself to promote. For my affirmation to be meaningful it had to have some content. I had to affirm a particular being complete with a face, a language and a particular culture. Until now, all that I could discover in common with my people was a questionable past, our eternal misfortune and our sad solidarity. I perceived with terror that our famous culture was but one long tenacious nostalgia, the deceptive shadow of distant splendors. And now the best we had were bits and pieces scattered throughout other peoples and other civilizations. I still lacked the courage or the strength to draw the obvious conclusion. If Jewish existence was nothing more than common misery and endless defense, why insist on it? Because the others forced me to? Because the Jewish fate is objective? Yes, but wouldn't honor consist of self-rejection rather than self-acceptance, to overcome this strange defeat imposed on me from birth? It was a vicious circle.

Meanwhile the same dilemma which paralyzed each whim of Jewish culture was everywhere apparent. Not only had I failed to discover any specific culture, but the culture of the Jew, living among others, seemed to me stamped by an unavoidable impossibility; the more liberty we secured, the greater the impossibility became. The Jews who are grouped together, encysted, more or less consenting prisoners in a ghetto, real or symbolic, are able to maintain some degree of specific culture. But has it any value? It is a scholastic, sterile and inadequate culture—the ghetto culture of oppressed and broken people. . . . Do we have to live forever in a hothouse just to protect this plant? When the Jews can at last cease huddling together, living on top of each other and on their memories, when they are at last permitted to open their minds to the culture of the world, they progressively cease to exist culturally. I have already emphasized that the Jew was an abstract being, disembodied socially, politically and historically. Now, despite appearances, I had to admit that the oppression encompassed the Jew's cultural life as well.

For we are continually confronted by the same evidence. Jewish history has never ceased to be the history of one long oppression interrupted by short periods of liberty or semi-liberty, and by a few rare but never victorious uprisings. Bar Kochba, the last Jewish hero to emerge before the Zionist resurgence, was defeated by the Romans. My exposure of the multiple deficiencies of the oppressed has caused me innumerable problems with the oppressed themselves whom I was supposedly trying to help. Again I am aware that this inquiry into our cultural asphyxiation will upset many of my readers, Jews and non-Jews alike. All the more so since there is such a reassuring and carefully maintained illusion of our spiritual health which is supposed to compensate for our historical misery. Yet how can we forget that it is precisely since Bar Kochba's final defeat that the Jews have everywhere and at all times become a minority—even in Palestine? And how could serious damage or strange disturbances in their collective life have been avoided by a minority group so continually oppressed? Any other result would have been a miracle. And why shouldn't I speak of them when just such deficiencies, such inner destructions brought about by the oppression, are probably the most serious wrongs inflicted on the oppressed, those which legitimize his revolt?

This unending misfortune, these profound disturbances, are perfectly discernible in our collective spirituality, or those vestiges of it which have been left us. For what is Jewish art if not an art of misfortune, meditation on this misfortune, and on the means of delivery from it? A Jewish critic, Mamenyi, who did not perhaps see the full importance of his remark, noted that by far the two most frequently used symbols in Jewish art were the sacrifice of Abraham and the menorah. What do they signify if not defeat and possible death, followed by armed deliverance? Of course, they also have a metaphysical dimension, an enlargement or a cover-up, depending on one's viewpoint. The divinity requests the sacrifice and grants the liberation. But underlying the theological explanations and the picturesque quality of each story is the same infinitely repeated story of mortal danger, whether collective or individual, followed by some unexpected deliverance. So it was with Isaac, with Job, with Esther (whose sacrifice is not even exacted by God), with the Maccabees. . . . How many rescues, *in extremis*, in Jewish history! In short, far from being surprised that he has less and less specific culture, we must admire the fact that the Jew has continued to have any, considering the conditions of his existence. What oppressed group has really had a culture? What have women created up until now? Or the proletariat? Or, for many years, the colonized? Or even the American Negro? A culture cannot be fashioned with catastrophe alone or in continuous misfortune; you cannot create a great culture in a great oppression. There is really no need to look any further for the explanation of Jewish deficiencies in so many areas. It is not an unphilosophical head that prevented the Jew from having a philosophy, since there are today so many Jewish philosophers. But to all intents and purposes they could only philosophize when they ceased to present themselves as Jews. No ideological impossibility pre-

vented the development of a Jewish art; an impossible
condition was translated into multiple prohibitions. Like
any healthy organism, a free people, given time, can certainly digest anything. But the Jewish people never
ceased being socially and historically sick.

THREE

Here I would like to propose a distinction which has a
certain methodological importance: as a Jew, I received a
tradition. I do not have a *culture* at my disposal. It is
true that we have had an extraordinary cultural *past,* but
it is equally true that our present is at best mediocre.

I have previously insisted on the importance of the
Jew's heritage, his astonishing survival, and the mark he
has made on a great part of humanity. And try as I might
to avoid the curiously convenient recourse to the past in
which most men take refuge, I admit that I too could not
prevent myself from sometimes feeling this insidious and
comfortable pride. Then I was reminded of the frightening acculturation of the American Negro about whom
my colleague James Baldwin had spoken to me, or that of
so many other oppressed peoples reduced to literally inventing a past. But, I told myself, I belong to the people
who gave the Bible to the world! My heritage continues,
more or less clearly; it lives in me, to some extent regu-
lates my life, and even, sweet revenge, nourishes my oppressors. Thus, the tenacity of the illusion of the Jew's
cultural wealth.

"But all the same, there is the Bible! The Talmud!
You may reject their mystical value but you cannot ignore these cultural monuments!"

It was the answer to every objection, to every anxiety.
Each time I faced despair, whenever the facts were overwhelming, I too repeated, like every one else: "Yes, but
we have the Bible! The great Bible, last rampart, mag-

nificent vestige of a more abundant literature buried in the dark ocean of Jewish history!" Until one day, I noticed that it was this very recollection, this retreat to our past grandeur which confirmed our defeat and our present deficiencies. For if we are obliged to go back to the Bible to show that a Jewish literature and a Jewish philosophy have existed, it proves that we deemed negligible all that came afterwards. It wasn't even fair.

No tradition, no matter how fabulous, can ever replace a living culture, either in glory or in effectiveness. "In the world of the spirit there are no pensioners," said the philosopher Lévinas, and he was a traditionalist. All the temples and statues and mythology of ancient Greece could not have been a replacement for an adequate culture to the modern Greek; and all the history of ancient Rome could hardly have sufficed to shape the face of modern Italy. Culture is invention and renewal, renewal based on a certain tradition, but also constant adaptation. Culture is at least a *continuing* tradition. The rupture between his heritage and his culture is one of the more important signs of the multifaceted dichotomies which affect the Jew's existence. His culture ceased too long ago to be defined in relation to Judaism. Judaism ceased too long ago to enrich and transform itself; the grandiose tree has grown into its final form and the bark which protects it has become too hard. The Talmud has been closed since the fifth century, the Cabala, for all practical purposes, since the thirteenth century and the Bible for so long. . . .

What's even worse, this same solidity and the rigidity of this formidable tradition have contributed to the smothering of all Jewish culture. How do you go about reaching the height of such a monument? How do you dare to measure yourself against it? The guardians of the tradition have also led a veritable war—not always a defensive one either—against anyone who made the slightest move against the common rites and values: an almost constant condemnation of the plastic arts, a sterilizing disdain of music, distrust of all literature other than religious literature. Their persecution of all innovations in the domain of ideas was still more careful. The work of the great poet Judah Halévy is, in a way, a war machine against philosophy and philosophers. At the beginning of the fourteenth century (1305), the teaching of philosophy was quite simply prohibited. During the seventeenth century we see the frightful curse against Spinoza— "Let him be damned when he gets up!" etc. . . . —a curse which to all intents and purposes has been revived in our time, even by Hermann Cohen, a disciple of Kant! Martin Buber is the only one I am aware of who has tried to create a work of universal dimensions which is Jewish in its genesis and its extensions. Even this unique and great Jewish philosopher of ours was bitterly criticized by the traditionalists. (According to them, Hassidism, in which Buber said he found inspiration, is fictitious; therefore the consequences of his deductions have nothing to do with the "true" Judaism.) On the eve of his death, the city of Jerusalem conferred on him the title of honorary citizen only after some shameful discussions.

Of course the Christian church has also waged a war against philosophy and thought, and at times art, but on the whole it has lost. The synagogue, alas, has won its battle. A Pyrrhic victory, it is true. It has not prevented the Jews from philosophizing, but it has prevented the existence of a Jewish philosophy. Just imagine what Christian philosophy would be if the Church had been successful in silencing Descartes. Imagine what the magnificent Christian art would be if the Church had not, in the final analysis, tolerated and indirectly encouraged sculpture and painting. The synagogue combatted and discouraged to the best of its ability the birth of a Jewish thought and a Jewish art.

I do not want to put Jewish tradition on trial. Without a country, without an army, without political power, without any of these attributes through which a human group is embodied and identifies itself, what could the Jew do but hold desperately onto a distant past? A past in which he was at least sometimes relatively free and healthy. Oppressed peoples, no longer having a history, also stop having a cultural history. Therefore, whatever the cost, they must preserve their memories, fixing them into sacred rites, congealing them if necessary, in order to save them from the ravages of time and also to save themselves. But, at the same time, they are merely the living dead who are slowly transformed into phantoms and subsist only through this necessary remembrance.

I willingly recognize that doubt, critical examination, free inquiry, love of truth alone, would have imperiled the old edifice which was so stubbornly defended. For quite a long period in my life I wanted to pursue the path of philosophy with a single-minded passion; it was precisely during that period that I became furthest removed from Judaism. I wanted to become a philosopher so that I might experience an adventure which seemed to me the most exalting, the most noble and the most radical, one which demanded the courage and ability to question and dispute everything. Why would I have excluded Judaism alone from this general questioning? (Then I would have had to forget it, put it between parentheses, as many of my friends, apprentice philosophers, did. But wasn't that just one more insidious way of killing the tradition?) On the contrary, to the extent that I considered it seriously and made room for it in my life, the battle had to be declared. The shock was necessarily all the more rude as the law was determined to remain (and could hardly do otherwise) definitive, abrupt and always on the defensive. The philosophical approach is systematic and necessarily insolent vis-à-vis the estab-

lished spiritual order. Abstention or some respectful compromise towards my own tradition seemed to me an intolerable limitation or, worse, pitifully treasonous to the
very essence of the great project which I had decided to
embark upon.

If the only choice left to Jewish tradition was between
the rigorous maintenance of its position and its disappearance, our choice—that of the modern Jew—was between liberation from that tradition and death, smoth-
ered in the bands of the *tefillin*. On the other hand, how
were we to liberate ourselves without ceasing to be Jews
in the end? Tradition had become unlivable, but nothing
had replaced it nor could replace it. It was, I believe, the
drama more or less openly enacted by all the great Jews
of modern times who decided to face up to their Jewishness. It was probably one of the major conflicts of Kafka
who, without clearly saying so, fought throughout his career against the crushing heritage, which he nonetheless
accepted. I have shown in one of my essays how Freud
courageously accepted the challenge, how he dealt tradition—its institutions and myths—its hardest blows, while
always affirming that he belonged to it, even insisting on
what he might have owed to his Jewishness. Although the
accusations against Spinoza were vile, it is true that he
questioned the very foundations of Judaism without,
however, ever agreeing to break off his affiliation. The
ambition and the hope of them all was to accept themselves and simultaneously keep their distance from a tradition which had become unacceptable.

The impossibility of creating for myself a harmonious
Jewishness, reconciled with the world and with myself,
became apparent. As long as we remained a separated,
threatened and periodically bled minority, it was probably impossible for us to have healthy institutions and
a creative culture. As long as we had to accept and
strengthen our solidarity in misfortune, the tradition,

suffocating and crippled as it was, remained jealous and all-powerful, for it was still our only sanctuary and our only sign of recognition. The furious censors of Martin Buber, heirs of Spinoza's aggressors, would have been almost at a loss to define "true" Judaism and its "essential and eternal truth." However, their frenzied exclusivity, their a priori separation from the only specifically Jewish philosopher since Maimonides were illuminating: once again they expressed the ferocious and anxious defense of Judaism against every innovation. The tradition of the oppressed cannot tolerate, without grave peril to its own existence, anything but its own infinite repetition. However, the respectful rumination on the law and the encystment in its immovable institutions exclude all living culture and all social future.

I suspected that therein lay a disturbing truth, one that I would often encounter later on: *in an oppressive situation, self-affirmation generally runs the risk of becoming a confirmation of that oppression.* Perhaps in accepting myself as a Jew, I was in some ways accepting myself as an oppressed person. To defy misfortune, out of pride and as a tactical measure, I had decided to lay claim to my Jewishness. But the result was the hardening and the reinforcement in myself of just those traits of the vanquished that I was burning to leave behind. A few years ago a well-known writer coined an ambiguous formula, which for that very reason had immense success: "We must assume ourselves," people repeated with self-delighted daring. "We must assume our condition." Can one really accept oneself as a Jew? Can one really accept oneself as a proletarian or as a Negro? Really, this was a simple matter of not knowing the meaning of misery!

To assume myself did I, in turn, have to protect the obstinate survival of this mythology and these defense institutions which might be necessary as long as the threat lasted but which blocked, as much as they protected, the moral development of this eternally adolescent people? Did I have to content myself with such cultural poverty and terrifying dispersion? Did I have to give my willing consent or even contribute to my exclusion from the community of men which surrounded me?

It is too often forgotten that the oppressed person who accepts himself can only organize his life within the narrow universe which is left to him. Jewish existence, accepted or claimed by the Jew, was necessarily an existence which had been defined by others. Installation within the oppression molds the limbs and finally the mind and temperament of the oppressed. So I told myself that the only courageous, effective way to *assume* the Jewish condition was not to accept its moth-eaten positivity and its all-pervasive negativity, but, as is the case for all oppressive conditions, to transform it and actually devote oneself to the task of destroying it.

[AUTHOR'S NOTE, 1973.

These chapters seem to me to deserve several criticisms: I have not insisted enough in them on the *positiveness* of the Jewish culture. I am particularly anxious to point this out because the eclipse of its culture, by others and in its own eyes, constitutes a part of the condition of a dominated people.

I would therefore ask the sympathetic reader to refer to another of my writings, "Culture and Tradition," where I set forth precisely and unequivocally the essential points of my theses, namely:

(1) that there does not exist a people without a culture;

(2) that every cultural fact is a positive fact, even if it expresses something negative;

but (3) that culture among dominated peoples is almost always insolvent.

(See also the chapter "The Heritage" in *Portrait of a Jew*.)]

part three

THE WAY OUT

"If I am not for myself
Who will be?
If not now
When?"

Pirke Abot

The Jew and
the Revolution

15

The Jewish fate is an *objective fate*. I have
greatly insisted on this point, but it was a
long time before I really understood it. I
rejected, I accepted, I hesitated, I assumed
. . . as if my fate depended solely on my
own moods and my own decisions. Actually,
whether I accepted or rejected made no
fundamental difference to my situation. I
had added up the bill without the restau-
rant owner, and he was the non-Jew. I was
more than just a member of a Jewish community! Even as a Jew I was a citizen of a
certain type, an historical man among others.
In short, if I seriously intended to change
my Jewish fate I had to make a frontal attack on this net of *concrete relationships*,
often institutional, which tied me to non-
Jews.

Of course I did not see all of this quite so
clearly at that time. But a logic of human
conduct does exist. It was not just a whim
that, towards the beginning of my manhood,

I ceased being directly preoccupied with my Jewishness and threw myself into the political battle. I became of the Left, as we say in Europe—in other words, a determined partisan of a new society. In reality, since I had failed in my self-transformation, I undertook to transform the world.

I might as well say right away that the net result was that I beat my head against another blank wall, and discovered one more impasse. The failure was all the more serious as I was playing my last card. To avoid any misunderstanding, I wish to state here that my reaction differed from that of many of my old friends who became foolishly reactionary.

I have written in the past that a Jew can only be of the Left; this apparently astonished and irritated some readers. I still maintain that this is so. It has always seemed to me that a Jew is conservative only out of blindness or some short-sighted caution. I can today understand the temptation to defend oneself by economic success, and that money can have a true sanctuary-value. I had perhaps underestimated the feeling of security which money procures and its real power in many circumstances. But I maintain that, for a Jew, it is in the final analysis an illusory shelter; the Rothschilds themselves supplied their quota to the deportation camps. Whatever kind of insurance he has, the Jew remains a dominated person, in other words, permanently threatened. If he gives any thought to the matter at all, if he has the courage to admit it to himself, how can he fail to want a new arrangement of a society which is so continuously hostile to him? Certainly, theoretically, this improvement might come from the Left or the Right; practically speaking, the alternative was an illusion. The government of the Right, cultivating the myth of the homogeneity of the nation, of the people or of the race, naturally tends to exclude the

Jew, or at least limit his participation. Only the Left was, in some ways, philosophically for us.

It is true that the parties and governments of the Left very quickly gave us reason to doubt their ability to resolve our problem. Relatively speaking, we had certainly furnished the different parties of the Left with the largest contingent of hard-core militants, but this did not put an end to the hesitations and muddling of the European Left with respect to us. The Left did not defend us against the vile racist aggression with the complete strength and decisiveness which we had a right to expect from it. I have already spoken of the enthusiasm with which many of our youth movements followed the Soviet experience. We often wore Ukrainian-style shirts, and sang in Slavic rhythms (which have contributed much to Israeli folklore). Our expression became almost religious when we said "the country of the workers" or "our comrades in the U.S.S.R." Did all this prevent an anti-Semitic brochure from appearing in Kiev as late as 1964? Did it prevent Russia from feigning ignorance of the kibbutz, the only true collectivist experience in the world? I will never be able to rid myself of a terrible doubt: would the Red Army have stood immobile at the gates of the Warsaw ghetto if it had not contained Jews alone?

In spite of everything, I persevered at first in thinking that these were only errors, side issues, at worst the recurrence of an old illness which socialism itself would cure. It was a long time before I discovered, or admitted to myself, that here we were faced with a new and perhaps real impossibility. Whatever our deceptions, I repeated to myself, the Left was necessarily in our favor, since it was in favor of all victims, and we were incontestably victims. This logical assurance was already considerable.

But I also had to conclude that such a constant de facto failure of socialism on our behalf could not be without significance. Perhaps it revealed another equally compelling necessity. I wanted to believe in facts and this was evident: the Communist revolution itself had not caused the disappearance of anti-Semitism. We were furthermore not the only ones to suspect this and we murmured discreetly ("so as not to embarrass the new-born socialism"). The Russians themselves began to recognize it.

"Anti-Semitism is a problem, Nikita Sergeievitch. It cannot be denied or ignored. . . . We cannot march towards communism carrying a load as heavy as judeophobia. Neither silence nor negation is appropriate." (Yevtushenko to Khrushchev.)

I continued, I continue, to think that socialism is the only honorable, probably the only effective, road open to humanity. But I also believe that this path cannot be salutary for the Jew unless he takes it in his own way and at his own speed. Later on I will state on what conditions. Meanwhile, as long as he lived among others as a Jew, even their socialism was unable to raise him out of his misfortune. We had to remain partisans of the Left for reasons of political morality, and because the Left was all the same our most effective lightning rod. We were, in a way, condemned to the Left. But if we had to be historical cuckolds, we could at least refuse to be complacent or stupid, and above all accomplices in our own destruction. After the war one of my friends, a really broad-minded person intensely devoted to all humanity, began to inquire, even of the most just causes: "All right, but now tell me if this is also good for me?" It was clear that the revolution had not been especially good for us. I began to think that the tacit maxim of many Jewish revolutionaries—"Let the Jew perish if necessary, as long as the revolution is triumphant"—was at least as scandalous and silly as that of the believers: "Let the Jewish people perish as long as Judaism lives." I will not abandon socialism, but if it is to have a meaning for me, it must also resolve my problem. I asked myself then if it was really possible, without being fooled, to be a Jew-of-the-Left?

TWO

A portrait of the Jew-of-the-Left would be easy to paint. Under a dogmatic and assured exterior, he would be emotional, easily disturbed, both Manichean and Rousseauist; determinedly logical, but blind to the obvious, a mixture of desperate intellectual severity and annoyingly naïve sentimentalism; stubbornly insisting on seeing as friends people who would watch him being tortured with indifference; believing in the fundamental goodness of man and in the irremediable evil of some men; clearly dividing humanity into two imaginary lots: on one side the dirty skunks—reactionary, racist, incomprehensible monsters, or those reduced to thoughts of their wallets alone; on the other, their victims—the good and the pure who happily make up the great majority. Though they are at present mystified, one day they will certainly carry out the revolution because they have already done so in their hearts. Then, that which comically betrays, better than all the rest, the Jewish note: a touchy disinterestedness. On no condition can anyone suspect him for a moment of thinking of himself or his people. He fights unconditionally for all humanity; a trait which everyone uses and abuses; perfectly abstract, in reality laughable and touching; in the final analysis always ridiculed and in fact he is a sort of cuckold.

Exactly what does he want? Who is he? The difficulty begins with these words: "Jew-of-the-Left." On closer inspection these words look somewhat ill at ease, they

seem to clash: of the Left, certainly, but Jew? Why Jew?
Jew how? He is uncontestably democratic, more profoundly socialist, I believe, than the majority of his com-
rades-in-arms. But does he really want the salvation of
the Jews? Yes, of course, but you have already embarrassed him by obliging him to define what he means. He
is of-the-Left precisely because he wants to abolish differences, to fight against everything that separates men. In
the same breath he manifests his suspicion of all particu-
larism, exclusivity, folklore, anything which smacks of
obscurant reserve. So what about the Jew, as a Jew! . . .
In reality, he would have preferred that Jewishness not
intervene in this vast combat. Naturally he would have
wished, right off the bat, to be a combatant for the universal, the partisan of all humanity, and not, he thinks,
without saying it aloud, a sort of shopkeeper of socialism.

But you insist: he is a Jew-of-the-Left and not merely a
man of the Left; he even contemptuously recognizes himself as such. Moreover, he admits that a Jew is what he is,
with all his qualities and faults, his collective habits and
his preconceived ideas. Does he feel it necessary to liberate him as such? Would he fight openly for him? You
quickly discover the ambivalence and contradictions
which cause a confusion the Jew-of-the-Left is never
totally able to dissipate. He has no clear conception of
whether he is struggling for a world in which all particularisms must disappear, harmoniously fused in a homogeneous whole like a Gregorian chant, or for the salvation of all particularisms, each one entirely respected,
each one contributing its own voice to the general con-
cert. It is true that this hesitation is common to all men
of the Left who vacillate between a desire for total but
abstract fraternity and a suspicious recognition of concrete diversity. But in the Jew-of-the-Left the distress be-

comes acute, multiplied by the usual coefficient: self-rejection. For isn't the acceptance of differences equivalent to the recognition of oneself as different? Wouldn't this be opening the door to every kind of danger?

"Even before the war I was afraid to react as a Jew to political events. As a pacifist I was happy to oppose the 'bellicosity' of most of the others. During the summer of 1940, I told myself that it was better to save forty million Frenchmen than five hundred thousand Jews! The first racial restrictions reinforced my saddened acceptance. . . . I was even ready to accept the slaughter of the Jews if salvation for the rest of the French was to be bought at that price—if the fatality of History exacted it." (Edgar Morin, *Autocritique.*)

With the uncompromising or rather unconscious cruelty of youth I viewed this flight disguised as choice, this weakness masked as nobility, without indulgence. At that time I began to receive a few invitations to salons of the liberal Left, many of which were predominantly Jewish. Far from participating in this convention of selflessness, instead of rushing towards this grandiose horizon, I immediately laid down my cards. In reaction, in an effort to provoke, I spontaneously revealed the Jewish dimension of my motivations. I attempted to explain several political or aesthetic preferences by the Jewishness of the Jews or the racism of the others. I said, for instance, that I was convinced that the failure of Mendès-France was due in part to his origins, that if Léon Blum had been so detested, it was because he was a Jew. I developed the idea that the division of the political chessboard, with the anti-racist Left on one side and the racist Right on the other, was contrary to the facts. The good people, including the proletariat, had never been all goodness for the Jews.

The Left also had its racist theorists. And it was strange to observe the absence of Jews in responsible positions of the French Communist party.

The distress, the icy embarrassment which I provoked, taught me that I had committed a terribly tactless *faux pas*. It was almost obscene to talk so much about Jews and Jewishness. "But you're a Jewish racist!" they told me, only half jesting. "Doesn't anybody interest you but the Jews?" Far from it, I was interested in a lot more than just the Jews; but I did not see why I should be disinterested in them. When the proletariat fights, it fights quite naturally for itself; who would have dreamed of reproaching them for it? One could argue with the colonized concerning the opportuneness of his battle, never about the meaning and the legitimacy of his liberation. If I am a democratic Jew, should I never announce myself as such, or openly put in a claim for myself and my people? Why would I have been of the Left if I myself did not suffer from serious injustices? Certainly other men suffered under diverse oppressions, and I was determined to participate in all these just causes. But was there a more foolish or artificial policy (more non-Marxist in the final analysis) than to ask someone to fight only against an injustice of which he is not a victim?

Here again we are up against a very old and very miserable argument. The Jew-of-the-Left does not deny that the Jew is a victim and that he must also fight for him. But this battle must not be "provocative." His discretion and his silence are *tactical measures*. Ah! A fine phrase, one that we have found convenient for a long time! It deserves a place of honor among the comic phrases of our time. Anti-Semitism is supposed to be a slander, an aberration of the anti-Semite. The anti-Semite believes, or pretends to believe, in the existence of a repugnant, harmful character, who is the Jew. Must we, they ask, by speaking of it, give substance to this delirium? Aggravate it by heralding it? Isn't it better, *tactically* speaking, not to discuss it? Moreover, the non-Jewish masses do not understand this particular battle in favor of the Jews: *tactically*, isn't it perhaps better not to usurp their attention from more decisive battles?

I have never been a card-carrying Communist or Socialist. Other matters preoccupied my attention too early in life. However, had I been moved by the slightest desire, the spectacle of the militant Jews would have finally deterred me, precisely because of their attitude toward our common problem. Considering the average primitiveness of the troops of most of the political parties, their endemic xenophobia, their latent racism, the impossibility for the Jew to function as such inside these parties, perhaps it served no purpose for them to announce themselves. But then why participate if they had to renounce that prime dignity: the right to be oneself?

Tactically it is better for the Jew to fight with a party of the Left. Granted. But then you must admit that the situation was hardly gratifying. I have known many Communist and Socialist Jews, which is not surprising since half the intellectual and bourgeois Jews in Tunisia were either one or the other. Was it this famous tactic which made them appear shamefaced and embarrassed about themselves as soon as they had to deal with the Jewish aspect of their lives? Or was the so-called tactic not just one more expression of the banal self-rejection of every Jew? Whatever the cause, it resulted in their absolute uselessness for everything concerning the affairs of the Jewish community. And as they never had the slightest influence on the other communities, you can measure the amplitude of their success. This was because they were Jews, because of this Jewishness which they pretended to ignore and which the others, those for whom these men of good will and undeniable courage labored, never ceased to consider. Later on during the colonial agitation and after independence one saw it clearly: they were eliminated, quietly but radically, from every responsible post in their respective parties.

It is amusing, or tragic, to rediscover another abstract quality in the Socialist or Communist Jews, as if some fatality condemned the Jew to abstraction. They read only the Communist newspapers, the books by "comrades," or maybe those of fellow travelers; try to work in a profession which abounds in Party militants; marry comrades or convert their partners. For it is still a question of the same profound desire: to construct a protected universe which cannot be penetrated by the hostility of the world. And in some ways, by installing themselves in the warm bosom of the Party, they almost succeed; all the harmful and despicable forces remain on the outside. And supported by the framework of the Party, they can even censor and combat them. "It is very easy," declared the late, lamented journalist Georges Altmann. "I only see people of the *tripe républicaine*." He forgot to mention the severe conditions imposed by this frequentation: the Jew-of-the-Left must pay for this protection by his modesty and anonymity, his apparent lack of concern for all that relates to his own people. In the hope of a future victory he must first agree to lose everything. Like the poor man who enters a middle-class family: they demand that he at least have the good taste to make himself invisible. As if this obligatory discretion were not already a very nasty symptom of the real meaning of this admission.

The Jew-of-the-Left, if he recognizes himself as such, is under the impression that he is playing a game of billiards: he hits one ball in the hope of its hitting another. He hopes for the salvation of the Jews (for in any case he desires the salvation of all men), but he believes it is possible only indirectly; he wants to fight for the revolution and believes that it in turn will save the Jew. Apparently the reasoning is not absurd, but from a practical point of view can we expect our salvation to come from others? What could we expect from the forces of the Left?

THREE

I will say it loud and clear: not much. In any case once and for all I convinced myself that *an oppressed person must never expect others to hand him his liberation.* Jean-Paul Sartre asked the Democrats to help the Jews, just as he demanded that they fight for the Algerians. Generous intentions, as are almost all the opinions of that great French writer. But why should they? From a sense of humanitarianism? We know what such sentiments are worth in a long, difficult and confused political battle. Sartre, who was well aware of this, sought a more effective argument: the combat of the Democrats, he stated, coincides with that of the Jews or that of the Algerians.

But is it true that the interests of the Democrats coincide with those of the Jews? Is it quite exact that the interests of the French workers coincide with those of the Algerians? In fact, the contrary. The hypothesis has been regularly proved to be false, and always for the same very simple reason: the objective conditions were not the same. The combat could not be identical because the risks run were not identical. The typical Democrat, who is neither a writer nor a romantic militant, knows this. When the man in the street evokes the somber period of the war, he willingly admits: "The Jews were miserable! The most miserable!" He saw perfectly well that the Jew had been abandoned by almost everyone, and that he paid an infinitely higher price than all the rest. Without wishing to minimize the involvement and the generosity of the writers, for example, the best of them, the most daring, were all able to continue working while we were exerting the utmost control over ourselves so that we did not breathe too noisily. Simone de Beauvoir calmly tells about it in her courageous *Memoirs,* and there is unfortunately much truth in this bitter remark of a Jewish writer:

". . . Apart from ourselves and the unhappy gypsies, Europe's brilliant culture, its eminent and outstanding representatives, its eternal or temporary values, its prejudices, its aestheticism, were in no way threatened and hardly inconvenienced . . . in France, Sartre and Camus were published and staged under the occupation. . . . Aragon and his poems were in good health, Cocteau's box office receipts in the Paris theater left nothing to be desired; Claudel, Mauriac and Gide were published, read and glorified. Not one of them was our companion in misfortune. . . ." (Arnold Mandel.)

It would be absurd to reproach people with not having been as threatened and unhappy as we. I simply say that, because the stakes were never the same, the Democrat's fight for the Jew always had overtones of "in favor of the Jew." At best, he fights for the Jew because he fights for all the oppressed. But it is always graciousness on his part. The Jew must depend on the good will of the Democrats for his security, his safety. The Jew must hope for his salvation indirectly and the Democrat will give it to him indirectly.

Alas, that is not all: the history of our relations with the Left—of our messianic hope of being delivered by the Left—is the history of a great derided hope. Forty years after the Russian revolution anti-Semitism remains a fact in Socialist countries and among the militants of many political parties and unions of the European and American Left. When I pointed out this fact in *Portrait of a Jew* I was told indignantly that I was repeating calumnies perpetrated by the adversaries of democracy. Except for a few tirelessly stubborn or blindly unconditional advocates no one denies this any more today. At most they try to explain that it is not exactly racism, that it is not a deliberate desire to hurt the Jews, but a question of certain inevitable social and historical difficulties. Maybe so; in any case, it looks savagely like anti-Semitism to me. And whatever the explanation, dialectic or otherwise, for the Jew, cut off from certain professions, or prevented from a political career, the result is the same. We can at least say with Professor Hyman Levy, one of the founding members of the English Communist party:

"To be frank, we must say that the [Jewish] Marxists looked confidently towards the Socialist camp, persuaded that the problem would find a solution in this part of the world. But we must also declare with equal frankness that, up to now, our hopes have not been fulfilled. . . ."

Can this be accidental? One of the many perversions of the revolution? A personal antipathy of Stalin's? (It has been said that his Jewish wife and conjugal difficulties are the explanation of his anti-Semitism.) Alas, no; alas, not at all. It goes much further and much deeper: I maintain that a certain rejection of the Jew, be it clear or confused, is part of the thought of the very great majority of Occidental Socialists. I add that it is not even an aberration or contradictory to revolutionary practice as it has in fact existed in Russia and elsewhere. And I am perfectly aware of the gravity of what I am writing: *the failure of the European Left, with regard to the Jewish problem, was no accident.*

The fact is that there exists in the Marxist tradition, with regard to the Jewish problem, an original sin: it is Marx himself. I am not talking only about the individual

psychology of the man Marx. (Although here again a
study of his Jewishness would be fruitful. We are in the
habit of repeating that Marx was born the son of a convert; that is false. He was eight years old when his father
converted, probably for professional reasons.) The conflict was also ideological and objective. Certainly Marx,
in his turn, passionately sought, like all of us, a solution
to the Jewish drama. But for the sake of convenience,
coherence with his own philosophy, and because of his
dogmatic approach, he proposed an abstract image of the
Jew and of the Jewish fate. Wishing to define the Jew in
opposition to his contemporary Bruno Bauer who charac-
terized him by his religion, he reduced him to an economic figure; the Jew became practically synonymous
with the bourgeoisie. The Marxist solution is easily derived from this process: the end of the bourgeoisie, in
other words, the revolution, will put an end to the Jewish
drama through the disappearence of the Jew himself. In
reality Marx is illustrative of one variety of self-rejection
and even self-hatred, this time involving the objective
Jewish fate.

In any case, a new aspect of the Jewish misfortune
evolved from this original attitude of the father of Marxism. I will not dwell on the economic aspects of the Jewish fate again here; I have already spoken of it at length
in *Portrait of a Jew*. Contrary to what the Jews and their
defenders cautiously maintain, I believe that this aspect
does exist. It is only one of the manifestations of the oppression: the Jews are concentrated in certain branches of
the economy because they are excluded from other
branches. The economy is, as I have said before, one of
the Jew's sanctuary-institutions. But extending this observation to the absolute, Marx condenses all Jewish existence into its economic aspect. (In passing, it is interesting to note that the Marxist reduction coincides with the
anti-Semitic accusation, which also makes the Jew out to

be an absolute economic figure.) And, most unfortunately, Marx's essay "The Jewish Question," which is his
worst sociological work, has become the Marxist Bible for
everything concerning the Jews. This has resulted in the
immense dilemma of post-Marxist thought on this subject, and a plan of action, or rather non-action, which is
perfectly sterile.

If the Jew is an economic figure, synonymous with the
middle class, how can we still class him with the oppressed? Why would anyone fight for him? Despite the
efforts of a few theorists like A. Léon, for whom the Jewish people are a class-people, or Lenin's late discovery of
the Jewish proletariat, this hesitation will never be completely removed. It will torment the Jew-of-the-Left. In
fact Marxism proposed to the Jew-of-the-Left an image of
himself which at best is doubtful: the Jew-of-the-Left
cannot like himself as such. From a practical standpoint,
what then can he do? The truth is that he doesn't want to
do anything. Moreover, nothing can be directly done for
the Jew since the final goal is his suppression. There can
be no particular policy in favor of the Jews, neither before nor after the revolution.

Here is something more serious than the ideological
deficiency, and a tragic confirmation of it: Marxist *politics*, derived from Marx's theses, have failed totally in
this sphere. The obstinacy of the Jews in existing did
not diminish in the least, even after the revolution. And
the anti-Semitism of the non-Jewish masses, even in the
Socialist countries, has hardly been reduced. They tried
to blame the Jews: they were wrong not to mix more into
a society which was no longer hostile to them. That is
debatable. But even more wrong were those social theorists who became impatient as soon as they were faced
with a social reality which did not conform to their ideas.
Shouldn't they have concluded rather that the economic
dimension of the Jews was not alone responsible? For

their part, the non-Jewish masses have, to a great extent, preserved their racist reflexes. What could the Jewish masses do if not, at least for the moment, take this into account? What could the French Communist party do in view of the xenophobia of its own forces during the Algerian war, if not take it into account?

The same type of simplification had led the Marxists to see only economic revolts in the demands of the colonized people and purely economic motives in the psychology of the colonizers, which were insufficient explanations in both cases. (See my book *The Colonizer and the Colonized*. The Communist parties of South American countries, Cuba in particular, have probably fallen into the same error by underestimating the national aspect.) In the same way they knew neither how to go beyond the Marxist plans for the Jew's assimilation as an economic figure, nor foresee that "the workers' paradise" would remain a country like the others, a nation which would continue to treat the Jew like a bastard, which would feel the same repulsion and prejudice as it would towards an illegitimate child. In reality, the Marxists, after Marx, failed to understand the Jew's real, total and objective situation.

The result is that the Jew is still the bone in the throat of the revolution. And Khrushchev, marching on the heels of Stalin and Lenin, in his turn found the Jewish problem humiliating and almost intact: a malignancy in the doctrine and a constant clog in the wheels of political action. It is true that had the Russian frontiers been open, great numbers of Jews would have left Russia; and it is equally true that the Jews were progressively eliminated from positions of authority in most of the Soviet Republics. To say that it was necessary to draw the elite from the native people is either a shabby or naïve argument. Thus, the revolution and forty years of Soviet rule have failed to make the Jew equal to the other citizens.

The result is a sort of reciprocal despair. We are insistently asked not to accuse this government of intentional anti-Semitism; granted. But what follows is even worse: it has become, in spite of itself, objectively anti-Semitic, as if by some internal fatality. The government which by nature and doctrine wished to put an end to all oppressions finds itself in an insoluble conflict with its own Jews. And so, not knowing how to act effectively, it becomes exasperated; periodically it seeks to reduce their number, to make them disappear. So we have the repeated attacks against Jewish culture, the elimination of Jews from key positions in the Party and elsewhere. When, after the war, a campaign was launched against cosmopolitanism, the Jews were almost openly pointed out. Thus also the changing and contradictory policies of Lenin, then of Stalin, the gathering in the Birobidjan, then the abandonment of the formula of a distinct nationality. It has even been said that Stalin, at the end of his life, megalomaniacal and delirious, seriously thought of deporting them all, and even of exterminating them, like Hitler.

Sooner or later the Jew-of-the-Left discovers he is faced with the impossibility of two equally disastrous alternatives: frankly accept the complete disappearance of the Jews, or cease to be a Communist. These two solutions were adopted by men I have known and whose sincerity I cannot doubt. For them it was always surgical and dramatic. For some their resignation from the Communist or Socialist party was the most serious act of their life. In one fell swoop they had to break with a philosophical ideal, a social morality, a course of day-to-day behavior, which were painfully, incomprehensibly contradictory to the salvation of their people and themselves. Others, by gritting their teeth, were able to face horrors which to them seemed necessary. During the trial of the Russian

Jewish doctors one of my colleagues, a sweet, shy woman, finally recognizing that the condition of the Jews in Russia, and above all in the Soviet Republics, was not what it should have been, ended up by telling me:

"Since Socialism does not seem able to resolve our particular problem we must therefore cease presenting it to others. Many will not be able to; there will be some falling off, but never mind . . ."

It was that horrible policy which we call "the omelet," here applied by the Jew-of-the-Left to his own people. Of his own accord the Jew had to accept being among the broken eggs. The Communist writer André Wurmser even dared to write openly that a Jew's only duty was to disappear. From what other people could one ask such saintliness? And, what's more, such perfectly absurd and ineffective saintliness? Why such historical masochism?

I repeat, I continue to think that the Jew, as a threatened minority, cannot allow himself, even today, even in Israel, to break with the forces of the Left. For us, the triumph of democracy, humanitarian and egalitarian ideals in the world, is a question of life or death. But we are here talking about a minimum—a defensive alliance. At best a powerful Left protects us; it does nothing to advance our cause.

On meditating on this incapacity I discovered a notion which for me is fundamental: that of the *specific liberation* of each oppressed people. It is no longer enough to shout "We must liberate the Negro!" Many white Americans honestly think it should be done but do not know how to go about it. The particular and probably the only adequate mode of their liberation must now be discovered. The social revolution was in fact a specific solution to a particular oppression: that of the workers. Its dynamism, the imperialism of every doctrine, led to the belief that it was a universal panacea. The European Left has already made a serious mistake in wishing to apply it to the oppression of the colonized, which first called for a *national* liberation. Even in China, even in the countries where Communism came to power, the liberation had a particular character which was not exclusively economic. It would be ridiculous to expect the liberation of the American Negro from such a social revolution. The oppression of the Jew still being a particular oppression, I had to discover a *specific solution*.

The Christian Rejection

16

The conflict between the Christians and the Jews was worse: it was one of doctrine, inevitable in the very nature of the two religions. It has for some time been pleasing to insist on their cousinship, their filiation and even on the anteriority of Judaism. What is supposed to be forgotten is that this logical and chronological relationship was also at the root of another of Israel's great misfortunes. The Jew found himself a part of the negative mythology of Christianity.

There can be no question that theologically the Jew is a disastrous element in the Christian drama: at his hands Christ suffered and died. We can look for extenuating circumstances: he played this role against his will. In some ways he was even useful in this melodrama: it is thanks to him that the Passion of Christ was made possible; the play required a traitor and an executioner. It remains that the Jew did play these parts and such is his function in Christianity.

"We can, *historically,* extenuate the responsibility of the Jewish people in the crucifixion and reinforce that of the Roman occupants; however, *theologically,* it is the Jews who made Jesus die and it could not be otherwise." (Jean Pépin, *Le Monde,* Paris, February 4, 1961.)

This paradoxical conflict is not limited to believers alone. It can be said that Christianity was the historical triumph of Judaism, its crowning and its conclusion. The derisive survival of the Jews, a handful of humiliated and crushed individuals, magnified even more strongly the outcome: from the little national church of Judea to this universal temple. Yes, of course, but the unbelievable survival of the Jew is also a painful sign of the non-fulfillment of the Christian movement. It is living proof that Christianity did not succeed in conquering the world. This defeat is infinitely more disturbing, more irritating than that of the missions to primitive and distant tribes. Here Christianity is up against a familiar presence, in the family you might say, more liable than anyone else to understand it, to assimilate it, and which nevertheless rejects it with a tireless, impenetrable obstinacy. More serious, in reality, than any external setback, the existence of the Jew is the reagent of the intrinsic impotence of Christianity, witness to its perpetually disappointed ambitions, ironic reminder of those marvelous adolescent projects drowned in historical mediocrity: in place of an only God, the Trinity; instead of strict monotheism, idols and magic; and above all, in place of love, violence and war. Not only did the arrival of the Christ-Messiah, the cardinal point in the divergence between Jews and Christians, not increase the rigor and the purity of the old faith (on the contrary, perhaps), but it also did not change the misery of mankind. The Jew is the Achilles heel of Christianity, as Manes Sperber so nicely expressed it.

From this stems, among other things, the astonishing resentment of the Christians with regard to the Jew, a subject which also deserves a psychoanalytical study. One of the most interesting Christian discoveries, or rather persistencies, is certainly the notion of *savior*. When you realize the generality, the depth of guilt in most men, there can be no doubt that the personage who takes upon himself all the sins of others is infinitely precious. Now, in denying the arrival and the authenticity of Christ the Savior, the Jew prevents the guilt from being absorbed. On this point again, he is literally the despair of the Christian. That is probably one of the sources of the negative myth: this disturbing obstinacy of the Jew in continuing to exist as a Jew is psychologically disastrous to the Christian. It was only too tempting to suspect him of wickedness and perversity, and of increasing the amount of evil in the universe. In the same way that the Marxists, because of the very demands of their philosophy and of their action, should have been able to resolve the Jewish problem, and in the same way they have, until now, come a cropper. The Jew was, and remains, a thorn in the body of Christianity.

In a word, I have never believed in a profound correctness of Christianity with regard to the Jews. (And I am convinced that no one sincerely believes in it.) There has been some talk of expurgating Christian teaching. But the whole doctrine, the entire Christian perspective, would have to be dismantled and reassembled! All the tradition and the dogma, the credo, the crucifixion! They would have to forget too many events and abandon too many symbols. How do you separate the Passion of Christ from his torture inflicted by the Jews of his time? How do you go about relieving Judas of the onus of representing the Jews? Christianity is an historical religion, based on a dated and situated event: the apparition of Christ and his death in opposition to Judaism. You can try to explain, to attenuate this opposition, but you cannot abolish it. It is not a matter of detail or presentation; its very essence and meaning are involved. Christianity is also a culture. How can you expurgate such quantities of religious texts, all secular literature, all art, either Christian or born of Christianity?

I am well aware of the workings of the Ecumenical Council. I do not wish to minimize the hopes which it has aroused, in spite of the fact that there is something humiliating about this expectation, as if we eternally hoped for our acquittal! As if it were merely a question of appeasing the resentment of the Christians, while our own resentment is a thousand times more founded and just as strong! However, it is never mentioned except as proof of our wickedness. In *The Pillar of Salt*, I described my childhood experiences in a summer camp. I told my friends the story of a man called Jesus who was a traitor to his people and to his religion. But all the same I had just received, because of him, an extraordinary thrashing in the little church of that mountain village. For two thousand years Jesus has been, for the Jew, a pretext for a continual bullying, a working-over in which he often meets his own death! But I must also admit to having been troubled by the Council, as I was during the Twentieth Congress of the Russian Communist Party. It is possible that we have at last entered a new era; that these two major events are the undeniable sign of an ideological and spiritual thaw of the West, and that the Church is sincerely beginning to show somewhat less hostility toward the Jews.

But how could I take in all seriousness these Christians, suddenly so generous? By the same token I remain distrustful of those Communists, smelling like fresh roses, whose tune has suddenly changed to affirm the baseness, the cruelty, the imbecility of the same Stalin whose genius and goodness they had previously proclaimed. It is not so much that I doubt the actual sincerity of all my new-found friends. I am sure that all are not cold-blooded tacticians, for whom these concessions are only the latest plot of the Church, and that many of them rejoice that events have at last taken a turn which better suits their individual sensibility. It is only that I can no longer blindly consent to place my destiny in the hands of anyone, and precisely not in the hands of men capable of complying to such an extent, and then of reversing themselves on command. What assurance have I that tomorrow they will not once again maintain what they defended so categorically yesterday and what they reject so firmly today?

The estimable (and I esteem him) president of the Judeo-Christian Friendship Association, Jacques Madaule, in his preface to *Les Ténèbres Extérieures* wrote: "For anti-Semitism cannot be exterminated any more than can Israel itself. Together they persist in their blindness and their complementary error. The anti-Semites are as necessary to the continuing passion of Israel as the Jews were to the Passion of the Messiah." Daniel-Rops, the most widely read and recognized Catholic writer, tirelessly repeated that nothing, ever, could efface Christ's bloodstains, spilled through the fault of the Jews, and that this blood would cry out eternally against us. He even went so far as to write, horribly, in *Jesus in his Time:* "It is perhaps not possible for Christian charity to undo what the horror of the pogrom cannot compensate for, in the secret equilibrium of the divine will, the indefensible horror of the crucifixion." Have I misunderstood or was it really an excuse for murder? The most admired, the most respected Catholic philosopher, Jacques Maritain, wrote apropos of anti-Semitism: "It is an illusion to believe that this tension can disappear. . . . The only way is to accept this state of tension . . . ("The Impossible Anti-Semitism," in *The Jews*.) And there is no end to the possible citations.

And all that is past! Finally over! After a Council, certainly important, but whose hesitations, postponements, the subdued violence of its discussions and the mediocrity of the final resolution, revealed, along with their new-found benevolence, the depth of the Christian rejection. Come now, let's be serious, at least prudent. The Jew's liberation begins, the Church is just beginning to admit it (barely: I remind you that the Vatican still hasn't recognized the state of Israel, that the Pope says his Easter Mass in fifteen languages, but never in Hebrew), but we still have a long way to go. That is why, on a theological level, the liberation has barely started, if it was even possible. If not, could the Pope himself have been so thoughtless, on April 4, 1965, at the time of the meetings of the Ecumenical Council, in a church outside Rome, to reaffirm once again, referring to the Gospel text for that day:

"It is a grave and sad page. It narrates, in fact, the clash between Jesus and the Jewish people. That people, predestined to receive the Messiah, who had been awaiting him for thousands of years and was completely absorbed in this hope and in this certainty, at the right moment, that is to say when Christ comes, speaks and manifests himself, not only does not recognize him, but fights him, slanders him, and finally kills him." (Pope Paul VI, Homily Sermon, April 4, 1965 in the parish church of Notre-Dame de Guadalupe, in a suburb of Rome.)

Nor is it a matter of indifference to note that this text was reproduced by *L'Osservatore Romano,* on April 6, 1965.

I must note that I am writing in a Catholic country and I am examining here our relations with the Catholic Church. The Protestant churches are, alas, on a par in their accusation and their rejection of the Jew. I live not far from a Protestant church called the "Billettes" which needs to be restored. Taking me for a parishoner, they appeal to the goodness of my heart by sending me a brochure in which I read: "In 1290, in the rue des Jardins in Paris, lived a ragpicker by the name of Jonathas. In return for the cancellation of her debt he asked a poor woman to bring him a Host. The poor woman went to the early mass at Saint-Merri, communed and returned with the Host which she had received. Immediately the madman repeats upon the Eucharistic substance all the tortures of the Passion: flagellation, nailing, lancing. Then he throws the Host, streaming with blood, into a kettle of boiling water; but the Host escapes from the kettle and the image of the crucifix appears. . . . A chapel was built, etc. . . ."

Drawings go with the story: a Jew complete with hooked nose, enormous ears, leaning up against a pile of moneybags coldly dismisses a poor woman in tears.

Granted, this apparently happened in 1290, but the prospectus which exploits the situation was printed and sent out in 1964.

TWO

The truth of the matter is that in Christian terms the Jewish problem has no solution. And there are at least two sides to the Ecumenical movement which claims to be agreeable to us by strengthening each one in his religion. Everything that strengthens religions perpetuates the differences and the separation and our exile in the midst of our fellow citizens. And I would like anyone to prove to me the contrary! Does anyone know that in response to the Christian rejection the Jew opposes his own theological rejection which is just as categorical? They make use of the same language, the same prejudices and the same so-called opacity of the others!

"The Jew is incomprehensible to the Christian. He obstinately refuses to see what has happened. And the Christian is equally incomprehensible to the Jew. He has the presumption to maintain that the redemption is an historical fact in a world which is not redeemed. *No human power can bridge this schism.*" (Martin Buber to The Conference of Christian Missionary Societies, 1930.)

Fortunately the Jewish destiny is not a "theological destiny," as believers on both sides would have us believe. Then we would really have to give up in despair! Fortunately the Jewish fate is not totally dependent on the believers! If the end of anti-Semitism depended on our acquittal by the Church or on the prayers of our faithful alone, our lot would have been really tragic. In the final analysis I reproach the Ecumenical Council's effervescence, valuable though it may be, with the same thing that I reproach the renewal of Jewish exegetics whatever its interest. They both distract our attention from the essential which is the *real behavior* of peoples with regard to us and our often necessary response.

That is why even attempts such as the one Jules Isaac made leave me skeptical. Whatever the prestige of the man and his persuasive generosity, his effort was condemned to remain peripheral. He was himself aware of it: "This can last for years, a century, centuries," he confided to an interviewer (*L'Arche*, October, 1962). This did not bespeak any great confidence in the *effectiveness* of his own action; for he too saw anti-Semitism as the result of the confrontation of two mythologies. His ambition was to disarm the dominating Christian mythology, to show that it has been wrongly understood by the Christians themselves and that the primitive texts did not contain, at least in the beginning, so much ill will towards the Jews that it was now necessary to expurgate the subsequent texts of the accusation. The Jewish misfortune being the consequence of this ideology, it would be sufficient to correct the ideology to make the misfortune come to an end.

The reasoning was plausible. But Jules Isaac does not tell us *why* the Christians would disarm and correct their texts. (Is it out of pure benevolence which they have not shown us for centuries?) Nor does he tell us how the fundamental conflict between the two faiths can be resolved. Christianity was and remains a heresy of Judaism. It stems from, and is based on, a questioning of Judaism; it exists spiritually and socially only through this quarrel. Between Christianity and Judaism there is a dogmatic, historical and psychoanalytical impossibility. Neither of the two doctrines, neither of the two groups of believers, can pardon the other. And, contrary to what has sometimes been affirmed, it is practically the same for Islam. The Moslems are themselves mythically situated from the episode of Hagar, the servant-wife of Abraham, driven with her son Ishmael into the desert. The birth of the Moslem group coincides with a cruel injustice inflicted on its founder by the Jews. How could it ever be effaced?

In one sense, fortunately, the problem lies elsewhere! Fortunately anti-Semitism is not purely a matter of Christian or Moslem theology. The Christian opponents of Jules Isaac were in this case correct. Anti-Semitism existed before the triumph of Christianity and it has often increased in violence where Christianity decreased in influence. To say that it is no longer the same anti-Semitism is perhaps true, but this also signifies that each society makes its own adaptation of the rejection of the Jew, translating it into its mythical and symbolic language.

The real problem is therefore to unveil in each case the *real basis for this rejection.*

What we really want to find out is why the Christians have persevered in this ideology, why the myths subsist, why they are elaborated and consolidated in one direction rather than in another; why Christianity has become what it is today. That is the question the historian Jules Isaac ought to have asked himself. For the historian knows full well that there is no immutable ideology; all ideologies become curiosities in the museum of ideas, or are so transformed from their origins that they become unrecognizable. Perhaps he would then have seen that the Christian's dogmatic rejection of the Jew is only the expression of an ever-virulent objective rejection; that the mythic condemnation of the Jew is only the final expression of the perennial social and historical hostility which Christians bear us. And he would have concluded, more effectively, that the liberation of the Jew depends on something other than this ideological transformation, however indisputable its utility.

The proof is that the Church is beginning to change on this point as on others—it certainly did not do so as a concession to the pathetic exhortations of Jules Isaac and the Judeo-Christian friendship associations. The dogma is relaxing or pretending to because the Church is historically obliged to retreat. It has tactical reasons which are now evident for all to see. I have already pointed them out in relation to the colonized. Decolonization was carried out to the detriment of the Church, which was too closely allied to the colonizing West. At least momentarily there is no future for the Church in Africa or in Asia. And in Europe the progress of Communism, the birth of the popular democracies, has seriously diminished the scope of Christian expansion. Reduced to Europe, and a Europe which is itself eaten away, the Church has slowly realized the immensity of the danger. In spite of the

shortsightedness of its integrationists, it has therefore let
go of the colonizers and, in Europe, it has decided to reduce its pressure against the Protestants and the Jews.
Next to the Communist danger—the most serious danger
for the Church—its harassment of non-Catholics became
far less urgent. On the contrary, since the Catholic religion has not been a strong enough rampart against Communism, is it perhaps wiser to strengthen the other religions?

Having said this, however, I still do not relish political
cynicism. Whatever the initial and hidden calculations of
the Church, I too am delighted with the result. Moreover,
I do not believe in the autonomy of tactics, and a little
ideology always follows in their wake. What is most important is that the Church's attitude towards the Jews is
evolving. But as I refuse to succumb to any illusions, and
as I coldly consider these changes of the Church, I must
also set forth the reasons for and limitations of this transformation. The "mystery" of Pope Pius XII's behavior
has tortured many minds. Isn't it much simpler to suppose that he believed in the victory of Germany and that
he had acted prudently as a consequence of this and, very
probably, I believe, with disgust and in spite of himself?
If the Church is changing once more today it is because it
is taking social and historical realities into consideration, still with reservations and in spite of itself, as the
Ecumenical Council showed us only too well. It will not
go beyond such realities, and why would it? To expect a
sudden and superabundant generosity would be worse
than naïve. This is the situation: the Church is losing
ground in the world, but on the other hand, the very
great majority of the Church's clientele remains anti-
Semitic. The Church will keep these two imperatives in
mind. It cannot force the non-Jewish masses suddenly to

cease being anti-Semitic; and they are still profoundly so. Another Catholic writer warns us of it:

"I tell you, do not trust in the end of the horror; do not believe that the number of yesterday's martyrs has even slightly diminished that of your tormentors in power. They have learned to hold their tongues. Their hatred has turned into a silent demon, careful to hide its name, the more terrifying perhaps since it has been repressed. A neighbor of mine in the country assured me that in country houses good folk were to be found who secretly went into mourning for the death of Eichmann. The swastika has reappeared on the walls—the spider, surfeited with the blood of your race, who has fasted for nearly twenty years." (François Mauriac, *Le Figaro Littéraire*, June 9, 1962.)

Perhaps the reader finds me once again too pessimistic. In describing anti-Semitism as a phenomenon which greatly transcends Christianity and for that matter all ideologies and their ensuing conflicts, I am making it more complex and more durable. It is true; for me the doctrinal Christian rejection is only the expression of a very real rejection by actual Christians of living Jews. Clerical, theological anti-Semitism only expresses the condition of oppression which overwhelms the Jew, and not the reverse. Christian anti-Semitism merely translates the impossible existence imposed on the Jew. Having said this, however, I am infinitely more optimistic on a long-term basis. If Jewishness is not a metaphysical decree but a condition, then it can and must change at the end of the battle which we must undertake.

THREE

Meanwhile what did the Christians want and what do
they still want? The disappearance of the Jew. In this,
curiously enough, they are in agreement with the Marxists. It is not an accident that the two greatest forces of
our time regard the problem in the same light and propose the same solution. Traveling parallel routes they
have been stopped by the same obstacle: the objective
condition of the Jew. (In other words by this double evidence: the existence of the Jew and the anti-Semitism of
their troops.) And both have shown themselves to be in-
capable of eliminating this condition in any way other
than by the suppression of the Jew.

For in effect what does the revolutionary ask of the Jew
if not that he cease to be different, and thus to embarrass
his revolution? What does the Christian demand if not
that the Jew cease to be a Jew, and thus bear witness to
the insolvency of Christianity? Of course, each one envis-
ages the future of the Jew after his own fashion. The
Christian is a conservative who hopes to integrate him
into a tradition; the Marxist demands his future transparency. But both of them feel that the Jew must renounce his Jewishness so that the non-Jew can forget
about it too. The Christians have tirelessly proposed
their identity to the Jew—conversion—as the only path
to salvation.

But, the reader will again object, what about the Ecumenical Council? Not enough attention was paid to the
fact that on this point the Conciliary Fathers remained
discreet. Commentators or religious figures without real
responsibility heedlessly expressed opinions on the subject. The ultimate and necessary terms for any Judeo-
Christian reconciliation remain conversion. In 1963 when
the work of the famous Council was well underway Father Daniélou, one of the most well-known French Jes-

uits and a founding member of the Judeo-Christian Friendship Association, could still affirm his "conviction that the whole of Israel will one day recognize in the Christ the accomplishment of its hope." He was only repeating an idea which he had developed even more clearly a few years earlier: "The Jews and the Moslems will be saved, but not by Moses nor by Mohammed, but only by Jesus Christ. . . . No compromise is possible. . . . There is an irreducible antagonism which we do not have the right to minimize through our desire of reconciliation."

I set a limit to the number of citations I would use in this book for it seems to me an easy and merely illustrative exercise, but here the mass of texts is such that it becomes a proof. The latest Christian book to make a maximum effort at mutual understanding, that of the Abbé Jean Toulat, unavoidably concludes with the need for disappearance through conversion of all that is not Christian. We are certainly not dealing with a well-accepted doctrine:

"There will be no more Greeks, nor Jews, nor men, nor women, nor slaves, nor free men, but a single humanity wholly united in Christ. Thus will Holy History end."

I admit that I prefer a thousand times this honest frankness which exactly states the problem.

The only trouble is that to date the Jew has refused to convert. (Rightly or wrongly; see the chapter on conversion.) He continues to exist in spite of the hatred, and the hatred around him remains intact. (And the one explains the other.) Faced with this double opacity, this double knot, the Christians concluded that there is no solution. And it is true that they find themselves faced with an impossibility of fact, a sort of mystery as they put it, in any case an historical drama. So pushing things as usual to the limit, they affirm that the drama of Israel is an eternal mystery. This simply means: we do not see any solution; we are powerless to resolve this problem; therefore the Jew will continue to live eternally in misfortune.

May I say, once again running the risk of being misunderstood, that, stripped of its metaphysical costume, the underlying analysis of the Christians is in the end correct? It would have been surprising if such a powerful assembly of men, led by leaders of such great talent, meditating on a matter which touches them so closely, were *totally* mistaken in their evaluation of reality. I am convinced that the Christians were right when they warned us: as long as the Jew lives among Christians he must choose between misfortune and conversion. And since conversion does not tempt him—whether because of his stupidity or his pride, his blindness or his perversity—he is condemned to misfortune. Thus in Christian thought the theme of misfortune is closely associated with Israel. This is not merely a Christian wish, a malediction. The Christians know and verify every day that the Jew actually lives in misfortune. And it is not my Christian readers who denied this statement when they read it in my last book.

Of course, they have recourse to their ideology to interpret this misfortune which is in turn reconfirmed: the Jew killed Christ. Then, misfortune feeding on misfortune, ideology comes in turn to their aid. The Jew becomes mythically that which he is in the Christian tradition. But first the real exasperation of the Christians is a measure of their real failure. I believe them when they write that the malediction of the Church is but the reverse side of a benediction which they wish to bestow upon the Jew. I believe them when they affirm that they pray ardently for the Jew while they behave hatefully towards him, depriving him of his ability to earn a living, keeping him outside their society or allowing him to be periodically massacred by frenzied crowds. They are like morbid lovers who kill the women they cannot possess. There certainly lurks, in Christians as well, the resentment of a disappointed love.

Christian exasperation is an echo of that of the Marxists; they originate from the same resentment. And our periodic massacre is, alas, only an exacerbation of this same resentment—let them die! Let them disappear physically since there is no way of convincing them to disappear spiritually! Lenin's rage against the Jewish Socialists' obstinate insistence on a separate existence, the bloody madness of Stalin in his last years and the Nazi delirium all carry on the tradition of the Inquisition and the Crusades. The absolute rejection of the Jew can be expressed as well by the myth of the Jew as it can by his extermination, just as the rejection of the colonized by the colonizer was expressed in the mythical image of the colonized.

Fortunately here again we come up against the automatic limitation of the *Nero complex,* which I described more fully in *The Colonizer and the Colonized:* a spontaneous curb on the persecution which is an integral part of the mechanism of annihilation of the oppressed and which automatically mitigates the massacre, for otherwise the oppressor would disappear along with his victim. The Christians have done *everything* they could to destroy the Jew; but at the same time, luckily, the Christians like the Marxists needed to be in the right vis-à-vis the Jew. The Jew has to be in the wrong for them to be in the right. Now, you cannot be right vis-à-vis a corpse. It therefore becomes necessary to call a halt to the molestations, allow the victim to catch his breath, pull himself together, dress his wounds, in order to begin again trying to convince him, torturing him. Fortunately the oppressor needs the oppressed!

In any event the only choice the Christians, as such,

were able to offer us was between misfortune and disappearance. The same holds true for the social revolutionaries. Both of them consider the condition of their forces. Why shouldn't they, for they are the expression and the relatively sincere leaders of these forces. For I must add that whatever their temptation might be to utilize us to their profit, whatever the wrong they have done us, I in no way accuse the Church or the Marxists of systematic and intentional perversity with regard to us. I refuse to answer a myth by a myth. I even believe that in a way they both represent the best of western spirituality and I am convinced that they sincerely wish to find a definitive solution to the problem which our existence creates for their activity and their philosophy. But if their analyses of our condition are relatively exact, I notice that they have always failed. And their failure itself is illuminating. They were unable to overcome this condition, except by our collective death. In reality, they never did anything but express the impossibility of our life among them.

An Impossible Condition

17

Yes, the Jewish condition was an *impossible condition*. No one will be surprised, I suppose, at this conclusion. My entire output to date is, in a sense, an inventory and an elucidation of this notion; and this whole book further illustrates it. *I define an impossible condition as a condition which can have no solution in its actual structure.* I did not find a solution to the drama of being Jewish in the Diaspora, neither in myself nor in the others, and I finally gave up trying to transform myself and others.

I am sufficiently diffident to know how much of my own personal experience was at the origin of this search. Even today I remain exaggeratedly upset by the spectacle of any injustice exercised against any individual or any people. And I have probably gathered all these impossibilities together because I lived through several unforgettable experiences simultaneously: colonization, poverty, Eastern Jewry . . . But I also know that if my personal life and my own sensitivity have made me more attentive to every kind of misery, that in no way, alas, excludes the existence of the misfortune which is the lot of the multitude. For, in the final analysis, the oppression does exist! Obvious, outside myself, generating unlivable human relationships, insoluble as long as the oppression endures. I had described the colonial condition in this way and concluded that there was probably no way out as long as the relation between colonizers and colonized remained unchanged. And I was accused of dogmatism, pessimism, not to mention perversity! We know what happened. I was only wrong in having been right too soon.

My Jewish condition was impossible to live, first of all because it was relentlessly imposed on me. It was more than a collection of impressions which were lived through, an inner experience. It could also be perceived from without, described by the non-Jewish observer, historian, sociologist, jurist, psychologist. It has been calculated that the Jews have suffered two hundred expulsions in two thousand years, on the average of one expulsion every ten years! Sometimes here and sometimes there, of course. But I have already said that the misfortune which befalls a local Jewry anywhere at all in the world reverberates throughout the entire dispersed body and propagates the same waves of anxiety. The collective Jewish conscience, periodically recharged with anguish, is thus a permanently suffering conscience. But I hope I have impressed the reader with the objectivity of the Jewish condition; otherwise my words would remain incomprehensible. I have pointed out the obstacles and the dilemmas, the inevitable laceration, the various and successive abstractions, the only too-real impossibilities. In this fashion I have constantly passed from difficulty to difficulty, hopping first on one foot, then on the other, without ever being able to rest in even relative equilibrium. I was neither able to reject nor to accept my fate without immediately discovering a new series of obstacles and ambiguities, just as unsurmountable.

The hero of *The Pillar of Salt*, who certainly represents me to a great extent, concluded that he first had to leave everything without thought of return—his family, his community, even the girl he thought he loved. "Oh, let me hear no more of Jews and Judaism and of myself as a Jew! Let me put an end to this inexhaustible torment!" And he goes to Argentina in the hope of starting a new life, this time anonymous. My Argentina was Europe, Paris to be exact, where it was only a matter of months before I discovered that one does not easily cease to be Jewish, and that self-rejection never solves anything. No mask, no compensatory tic could save me. The net result was, on the contrary, constant self-contraction, a veritable and painful distortion of the whole being which isolated me, singled me out more surely than the accusation of others. In short, self-rejection, far from being the best response to the oppression, rapidly appeared to me one of the most characteristic traits of the oppressed. Far from being a free and courageous act, it was the expression of his non-liberty, of his barely disguised submission to the accusation and the aggression. Complicity with the oppressor was not far off. Self-rejection was then perfectly useless as soon as the threat became clear.

Was it necessary to accept oneself as a Jew? That attitude was attractive to me because it offered the possibility of pride, an impression of facing-up. I decided that henceforth I would tell others and myself: yes, I am Jewish—what of it? Yes, to some extent and on several points I am *different* from my fellow citizens, from other men. In the future, far from trying to pass over these differences, I would immediately recognize them—without provocation of course, but spontaneously. And I would even demand that others recognize them and take them into consideration, that they allow me to live as I please and as my nostalgia, my childhood memories and my sympathies dictate. All of this continues to be my firm belief. I have sufficiently stressed these demands and this respect towards differences.

It was soon clear, however, that though this affirmation was certainly more honorable and perhaps more soothing, it could not save me any the better. Later on I will come back to the intimate difficulties of this acceptance, the inevitable and dramatic confrontation with a half-obsolete tradition which, for that very reason, was all the more exacting and captious. What was even more serious was that in proclaiming myself a Jew I was also recognizing, in reverse, the separation and the exclusion. In fact, it was again a matter of agreeing to the oppression. Oddly enough, no matter which way I turned I always found myself an accomplice of the established order, of the reigning iniquity. *It was just as impossible, within the oppression, to reject as it was to accept oneself.* Neither attitude could negate the obsessional and opaque reality which was my burden as a Jew. Within the framework of the oppression there was no way out for the oppressed.

Here we have the prototype of the condition of conflict, one which is also neurosis-inducing. I know full well that man, a tenacious beast, can bear anything and always survives as long as he has not been systematically exterminated. (From time to time, however, a Jew does decide to put an end to himself. Stefan Zweig committed suicide after the arrival of the Nazis, because he had realized that his life was finished in any case. The hero of Israel Zangwill's *Had Gadya* slides into the Thames: the *Adam* of Ludwig Lewisohn could be cited as another example. From time to time the Jewish fate appears absolutely unlivable.) I am also aware that the oppression is maintained in a state of continual paroxysm, that it is not intolerable at the same time in every place, that each temperament gets used to it in its own way. The fact remains that the Jewish condition contains, probably in every case, a high coefficient of suffering in the clinical sense, a costly effort of response to this painful stimulant.

Had I not forbidden myself any detour in these books I would also have developed the undeniable correlation between neurosis and Jewishness. "Isn't being Jewish also a mental illness?" was the hardly amusing title of a Jewish journal. Fortunately every Jew is not psychically fragile, and it might even be that the Jews are by now better able to cope with the hazards of history. But too much so; it's too much. The number of psychic disorders, admittedly neuroses rather than psychoses, is assuredly much greater among Jews than among non-Jews, even considering the fact that they are more apt to seek help, in other words more liable to reveal themselves as ill. A psychiatrist who had practiced for twenty years in Tunisia summarized his experience for me in these words: "The specific malady of the Jews was anxiety and its corresponding depression." I would not have needed to do much research to bear this judgment out. I was certainly not surrounded by numerous examples of calm and serenity. At seventy, impotent, half blind, my father started every time the bell rang: "What could they want from me now?"

When I mentioned these facts to a Jewish audience they objected that this was not a Jewish trait but a consequence of anti-Semitism and transplantation. The observation is perfectly correct. The sons of immigrants, whether Jewish or not, probably comprise a high ratio of the mentally ill. But since when have I pretended that the Jewish condition was an absolute, immune to all analysis? On the contrary, all my efforts have tended to show what it has in common with other oppressive conditions. The neurosis of the Jew is not essentially different from that of others. If the Jew is more frequently disturbed, it is because he is more often, more continually assaulted by society and by history. Mental illness is an illness of inadaptability. Now the adaptability of the Jew is constantly questioned, not to mention the hesitations and the guilt of a too-difficult and yet necessary assimilation.

I had written that the Jewish condition humiliated, corroded and destroyed the Jew; this shocked everyone at once—the laymen because they denied the existence of a particular Jewish condition, the believers because they mythically transformed this misery into a supernatural mission. It is, however, profoundly and unfortunately true of all oppressions. I was informed by a Canadian reader that depression is widespread among the French Canadians. In my opinion the main interest of Franz Fanon's work is probably his sketches of a psychopathology of the colonized. If the objective qualities of a too-difficult situation cannot be transformed there are really only two results: criminality or neurosis. In other words, there is aggression against the others or against oneself. As criminality is, practically speaking, forbidden, the Jew, an observed and threatened minority, is left with nothing but neurosis. The Jewish condition, I firmly believe, is a pathogenic condition.

The Jews themselves admit as much. And if I have restricted myself to the facts of my own personal experience, I have constantly compared my experience with that of my coreligionists. The Jews have certainly formed this image of themselves, over and above deformations of the imagination or interpretations which are, moreover, significant. My only merit consists perhaps in having pushed the investigation to the extreme, co-ordinating the results and daring to transcribe them. For after all what do all these dissertations on the Jewish "destiny"

signify if not this impossibility? If not a resigned or indignant confirmation of the fact that so far there has
never been a possible solution to the Gordian knot of the
Jewish condition. Does Jewish theology do something
other than express the Jew's anguish when faced with this
insurmountable problem? What does it offer if not an
almost desperate hope and an infinitely postponed liberation? Of course, it transforms this very difficult destiny
into one of the conditions of intercourse with God, but it
must first supply a drama! What are the Zionists saying,
even the most positive among them, when they inexor-
ably, almost naturally, link anti-Semitism to the presence
of the Jew?

"I believe that the only fundamental cause of anti-
Semitism . . . is the existence of the Jews. We carry anti-
Semitism around in our packs everywhere we go."
(Chaim Weizmann.)

TWO

Yet in spite of everything I do not consider the results of
this somber itinerary hopeless. The reader will have noticed that I have closely linked the impossible condition
to the oppression; it will therefore bear the fatality and
the weight of the oppression but *nothing more.* The Jewish condition seemed insoluble to me, but only as long as
the oppression of the Jew continued. It would therefore
be soluble to the extent that the oppression could be reduced, and according to the manner in which we are able
to free ourselves from it.

Here I would like to suggest one last distinction: for
me the impossible condition is not exactly a *tragic condition. I call a tragic condition one which is definitively
contained within itself from the start.* On the stage, for
example, a condition only appears fluid because of an ar-

tifice of development which relates the story as if the ending were uncertain, in order to sustain our interest. However, one discovers along the way that, the characters and the situation being what they are, a favorable outcome is excluded. It only responds to its own duration, that of a crisis, over which external events have almost no influence if not to accelerate the catastrophe which is incribed within it.

In a sense it is true that the Jewish condition until now has behaved like a tragic condition; death was the monogram inscribed on it as it is on most oppressive conditions. I have already said that murder and the crematory ovens were only the exasperation of anti-Semitism, the ultimate effort of the oppressors at annihilation of the oppressed. But in spite of everything, it was a social and historical drama, a relative and not absolute impossibility. Nothing prevented one from thinking that in acting on the given facts of the drama one might not destroy the source of this torrent which periodically devastated Jewish existence. And I am now aware that I have never ceased to believe in this. Call it a resurgence of the old Messianic confidence in the Mashiah of my childhood if you wish, or simply Socialist optimism; I have always stubbornly thought that the fight was as possible as it was necessary.

The Jewish condition was insoluble, but in its present formation, in other words as long as the fundamental relation between Jews and non-Jews remained the same. This merely signifies that this relation had to be overthrown, that this formation had to be demolished and not merely come to terms with. I have already shown, apropos of the colonized, that impossible conditions are closely linked to revolt and revolution. In reality the Jewish condition was a potentially and permanently prerevolutionary condition. It called for revolutionary action; in other words, an action which must end this condition. *The Jew asked to be surpassed.*

Here is an ambiguity which must be cleared up. When I wrote that we had to end the Jewish condition, and, in a way, the Jew himself, a great hue and cry arose: I was ashamed to be a Jew, I wished for the disappearance of Jewry, I reveled in misfortune, etc. . . . Had I been in the least ashamed of being a Jew would I have signed so many books, written in the first person, in which I present and analyze myself as a Jew? Would I have associated my name as a writer with a book entitled *Portrait of a Jew*, which I almost called *Self-portrait of a Jew*? On the contrary, I think that we must summon the courage to face this condition head on, without any particular provocation, but we must draw up a very precise balance and dare to present it in public. I believe, it is true, that the Jewish condition must be abolished. What does this mean? I am not proposing the end of Judaism, nor the end of Jewry, nor the end of the Jew. I am aware of the exact weight and meaning of my words. I do desire to see the end of the misfortune of the Jew and the abolition of the conditions which perpetuate it. Will the result very probably be that the Jew, such as we know him, will change? I say yes; and why not?

Other readers have written: "In spite of everything I am proud to be a Jew! I want to remain a Jew in spite of everything!" Women readers have even warned me, provocatively: "I am happy to be a woman! I would not want to be a man for anything in the world!" "True courage," they cried, "is to remain what one is!" "To hold on with one's own people, etc. . . . " May my readers forgive me. I find little boldness in such courage and such preferences—they are even misleading if they stop there. Let me explain myself. You may choose, in spite of everything, to remain on the side of the oppressed, whatever the risks; *but you cannot prefer to be oppressed.* In any case I fail to see the glory in it. To uphold one's oppressed condition is an act of false daring and empty words, if it does not also mean an *action* to abolish it, the firm decision to do everything in one's power to cease being an oppressed person and to end the oppression.

For me the dignity of the oppressed begins, first, the moment he becomes conscious of his burden; second, when he denies himself all camouflage and all consolation for his misery; third, and above all, when he makes an effective decision to put an end to it. May all the victims of history forgive me. I know only too well how a victim becomes a victim. I understand the subterfuges which enable him to survive. I pity his inner ruin, but I do not admire his grimaces of pain or his scars. I do not find his suffering face the most beautiful in the world nor do I consider the plight of the victim to be very admirable. You will remember during the Eichmann trial the irritated and slightly scornful astonishment of the young Israelis at the Jews of the Diaspora who allowed themselves to be slaughtered, too often without the slightest gesture— even of despair. I must admit that whatever the naïveté, the ignorance, the insolent thoughtlessness of these young men so freshly minted, I am in the end more on their side than on that of these perpetual victims, complaisant towards their pitiable fate, which the immense majority of us were.

The ambiguity stems from this misunderstanding: when I say that we must put an end to the feminine condition, people retort with indignation: "I am proud to be a woman!" As if I were denouncing women as women, as if I were attacking some eternal femininity. When I say that the Jewish condition must come to an end many of my Jewish readers feel in danger of totally disappearing. Now I was in no way attacking women as such, but the oppression endured by women. I was in no way seeking to question everything which constituted a Jew but only that which crushes him, humiliates him, deforms him and kills him; the Jew as an oppressed person, and not the Jew *per se*.

It is true that his oppression was so familiar to the Jew, so much a part of his own traits that he ended up by fearing that if it was tampered with he would himself be disfigured. Thus we see the extraordinary and pitiable spectacle of the oppressed often cherishing and defending his own misfortune. One more example will better illustrate my point. When I wrote that the colonized rejected himself, and should reject himself, I in no way wished to say that the Algerian must cease to be an Algerian, and the Tunisian cease to be a Tunisian (as was sometimes understood); but that the Algerian must cease to be this colonized man that he had become, that the American Negro must cease to be this dominated being. The concept of oppressed, in short, does not exhaust that of the Algerian, the American Negro or the Jew. But I maintain that only the end of the oppression, of the negativity, can, on the contrary, restore the Jew to himself, the woman to herself, just as the Tunisians or the Algerians are beginning to be reborn.

Finally, my real problem was that since my Jewish condition was unacceptable, I had to cut myself off once and for all from this image of myself which had been imposed on me from birth by others and by my own people, and which had become second nature. And yet, in doing so I had to avoid rejecting myself or my people, or scorning their universe which was to a great extent my own. For self-rejection is just as disastrous as the worst encystment. If it is pernicious and stupid for a people, as it is for an individual, to extend its values to an absolute, to hang on desperately to its mythified past, it is just as destructive, and perhaps unworthy, to exhaust one's energies in a battle against oneself, to be ashamed of one's people, to despise their tradition, their culture and their institutions. Again in the last pages I insist that for me it has never been a question of some ultimate weakness, of any sort of mystical complaisance. Although I do want to abolish the condition imposed on me as a Jew, I do not wish to deny automatically every opportunity to the Jew which is in me. Or, to reverse the proposition: I want to accept myself as a Jew while rejecting conditions made by the others and imposed on my existence.

I am not exactly sure what this opportunity will be. I do not know how my Jewishness or Judaism and Jewish values will fare in this battle. What can remain, will. Huge portions will probably evaporate; in all probability the Jew, newly freed man, will discover an unexpected sequel (and why not just as beautiful?) to his admirable beginnings. But what seems important to me now is to fight to make him, at long last, into a free man so that I myself can be a free man with my people. My real problem, in short, was to discover a specific liberation for my oppression as a Jew and not just any liberation, since a general liberation would not be one for us. In reality the question can be thus defined: what was the specific solution to the Jewish drama? What were the specific conditions for the liberation of the Jew?

THREE

The first condition of a *specific liberation* seems to me self-evident: the oppressed person must take his destiny into his own hands. My life must no longer depend on any treaty, often signed with other ends in mind, by anyone with anyone. Not that alliances or the aid of generous friends must be refused, but neither Socialist planning, nor the abstract humanitarianism of the Democrats, nor Christian charity are essential. Better still, no one owes us anything. I became adult, I believe, the day

I understood that nothing was owed me. It was high time we became adult; in other words, non-dependent, neither in fear nor in hope. We should not have had to ask ourselves piteously and in vain why the Pope was silent or why the Americans abandoned us, why the Russians didn't budge. And why not the Red Cross! And the A.S.P.C.A.! Liberty is not a gift; bestowed, conceded, protected by someone else, it is denied and vanishes. Our liberation must depend on our own fight for it.

It was, therefore, obvious that we first had to desire the end of our oppression, well understood as such, before we could act to destroy it. It was first necessary to stop being deceitful with the consciousness of our misfortune. God alone might be able to ferret out and count all the inventions which the Jew used to become accustomed to, deny or explain his misery. But, what is the use of hiding it, they were never anything but the remedies of slaves. Even today when I am asked "Of what misfortune are you speaking? What oppression?", I know that I have again encountered the mentality of a slave or a freed man, whatever the richness of the costume or how gold the braid. I know that my questioner is in need of a long and difficult cure before he earns his liberty.

I willingly recognize that a situation is all the more dramatic when one is conscious of it; that the consciousness of it renders it really unbearable; that a condition is never absolutely unlivable as long as one is not aware of it as such. And that, as a consequence, it is perhaps better to leave the oppressed in peace, in a relative ignorance of his misfortune. All that, of course, I have often told myself. Why upset these men who are already at such pains to come to terms with their misery? Why insist on this misfortune which they find it so hard to come to terms with? But an immediate answer was that their lucidity is prerequisite to their liberation. And I told myself once again that the oppression of the Jew does not exist merely within his own consciousness, but it exists concretely in the institutions, in the day-to-day relationships between Jews and non-Jews; that the mutilation of the oppressed is a *real* mutilation and that the refusal to see his oppression is probably one of the aspects of this mutilation. If a clearer awareness of the oppression increases the uneasiness, it alone can be the beginning of the cure, the revolt and the liberation.

A *transition to action* had to follow; in other words, an effective transformation of the concrete conditions of the existence of the Jew among non-Jews. Any solution which does not undertake this radical reversal in the relations between Jews and non-Jews will remain illusory and a hoax. The Jewish condition is an impossible condition— in other words impossible to live as such. To be Jewish was not to live, it was catch-as-catch-can to survive. From time to time, when history permitted it, we could place our Jewishness in abeyance, forget it a little, and above all remove it from the eyes of others. We could give ourselves a marvelously flattering and reassuring interpretation of it, lend it a wonderful meaning. Still we had done nothing since we had not attacked it concretely. As soon as we gave it a second thought, as soon as we felt it, as soon as we let it come into our relations with others, it imposed its truth once again. It was rejected, humiliated and threatened by the others. Strictly speaking, if we wanted to put an end to the misfortune of being Jewish, while maintaining the Jewish condition intact, we would have had to cease being Jewish. Since we have been unable to do so, since the majority of our people have not resigned themselves to it, we had to put an end to this condition.

Still none of this was specifically Jewish. All impossible conditions call for a radical solution, all absolute misfortunes demand an absolute revolt. How were we to discover the specific conditions of each liberation? Here I proposed another criterion: *the liberation of an oppressed person must be made as a function of the specific conditions of his oppression.* In other words, our starting point had to be the complete description of the Jewish condition, which I have attempted to give in my last book and in this book. The reader may now understand why I have dwelt on this problem; it was not only because I needed to free myself of it, or to exorcize my own ghosts. The liberation of the Jew must be deduced from his particular misfortune.

The misfortune of the Jew is then a *total misfortune;* in other words, it does not encompass only one aspect of his life, his political autonomy, his economic function, his culture or his religion. It concerns his whole existence, his relations with himself and with others; it affects the unity of his personality, divided into a private individual and a public person; and his whole dimension as a questionable citizen and an historically impotent man. It is true that all oppression has a strong tendency to become a total oppression, but it is a question of degree and nuance, of generalities and accent. The specific conditions of each oppression consists precisely of such degrees and particular intonations. The Jew is not oppressed as a member of a class, which distinguishes him from the proletariat, for example. Nor is he oppressed as a member of a biological group, which distinguishes him from Negroes or women. He is affected as a member of a total, social, cultural, political and historical group. In other words, the Jew is oppressed as a member of a people, a minor people, a dispersed people, a people always and everywhere in the minority (which distinguished him from the colonized, also oppressed as a people, but a people in the majority).

Therefore the Jew has to find a *total solution,* one which answers every aspect of his threatened existence, which guarantees his present but also rehabilitates his past and restores to him possession of his future. In other words, *the Jew, oppressed as a people, must find his autonomy and freedom to express his originality as a people.* Therefore to overcome absolutely, the revolt of the Jew must include that particular aspect which will necessarily rehabilitate and recognize him as a major and majority people.

In effect, if the Jews do not pull themselves together as a people they will necessarily remain a separated minority, threatened and periodically exterminated. If they do not defend themselves as a people they will remain subject to the benevolence of others, in other words, to the fluctuations of their moods, more often bad than good. They will remain condemned to serve as a too-convenient scapegoat, a target for other people's economic and political difficulties, to live in ambiguity and by subterfuge and in fear—his own and that of others, to which he strangely clings, like a hated ghost.

Only this collective autonomy will give us at last the daring and the taste for liberty which alone are the foundations of dignity. I admit that I have never been able to forget the extraordinarily fearful timidity of our community in Tunis. We were taught to be nice to everyone— the French who were in power, the Arabs who were in the majority, the Italians who were quick on the draw, the Orient which had a hold on us, and the Occident towards which we aspired. And if a young man, insufficiently trained, or too hot-headed, rose to the provocation and began flexing his muscles, the commotion had to be seen and heard to be believed: the death screams of the women, the panic of the men, the barricaded doors. . . . Unfortunately this ridiculous and pitiful drama made an impression on us. . . . We were neither more cowardly nor more weak than the others, but we were already emasculated, castrated by the collective anguish.

"As late as 1791," says La Condamine, "a Jew who hit

a Moor, even in self-defense, even to avoid his blows, was burned." It is perhaps because of these humiliating memories that my whole life has since become an undertaking of liberation. And when for the first time I witnessed a bullfight, I was annoyed at my disgust, my desire to vomit, my moral distress before the obvious collective satisfaction of the most evil, the most aggressive instincts of humanity. How tempting it was to say, once again, that we, the Jews, had gone beyond all that, on the long path which must lead man from bestiality to humanity; that we had already stopped loving the sight of blood, that we refused to be part of the death of others! But then I told myself as you might pinch yourself to keep awake: progress obtained by and in oppression is worthless. Progress of the vanquished is suspect progress. The rejection of drawn blood is also the fear of blood: sanctuary-value. It is a progress which must be remade, this time in liberty. Humanism yes, but humanism after the liberation and not this fake humanism, a one-way street where I must consider all men as saints in a humanity in which I still have no place.

The Way Out

18

ONE

Here we are before the last, the ultimate question in this cascade of problems: what can we do today to become an autonomous people, so that we may function freely and completely as such?

Let us pause a moment before going any further. In *The Colonizer and the Colonized* I made an important distinction between what I called the *inquiry* and the *wish*. Practically no one paid attention to it. I meant and still mean that we must clearly distinguish between the inventory of a reality (psychological, social, political) and the different plans which can be formulated concerning it (wishes, decisions, opinions). For me, this distinction was more than a working precept and a precaution against confusion; it was the expression of different aspects of the truth.

Thus all that I have written on the subject of dominated men—the colonized, the Jews, the Negroes—is essentially descriptive.

In my opinion, the great merit of these descriptions is their fidelity to their models, and their coherence which exposes the mechanisms of the oppression. Although I certainly suggest solutions to these different misfortunes, these are always additions. Supplementary chapters, though I find them necessary, can, it seems to me, be rejected without contradicting the inventory itself. I can readily understand that the reader may hesitate to follow me to the end; that he may allow the diagnosis without accepting the cure, or even reject all concern. I am convinced, I admit, that he can hardly conclude differently, that events will see to it that he is shown and that it is therefore useless to distract his attention from the essentials of my argument. This is not only a tactical concession. If I am practically certain that I am not mistaken in my portraits of the Jew or of the colonized, because I have lived through colonization and Jewishness, I sincerely admit that my practical proposals may appear fantastic, since we pass from the inquiry to the wish.

At the time of publication of the *The Colonizer and the Colonized* it was apparently asking too much of the passions involved. I had warned that the last chapter was hypothetical in the literal sense of the word, since I tried to foresee the future; and I stated that the analysis of the colonized's condition was of greatest importance, for of that, at least, I was certain. My warnings, however, were to no avail, and everyone jumped to the conclusion which I had only formulated with anguish and timidity. I was often loudly applauded while I myself was terrified; I was more often blamed for it and called a provocateur, when I only foresaw with pain towards what catastrophes we were all heading. In short, what I feared most came to pass: almost all the discoveries which I had accumulated in that book were neglected! It was praised for the wrong reasons, or was rejected as excessive and false because of what had offended in the last pages.

Witness my naïveté: I am about to do the same thing again. Once more I emphatically state that it is my sincere hope that, at least for the moment, this long itinerary, this portrait of myself as a Jew, will be considered separately. My book, in some ways, ends here since I have completed the inventory of the Jewish condition.

I believed I had discovered, along the way, that the Jew is one of the major figures of oppression of our time. Jewishness was largely the negative result of my corrosive, destructive relations with non-Jews. Even its positivity, which still existed, was heavily mortgaged by the oppression. This condition, as impossible to reject as it was to accept, remained, therefore, unlivable, unacceptable, as long as these relationships remained unchanged. The real subject of my book, the real discussion which I would like to see opened is this: is this portrait a good likeness? Does the Jew recognize himself? Do the non-Jews recognize the Jew? Have I succeeded in showing the singularity and originality of the Jewish condition? I hope I will be better understood this time.

Having said this much and come this far, I must admit that once again I find that the solution seems to impose itself irresistibly. After this patient and systematic search it can be discovered at a glance. The oppression of the Jew, like all oppressions, must be understood in its specificity. This means that its solution must also be specific. In other words: what is the most adequate solution to the Jewish drama? Oppressed as a people, and living as such, the Jew must be liberated as a people; he must see an end to his insolvency and rediscover the full dimensions of his life.

We must now go one step further toward what appears to me equally obvious and equally obligatory: since a people cannot, even today, live and determine its destiny freely except as a nation, the Jews must be made into a nation. In short, *the specific liberation of the Jews is a national liberation* and for the last years *this national liberation of the Jew has been the state of Israel.*

First of all, no moral or metaphysical petition whatsoever is involved. The national solution stems from a purely sociological necessity. The Jews are what they are, a living people, a continual minority dispersed among others; on the other hand, the majority of peoples are as yet unable to put up with the presence of compact minorities among them. Thus, this relationship must cease. Since it is impossible for the Jew to live fully among others, the Jew must be removed from their midst (or merged with them of course if assimilation were possible).

With the same rigor and the same honesty I have tried to use in this methodical investigation, I must state precisely that these two propositions (necessity of founding a Jewish nation, and a Jewish nation in Israel) do not have the same logical value. The Israeli solution, in other words, locating this nation in Palestine, was in a certain way historically contingent. It might have been installed elsewhere and I will return to this question in a moment. Today, however, the debate is closed for it is out of date: history has also imposed the second proposition on us.

It is certainly easier to make people admit this double consequence now than eighteen years ago, official date of the birth of this state. Easier in any case than at the time of my adolescence when, in order to carry on our meetings, we had to use deceit as much with our parents and the leaders of the Jewish community as we did with the authorities. (Many of us had to abandon our family homes forever, or forge a signature to leave the country. One of our comrades, whose family suspected her plans to embark, had her head shaved and dyed with iodine to prevent her from leaving her room, which she did anyway, dressed as a boy.) Few Jews today regard Israel with anything less than benevolence; but that is no longer enough. We must now pursue the matter to its logical conclusion. It is now time to instigate and achieve a reversal in our perspective, a *radical conversion* of the entire Jewish people.

Only a few weeks ago one of the leaders of French Jewry, Elie de Rothschild, declared that there were henceforth two solutions to our problem: religion or Israel. He was still half-mistaken. The national solution is not one of several; it is the only definitive solution, because it is the specific solution to the Jewish problem: Israel is not a supplementary contribution, a possible insurance in case of difficulties in the Diaspora; it must be the frame of reference for the Diaspora which must in future *redefine* itself in relation to it.

Henceforth the relationship between Israel and the Diaspora must be reversed, to the profit of Israel.

Those who insist on holding on to the notion of the Diaspora, even cloaked in nobility, invested with a so-called mission throughout the world (which legitimizes the dispersion!) must realize, as we all must realize, that they are holding on to the misfortune, bringing up the rear guard, retarding the liberation of their people. To limit oneself to the reinforcement of the religion is in fact to maintain the Diaspora. What has religion done for this people to date? It has helped them to survive, which is already saying a great deal; but I must repeat that it has not loosened the noose by a single inch. On the contrary I greatly fear that it serves as an alibi: Israel or religion would mean Israel or the Diaspora aided by religion! To insist on the actual singularity of Jewry is only insisting on its misfortune.

It is always possible to reassure oneself with money, science, honors, universality, but without liberty all these things will give forth the tenacious odor of death. Neither the perpetuity of an improved Diaspora, nor Socialism, nor a more adaptable religion, more easily tolerated by

others, nor a *modus vivendi* with the Christians, nor
even an amiable pro-Israelism—Jaffa oranges and Tel-
Aviv singers—are real solutions. They are at best compromises which do not fundamentally change a condition
which demands a radical transformation. On the contrary, only this transformation will permit us to endow
these partial and laughable efforts with a semblance
of effectiveness. Those who today are again talking
about assimilation are not aware that it is again becoming possible just because of the birth of the state of
Israel which has already enhanced the Jew enough in his
own eyes and those of others to liberate him from the
unbearable mark of treachery which overwhelmed him.

We did not have a choice between the Diaspora *or* Israel, assimilation, religion, universality, socialism *or* Israel. There was no *either* . . . *or* possible in Jewish existence, unless it was the choice between oppression and
liberty. Even worse, this last balance never existed. Until
now there has been only one question: how to survive in
servitude? Only a Jewish nation finally allows us to pose
the problem and, at the same time, indicate a solution,
the only real way out. This is why we must say: if Israel
did not exist, it would still be necessary to invent it.

Sooner or later we must recognize the serious and practical nature of the consequences for the existence of the
Jew everywhere in the world. And we cannot put them off
indefinitely. For example, what will be the nationality
of the majority of Jews? Shouldn't we foresee, at least
provisionally, a double nationality? Shouldn't we think
about establishing a national tax, to be exacted from all?
The so-called experts will bring up their eternal objections: why insist on it? Why disturb our relations with
others any further? In so doing aren't we bringing grist to
the mill of the anti-Semites, etc. . . ?

I must be frank right to the end: I believe that this

radical conversion, clearly expressed, is indispensable to
the convalescence of this people. From now on they must
grasp the meaning of their true nature, the basis of their
identity, and of their future. The consolidation of this
young and fragile nation cannot wait. It must be immediate, or a catastrophe will ensue which will retard the
liberation by several centuries. It is a race against time, a
decisive trial into which every resource must be thrown:
strength, intelligence, money. Wise tactical measures can
only be used based on these principles, clearly affirmed
and consciously adopted by the entire people.

Of course we must also consider the residual complexity of our life. It is obvious that all Jews will not be able
to resettle immediately in this tiny country; many will
never wish to. We will for some time to come be tributary
to those nations which, willingly or otherwise, have welcomed us, and in many cases adopted us. I repeat: we owe
them the most absolute, the most courteous and the most
grateful loyalty. For most of us the effort will not even be
difficult: for beneath the misfortune of separation, the
suspicion of others, we too plunge our roots into these
lands, we too become attuned to their skies and, when we
have to leave, their imprint remains engraved in our
hearts. How can I forget what I owe Tunisia and France?
Therefore, no one will be surprised that I am a resolute
partisan of a policy of alliance and engagement in the
community where one continues to live. We do not have
the right to refuse our aid and our solidarity to the men
who live there. Activity in favor of Israel must not be a
final form of abstraction which always lies in wait for the
Jew: it's like taking an interest in Israeli elections, the
better to ignore French or English elections. In short, we
will be responsible for a *double involvement*. But, in any
case, we must never forget our final goal: the meaning of
Jewish presence outside the Jewish nation must change.
The Diaspora must cease to be a Diaspora.

TWO

I do not underestimate any of the difficulties, imperfections or errors of this young state. The actions taken by its governments have often shocked me. I have never denied myself the right to question them or denounce them; regarding the status of the local Arabs, for instance, or the North African immigrants, or their excessive clerical indulgence. But I only criticize what exists and ought to function better; I never question the existence itself; just as no scandal, no error can make us doubt the necessity of decolonization. I will go even further: I know and recognize the objections to the very principle of Jewish liberation. I have not tracked down so many myths in order to straddle this one with my eyes closed. But over and above the mythicizing of the endeavor, its exaggerated claims, inherent in all liberations by the way, its excesses and its injustices, henceforth it possesses a definitive historical justification.

I did not suddenly become nationalistic as soon as it was in my own interest to do so. I continue to think that nationalism is far too frequently an alibi for hatred and domination. I cannot forget that the Jew was always one of the first victims of nationalist crises. But history has convinced me, at least twice, that a nation is the only adequate response to the misfortune of a people. In the case of the colonized I had already discovered that their liberation would be national before it could be social, because they were dominated as a people. The Jew too was oppressed as a member of a total society which was neither completely real nor completely fictitious! He was considered and treated as a foreigner, or at best as a special kind of citizen.

For the Jew, it is true, the matter was extremely complex. The colonized were generally a people, reduced to impotence, but a compact and obvious mass—a majority.

What then could become of the Jewish people, scattered in a thousand fragments across the globe, not even able to understand each other in a common language? I am sorry to have to point out once again our sociologists' lack of imagination, one which leads them furthermore into a systematic error in their evaluation of reality. They can only conceive of peoples and nations on the basis of the completed models which they have before their eyes: the great European nations. The result is that no one has the right to conceive of a new type, either in the present or in the future. The same objection had served against the colonized: how dared they claim a national liberation for nonexistent nations? The Jews, it is perfectly true, did not comprise a nation, hardly a people in the usual sense of the word. Efforts, such as those of the Zionists, to demonstrate that a Jewish nation has always existed, apart from the abnormal conditions of its existence, are, I believe, useless. Today the Jew has become an anachronism, irritating to others, unbearable to himself. His dispersion, his crumbling, are part of his oppression. He must cease to be a three-legged sheep: the missing leg must be restored him, he must be allowed to remake an existence more adapted to the world in which he lives. He must be shaped into a people among peoples, a nation among nations.

In short, *the nation is before the Jew and not behind him.* Like the colonized, he has to fight for his national liberation and create a nation for himself, since history exacts it. Since the nation is still the most effective historical form, the Jew must adopt this form to rid himself of the oppression and live as a normal people among other peoples. The nation is not a preliminary, it is an ending.

I continue to hope it is a temporary ending. I will always hope and fight along parallel lines for a united, pacified and confident humanity, where only the differences of culture and need will be recognized. I am very sorry that we must pass through this national stage which represents a sort of contraction of a people within themselves. But what does one do? Were we obliged to accept continued servitude, dispersion, domination and the impossibility of ever developing ourselves? Did we have to continue cultivating our pained grimaces and humiliated subterfuge which disfigured our faces; consent to stoop our shoulders forever; survey the entire world in an effort to guess where the next blow would fall, and where, one day, we might take rapid refuge? Are we to blame if we have begun to resemble the nationalists, since most human groups are still nationalistic, aspire to become nationalistic or are compelled to be as nationalistic as we?

". . . only a common enterprise dear to the heart of Jews all over the world could restore this people to health. . . .

All this you call nationalism, and there is something in the accusation. But a communal purpose without which we can neither live nor die in this hostile world can always be called by that ugly name. In any case, it is a nationalism whose aim is not power but dignity and health. If we did not have to live among intolerant, narrow-minded and violent people, I should be the first to throw over all nationalism in favor of universal humanity." (Albert Einstein, *The World as I See It.*)

I also recognized that there was no necessary connection between the national regouping and the Israel nation. The Jewish state in Palestine was perhaps a catastrophic error. His devotion to the traditional dream was perhaps the last trick played on the Jew by his religion. Was it really necessary to return to that old country, Biblical yes, and omnipresent in the entire culture of the people, but which had belonged politically to others for so long that they had lost even the memory of their arrival? And contrary to the opinion of half the world? Even if we leave to one side this insoluble historical controversy, the consequences of this choice have been terrible: what price must we pay! What an extraordinary waste of energy in an endeavor which was of itself so demanding! It multiplied the battles against nature and men, men who were not even completely wrong! Since it was necessary to start from scratch in any case, why didn't they choose some fertile-soiled, perhaps subsoiled, Eldorado, uninhabited, rich in deserted expanses?

I made my trip to Israel! What regrets mingled with so much emotion and so many hopes! Unveiled, the Sabbath fiancée proves a great deception! Expanses? It's a hole in the wall; the country is about as big as a pocket handkerchief. The Israelis themselves make fun of it with an irony which barely disguises their anxiety. A deserted expanse? Israel is a real desert, a waterless desert of stones. And this tiny and disinherited domain, which you could almost cross in a single glance, is still disputed from within by its ancient inhabitants, suspicious and sarcastic, and is on all sides surrounded by hating populations.

For years we bartered, we played tricks, we fought to buy these pebbles in the sun for a very high price. And now that a little greenery may at last cover these pebbles, they must be, and will have to be for a long time to come, tirelessly defended by loaded weapons. In view of the extraordinary disproportion in populations, the inexorable reinforcement of the Arab forces, their humiliated remembrance of so many successive defeats, their at least partial feeling of having right on their side, the too-facile political diversion which a war with the Jews would constitute—in view of all this how can we avoid the anguish of asking ourselves if our gathering in the heart of so many hostile multitudes will not one day be transformed into history's final trap? Until now history has only suc-

ceeded in inflicting its cruel wounds on us, first in one
spot then in another. Has history now found the unique
opportunity of finishing us off with a single blow? Without a doubt, that is what several Arab leaders, aided and
abetted by the obstinate delirium of their Nazi advisors,
are hoping and preparing for. How else can we interpret
this news bulletin:

"The Afro-Asiatic Youth Conference, organized by the
Permanent Committee on Afro-Asiatic Solidarity, will
open in Cairo on February 2, 1959, and will bring together youth delegates from fifty-two states of Africa and
Asia.

"The highlight of the conference will be a large military
maneuver against Israel: 6,000 male students and 4,000
female students wearing the various uniforms of all the
Arab countries will participate in this little war. One
group will represent the Israeli army. The program gives
the following description of the spectacle:

" 'All the Arab forces march towards Israel. The Israelis
panic and take flight. In a victorious apotheosis the Israeli flag is torn down and replaced by the Arab flag.' " (*La
Dépêche Tunisienne,* February 1, 1959.)

There is some naïveté in this operatic performance,
and much self-persuasion; Israel will defend herself, and
at the moment has at her disposal the best army in the
Middle East. (And here I myself am overcome by the desire to say: "And then the great powers would never allow such a massacre." Is it so difficult to renounce the
protection of others?) But how could we avoid being wor-
ried by their smoldering and ever-wakeful hatred? Were
such efforts, sacrifices and courage necessary only to come
up against the same threat? Did we have to exchange one
anxiety for another, one danger for another, this time

perhaps worse than the others? Was that the promised
land, to which we so ardently aspired, was that the *way
out*, which I in turn am discovering?

"One more round, then another; then another . . .
until when! Is that life? Is it for this that we are Jews?"
sighed Israel's oldest fighter, Ben-Gurion himself.

And yet I too am able to see that this mythic delirium,
the aberration of founding the new Jewish state in Palestine, has perhaps contributed to the restoration of this
people's collective health. Let me explain: the choice of
this already inhabited, terribly exposed corner of earth
on which to build the nation so necessary to the Jew was
the effect of a slightly mad and a slightly unhealthy inspiration. The actual state of Israel was perhaps the result of a collectively neurotic choice, one of the last neurotic acts, let us hope, of this neurotic people. The reader
may be familiar with the extraordinary scene enacted at
the Sixth Zionist Congress: those delegates who rolled on
the floor, tore out the hairs of their beards, cried, accused
Herzl himself of treason because he timidly proposed that
they accept the offer of an immense African territory, really rich and really uninhabited: Uganda. Reason is obviously on Herzl's side; he had political sense:

". . . a temporary result is at hand: this land in
which . . . we can settle our suffering masses on a national basis and with the right of self-government. I do
not believe that we have a right, for the sake of a beautiful dream or a legitimistic banner, to withhold this relief
from the unfortunate. . . . Palestine is the only land
where our people can come to rest. But hundreds of thousands need immediate help." (Theodor Herzl, *Diaries*.)

Herzl's first aim was to save a people; the delegates
wanted to remain faithful to a myth: that of a chosen
people in a promised land. Unfortunately they tri-

umphed; they imposed their point of view, forcing us to claim a heritage long ago acquired by others, one which had to be torn from them by force of arms, so that blood flowed and will perhaps flow again. I angrily say to myself sometimes that the obsessional stubbornness of those daydreamers has perhaps made them into malefactors of our history, unconsciously responsible for many useless deaths and for the fragility of our national reconstruction! As if they still morbidly needed to prolong the misfortune!

And yet, this myth may have contributed after all, in some other way, toward the consolidation of our reconstruction. It has perhaps helped to reshape this diaphanous, bloodless people into a people of flesh and blood. Peoples probably need myths. The Israeli nation has renewed a cultural tradition, fossilized though it may have been, a language which was almost dead and a religion which had been arrested for centuries. One may be indifferent to such claims. However, it seems to be a general fact in most liberations that the oppressed's first need is to return to himself, in other words to his language, be it sick, to his tradition, be it a phantom. In this restoration of himself he is obliged to utilize the stones of his past. It is as much a question of reconstruction as of construction. In our case we also had to put an end to the *exile:* that theme which has become so painful to our collective consciousness, because it symbolizes and sums up our historical condition. The mad obstinacy of the delegates to the famous Congress of Basel stemmed in some obscure fashion from this: it was in fact a matter of a necessary *revenge* on history. The long defeat had to be effaced, and a victory under the same flag, the same insignia was a necessity; a victory in the explicit name of this people, in other words, of their God and their tradition, had to be won before they could at last agree to feel worthy to live again.

But let us call a halt to this interpretation which may or may not be a little wild. It is hardly necessary. Today we are no longer defending a myth, but a reincarnated myth, a dream come true—the most solid of realities. Today three million men live in the new Jewish nation, one quarter of the total Jewish population. It was perhaps folly to have led them there, but it would be an even greater folly to abandon them. The time for discussions of principle—historical, judicial, or even moral—is past, and now the young life of this state must be protected. Israel has been a doubtful wager; all that we can do now is win it. It is a hole in the wall; now it must be defended. Henceforth, we can no longer refuse to participate: our people's destiny is riding on this. This tiny corner is our only recognized bastion. Its destruction would be the greatest disaster of contemporary Jewish history, perhaps since the fall of the Temple, greater than the massacre of six million, because of its significance: it is the ultimate effort of a people to survive.

THREE

If Israel did not exist it would have to be created. If Israel should disappear it would have to be re-created. For Israel alone can put an end to the negativity of the Jew and liberate his positivity.

Only the territorial solution, a free people on a free territory—a nation—is an adequate solution to the fundamental and specific deficiencies in the Jewish condition: the Jew was an *absolute foreigner*. Any oppressed person can return to or feel at home in his native country, however tiny or crushed by the occupant. At any moment, if he wishes, he can cease to be a foreigner. One is moreover only relatively a foreigner. In whatever part of the globe the Jew may be threatened or menaced he can never *return* anywhere. Suddenly, periodically, he is again the same absolute foreigner which his father or his grandfather was before him. The reader is perhaps familiar with another good Jewish story which is hardly funny, where one Jew says to the other:

"I am leaving for South America."

"That's a long way off," says the other.

"From what?" asks the first.

I am convinced that this impression of a vacuum behind one, of no possible return, the absence of a stable frame of reference, has strongly contributed to our secular anxiety. It has also contributed towards the ghostly demeanor which we have in the eyes of others. The Jew is a man with no earth beneath his feet, a man from nowhere, an unhappy figure of misfortune who provokes pity but also doubt, suspicion, irritation and, should the occasion arise, punishment. "I've had it with the Jews," an employee of the Paris police prefecture said to me (and he was not excessively ill-disposed). "First it was the Russians, then the Poles, then the Germans, then the Hungarians, the Egyptians, now the Tunisians, the Moroccans, the Algerians . . ." It was high time that all this end; in effect, that the Jew no longer be the eternal and humble client of police prefectures seeking a room, a visa, a naturalization. It is misery to be a foreigner, Jung observed. It was time for the long misery of the Jewish immigrant to come to an end.

Only a definitive, *legitimate* national status could bring this about. Only the precise conjunction of a Jewish countenance with its own history and geography will make the suspicious conduct of the perpetual foreigner disappear (one would think this would be obvious), even if he continues to live abroad. The Italian can live in America, the Spaniard in France, and the Greek in Turkey. They still preserve a jurisdiction, a frame of reference by which they cease to be foreigners. I have in mind more than mere military power. It is enough that the

Greek recognize himself in Greece, and the Spaniard in Spain. Were it necessary for us to live and die elsewhere, Israel could become this jurisdiction and this frame of reference—our collective backbone.

"If you do not let your son grow up as a Jew you deprive him of those sources of energy which cannot be replaced by anything else. He will have to struggle as a Jew and you ought to develop in him all the energy he will need for that struggle. Do not deprive him of that advantage." (Sigmund Freud.)

Only a national solution can exorcize our shadowy figure. Only Israel can infuse us with life and restore our full dimensions. Only the liberation of a people can provide a real opportunity to their culture. Let me finally get to the bottom of this difficult problem—that of the culture of the oppressed. My treatment of it apropos of the colonized and apropos of the Jew has been much criticized. I will try to be precise.

A people must have a common culture; that is an observation, not exactly a wish. Perhaps it is deplorable that humanity is divided into peoples. Possibly one day it will become a unified body with one culture. Meanwhile, peoples do exist, and particularly thanks to their collective psyche. The Jewish people exist because they possess a religious and cultural tradition, institutions and collective habits of thought and behavior. (Here I differ from authors like Sartre who have only seen in it enormous negativity, above all psychological.) But all these assets are heavily mortgaged by the terrible oppression, special for the Jew, one of the most tenacious, the most ancient and the most insidious in history. And so I may say that *to be Jewish is a culture and a condition, a condition of oppression and a defective culture,* practically reduced to its traditional aspect.

What is to be done? For this people to regain their full dimensions the twofold misery had to end. The condition imposed by others had to be abolished and the culture freed from its defensive girdle. There was effectively a double oppression: an objective external oppression made up of the innumerable limitations imposed on our life, the incessant aggressions inflicted on us, *and* an auto-oppression, resulting from the other, but having its own weight, its own laws whose consequences were just as harmful—encystment, the retreat to a strictly defined front, the rejection of all experimentation, the condemnation of all innovation and research. In short, the very negation of a living and lively Jewish culture.

The doubly caused asphyxiation could only be remedied by breaking the yoke of the servitude and also the encystment. Then everything ought to be possible—the writer, the artist, the Jewish thinker ought to be able to say anything without being immediately suspected of treason, excluded or crushed and thus lost in every way as a creator. This is understandable in the case of a Jewry which is itself terrorized, which could not tolerate the slightest imagination around a law which was its only memory and its only frame of reference. But it was high time to restore liberty to Jewish culture for it is the *sine qua non* of normal development.

What will become of religion in all this? In wishing to liberate Jewish culture from tradition, am I insidiously ruining Jewish tradition and that which has, to date, been essential to it—religion? Not necessarily. My aim is to liberate my people. I do not seek to destroy any element which they hold dear as long as they need it and if I am free to exercise my right to open discussion, at last possible, in a collectivity at last free. I have been outspoken in stating my belief that the weight of tradition and religion in the life of this collectivity is excessive and harmful. I am convinced that everything is paralyzed, fettered and inhibited by it. In our rediscovered liberty each element of the convalescing Jewish collective consciousness—art, philosophy, the sciences, ethics and politics—will have to take its proper place.

In fact, far from marking the end of the Jewish religion, it is my contention that this liberation, this opening up to the world, might again offer it its real opportunity. Like the other disciplines, religion will at last find freedom of expression, a progressive adaptation to the needs of the modern Jew, without having to limit itself to the role of watch dog which was necessary in the dispersion. In short, far from declaring war on believers and religion, I am convinced that it will be to their advantage to lose the exorbitant rank they now occupy as some ghostly mummy. It goes without saying that the end of the objective oppression will allow Jewish believers to benefit from the same rights as those of the other religions.

Would the Jewish culture I envisage be deprived of the inexhaustible support of this old soil? Again, the contrary: de-sanctifying the Jewish tradition will restore the greatest fertility to it. I am thinking of what Christian tradition has become in the culture of the Occident: infinitely more than a religion, fortunately. The inspiration of every thought, secular and profane, of art, ethics, legislation and philosophy, and this just because it is no more than the inspiration, the source and not the guardian or iron collar of every moment, of every effort. Western art continues to drink at the well of Christianity just because it does not have to be religious, because it possesses the liberty without which no art is possible. I am thinking, above all, of the astonishing Greek people. Are they less important than we in the history of humanity? Greeks have survived too for twenty centuries. Do they talk about miracles and mystery? No, for they have lived on the same soil, in at least relative independence; they were able to live, in other words they changed while remaining faithful to themselves. Far from taking their prestigious past literally, they have retained the essentials, those symbols charged with meaning, marvelously convenient vehicles for present-day Hellenic culture. In monotheistic Athens you still meet people called Hercules or Ulysses and young directors put the gods and ancient fatality on their stages. The Greek people have not been afraid that they would lose sight of themselves if they took their eyes off Olympus for a moment, if they ceased to take this immense fabulousness seriously. The Jewish people, on the other hand, forced to struggle in the midst of perpetual misfortune with nothing to hold on to, not even the earth, or the same climate, or even the same food, held tightly on to the myths of their origin which hardened in their clutching hands. For without them they would not only have changed gradually like the Greeks, they would probably have disappeared.

But I have already examined these problems under different aspects. What is now important is the lesson which we might draw. Will this people, once brought together with the same secure ground underfoot, and rediscovering other foundations for their identity, set Yahveh down on the same shelf as Jupiter in the mythological museum of humanity? I don't know the answer. On the other hand, I am sure that when terminated, this great mutation will restore this people to history and to themselves, to historical health which has its risks and banalities, of course, but which is a thousand times better than this permanent alienation born of suffering and anguish. In any event, they will be able to distinguish between the profane and the sacred, celebrate the sacred if they so desire, but live the profane without being haunted by ghosts. Far from being lost, the Bible and the Talmud and the Cabala will at last become what they deserve to be, an inexhaustible reservoir of themes, designs and

symbols, inexhaustibly fruitful, monuments of world literature and not merely religious works; incomparably superior in my opinion to the *Iliad* and the *Odyssey*.

Have I made myself clear enough? Will someone still
find fault with me on some other grounds, claiming that I
have desired the destruction of the tradition, its values,
of all of Judaism? Actually, I am perhaps proposing the
only solution which can save them by allowing them to
bear new fruit which will not be immediately thrown out
as has been the practice to date, for there is no culture
other than a living and continuously renewed culture.

Paradoxically, even *assimilation* will at last become
possible. In the oppression it was not so because of the
rejection of the others and also because of the unbearable
anxiety it aroused in the Jew himself. How is it possible
to leave one's people in such a great misfortune? One
does not abandon a vanquished camp without unbearable distress. Henceforth the possibility for this people to
refer to a soil, to a state, to a culture will absolve the
assimilated. By becoming a free man the Jew gains at the
same time the freedom to cease being a Jew. If there is so
much talk about assimilation again today it is not merely
because of the temporary peace we are enjoying, but because the shock of assimilation has noticeably lessened in
the Jewish conscience.

I insist on repeating just as clearly that that too is a
gain. *Assimilation must be a legitimate way out for any
Jew who desires it.* The liberty to choose his own destiny
must also be restored to the Jew. The confirmation of his
belonging or the choice of another community must at
last become simple matters of temperament or self-
interest. Why should he be denied a right which is
granted to all other men? What is more praiseworthy
about Italians who assimilate with the French, or Germans with the Americans? Here again we must recognize

that the existence of a Jewish nation will at last permit the disappearance of Jewishness. Both the misfortune and the myth were opposed to a Jewish nation for in it the misfortune must come to an end and the myth of the world-wide mission will at last be dissipated.

The same historical promotion which makes the Jew a free man will also give him the freedom to leave Jewry.

Thus only Israel will, and has already restored our dignity. Until now I have not dwelt upon the moral aspects of the endeavor, because I am in general suspicious of such motivations which often prove to be fictitious and too-convenient alibis. It seemed to me presumptuous to demand brilliant achievements of the oppressed since he had precisely lost the bold taste for the riposte. I have preferred to relate the itinerary of a liberation step by step in order to demonstrate its logical and historical necessity. Certainly at the origin of my search there was a sentiment and a decision that liberty is better than servitude, that the subterfuges used to subsist are degrading and in every way destructive. But I was more preoccupied with healing the Jew than with judging him because one does not judge an oppressed person by the same criteria as a free man.

Having said this much, when the moment arrives which places liberation within reach, it becomes unworthy not to contribute to it to the maximum of one's capacity. Servitude becomes a shameful sickness when it is agreed to. Our future has taken a decisive turn, has been suddenly, unbelievably opened. How can anyone fail to see it, and refuse henceforth to accelerate it? The Eichmann capture was much discussed: had we the right to take him in a foreign country? Wouldn't it have been better to kill him discreetly? Once taken had we the right, we, to execute him? Shouldn't we have handed him over to his own country or an international tribunal, etc. . . ? (In passing let us admire the judicial reservations of all those good souls who had always forgotten to say a word in our favor when we were abandoned and despoiled by all the jurisdictions of the universe.) I find all this of minor importance, even a little despicable. On the other hand, it has a fundamental meaning. For the first time the Jews took revenge as Jews, by themselves, and in the name of the entire people. I do not especially like vengeance as such, but in order to renounce it with nobility it is first of all necessary to be in a position to execute it. For the first time we were able to, we will be able to again: we are, at last, historically adult.

In the past we had excuses—granted. We were in such despair that we hadn't even the idea and the strength for revolt. The young sabras cannot even imagine what state their people were in; they cannot guess how terribly wearing for the individual and the entire Jewish social body this secular adjustment to anxiety, injustice and periodic catastrophe had been. But what answer can we give them from now on when they will say, more and more harshly:

"For a long time to come our world will wonder about this episode in its history, and will hold its breath . . . Our face is still on fire from the magisterial slap. Can the Jews continue to live this double existence? Can they forget that they live dispersed among the peoples who did not step between them and death, among innumerable beings who, apart from some courageous exceptions, lent a helping hand to the assassins, or watched them with indifferent eyes?

The death of the weak is not shameful when there is neither sanctuary nor aid, but life can be dishonorable for the man who does not profit from the right to lead a different existence." (Chaim Gouri.)

Not long ago a delegation of students, confused by religious demands, and the useless flight of the democracies,
insisted that I write a sort of program of action for Jewish
youth answering the question of how to be a Jew today.
How to be of the Left without necessarily ceasing to be
Jewish? How to remain Jewish without necessarily being
a believer? I got out of it, of course, fearing ridicule; but
above all because I first wanted to finish this book which
would contain my exact answer. Here then is the answer.
The Jew must be liberated from oppression, and Jewish culture must be liberated from religion. This double
liberation can be found in the same course of action—the
fight for Israel. Had I dared to address myself to the
young people I would have told them: "I am happy to
have belonged to the generation which understood and
undertook our liberation. Your role, just as important,
is to complete it. Israel is henceforth your concern. It is
our only way out, our only real card, and our last historical chance. All the rest is diversion."